On Huron's Shore

linked stories by
Marilyn Gear Pilling

DEMETER

DEMETER PRESS, BRADFORD, ONTARIO

Copyright © 2014 Demeter Press

Individual copyright to their work is retained by the authors. All rights reserved. No part of this book may be reproduced or transmitted in any form by any means without permission in writing from the publisher.

Published by:
Demeter Press
140 Holland Street West, P. O. Box 13022
Bradford, ON L3Z 2Y5
Tel: (905) 775-9089
Email: info@demeterpress.org
Website: www.demeterpress.org

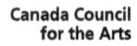

Canada Council for the Arts
Conseil des Arts du Canada

The publisher gratefully acknowledges the support of the Canada Council for the Arts for its publishing program.

Demeter Press logo based on the sculpture "Demeter" by Maria-Luise Bodirsky <www.keramik-atelier.bodirsky.de>

Front cover photograph: Dan Pilling

This book is a work of fiction. Names, characters, places and incidents either are the product of the author's imagination or are used fictitiously, and any resemblance to actual persons living or dead, events, or locales is entirely coincidental.

Printed and Bound in Canada

Library and Archives Canada Cataloguing in Publication

Pilling, Marilyn Gear, 1945–, author
    On Huron's shore : linked stories / by Marilyn Gear Pilling.

ISBN 978-1-927335-34-5 (pbk.)

    I. Title.

PS8581.I365O6 2014   C813'.54   C2014-901897-5

On Huron's Shore

for the cottage library!

Love, Mum & Dad

2015.

*For Sheena, Merrick, Philippe, Maurice,
Aimée, André and in loving memory of
Stéphanie (1987–2007) and Sari (1965–2013)*

Contents

PART I

i.
Tomatoes
3

ii.
Head-doors
16

iii.
Her Mysteries
24

iv.
The Fullness of Time
41

v.
Flies
48

vi.
The Accident
52

vii.
Blossom
60

viii.
Beyond Aunt Bea's Garden
67

PART II

ix.
Europe on Five Dollars a Day
79

x.
Her Mark on Men
96

xi.
The Discovery of the New World
102

xii.
The Sun is Out, Albeit Cruel
112

PART III

xiii.
On Huron's Shore
125

xiv.
Our Mother and Dorothy Goodman
142

xv.
Beneath the Mock Orange
153

PART IV

xvi.
Incestuous Ossuary
165

xvii.
Pilgrimage
173

xviii.
Puke Birds
187

xix.
The Dinner Party
193

xx.
This is History
205

xxi.
The Love Bites of Twenty-three Rogue Monkeys
221

xxii.
The Play of the Gods
227

xxiii.
The Mothers, the Daughters, the Sisters, the Brother
241

xxiv.
The Festival We Call Christmas
251

Acknowledgements
267

The truth that had just been revealed to me, and that Chekhov's Yalta exile revealed to him—that our homes are Granada. They are where the action is; they are where the riches of experience are distributed.
—Janet Malcolm, *Reading Chekhov*

PART I

She chews the bitter pieces of walnut in her ice cream and suddenly is no longer quite steady on her chair. A thought, a surety, has come to her that will make all the days of her life before this different from all the days that follow.
—"Beyond Aunt Bea's Garden"

i.
Tomatoes

LEXIE'S FATHER IS A TRUE BLOND. He's small. He weighs only one hundred and thirty pounds. He doesn't look like a man who would eat eight large tomatoes in a row, then look around and ask his wife what's for supper. He stands five feet eight inches, and his eyes are the blue of the chicory that blooms along roadsides in August.

Lexie's mother says that Lexie is a blond too, but not a true blond.

"What's the difference?" says Lexie.

"Your father's eyelashes will never go dark," says her mother.

Lexie files this answer in the large drawer in her head where she keeps her mysteries—those things she does not understand. Whenever she's bored, for instance in church, she opens the drawer and picks one of the items to ponder.

Lexie's father loves tomatoes. Fresh tomatoes only. Fresh means picked after Lexie's mother calls the family to supper. When her mother calls the family to table, her father drops what he's doing and gallops to the garden. He plucks eight or so large tomatoes from their stems, gathers them against his old shirt, runs for the house, crosses the kitchen with giant strides, comes to a sudden and dramatic stop at his place, and carefully rolls the tomatoes onto his white plate. Lexie has watched him do this many times. The galloping and the gigantic strides are because Lexie's mother objects to him waiting 'til the last minute to pick the tomatoes. It holds up supper, she says.

"God is gracious God is good Let us thank him For our food," says their father, at top speed, making food rhyme with good, though at all other times he pronounces the word food to rhyme with mood. With a paring knife, he cuts the tomatoes in slices, covers his dinner plate with their redness, and stacks the extras in high columns on his dessert plate. He takes the spoon from the bowl of white sugar and scoops sugar onto each slice, then douses each heap of sugar with vinegar, and sprinkles the lot with salt and pepper. "Down the hatch," he says.

Lexie's mother wears her black hair rolled up in small metal curlers until she must, for some reason, leave the house. She sits opposite her husband, and she is the opposite of her husband. Her mother's hazel eyes take in their father's tomato performance. She says, "I'm aghast, James." She says this, yet Lexie has heard their mother more than once boast to her sister, Aunt Bea, about how much their father can eat. Aunt Bea always says the same thing. "James do beat all, Irene. For all the size of him, too."

Lexie's father stabs the red circles one after the other, and swallows them whole. He folds a slice of soft white bread in half, uses it to mop the seeds and the juice, and eats that too. The whole family watches. Lexie's father keeps on until there is no sign that there has ever been a tomato at table. He looks across at Lexie's mother. "What's for supper tonight, Mommy?"

"You must be a bottomless pit. You must have a cast iron stomach, James. I'd be sicker than a dog if I ate one tenth the amount of tomatoes. And please don't call me 'Mommy.'" She shakes her head. "They're starving in Africa. And just look at you."

Lexie always looks at her father then, trying to see what her mother sees. She sees only a small man with eyes of chicory blue, a true blond whose eyelashes will never go dark, sitting at the table waiting for his supper. Another mystery for the drawer.

Every day, Lexie's father runs to and from the office where he works. He runs in his brown suit, brown fedora and brown leather shoes. Fridays, he runs as fast as he can. Even though the housewives in their neighbourhood are used to seeing Lexie's father run up the street, he's moving so fast on Fridays that they give him a second look. People who have never seen him before stop and stare. This is 1956. Grownups do not run in the street, only kids who are playing tag.

Lexie's father doesn't care that people stare at him. All he cares is that her mother has packed the suitcase and the supper, loaded the car, and made everything ready for blast off, so they can pull out of the driveway in their blue Austin no later than 4.22 p.m. Their father has figured out that it takes twenty-two minutes for him to run the mile home from work, take the stairs of their small city home two at a time, change his clothes, and be ready. He has trained their mother, Lexie, and Graham to be on high alert for his appearance.

Lexie is eleven; her brother Graham is eight. On this Friday afternoon, Lexie is leaning against the open trunk of the car, watching her father fly up the street towards her. When he sees her, he leaps into the air and kicks his heels together, then resumes his flat-out running.

Lexie's mother is ashamed of their father, running in his suit, running in front of the neighbours. "I'm appalled James. I can't hold my head up in front of anyone on this street."

Lexie wonders what the people who stare at their father are thinking. Do they think he's being chased? That the police are after him? Or do they think he's in a race, a strange kind of race they've never heard of, where grown men in suits run like greyhounds through the quiet neighbourhoods of medium-sized Ontario cities?

As her father blurs past his firstborn, he tilts his head in her direction and makes his eyes bug out. This means—hello, I haven't seen you since last evening, but greetings must never delay blast off. Lexie feels the whir she always feels when her father is near, like the whir within the wood stove at the farm, when it's going strong. Her father burns through all his days, running towards his next chunk of work the way a dog runs after a ball.

Lexie calls to her brother Graham. Time to get in the back seat. Their mother closes the trunk and sits down in the front, three year old Vivian on her lap, then leans over and fits the car key into the ignition. When their father comes running around the corner of the house three minutes later, they close the car doors. It's a hot afternoon, boiling hot for May. Their mother won't allow them to wear shorts until after the 24th. Anticipating the sticky heat in the car, Lexie slams her door harder than necessary.

"Please close the car doors gently," says her father in the polite voice he uses when they do something wrong, the voice that sounds like a robot. "To do otherwise creates more wear and tear on the car than necessary."

Lexie knows of no other father who speaks this way.

A few miles from the city, on their Friday journeys, are the purple hills. That's what their father calls them. He announces the hills in a voice different from his everyday voice. He sounds like a footman announcing the Queen: "The Purple Hills!!"

At the top of the first hill, their father switches off the ignition. As the motor dies, their mother asks him not to do it. From the back seat, Lexie sees her mother's left ear turn red. Her mother turns toward their father and starts the cross speech she makes every Friday at this time. "And now you're making the baby cry," her mother finishes.

Lexie's father says nothing. He always says nothing when their mother gets mad, even when she loses her temper and shouts. This makes Lexie's mother even madder.

"Vivy isn't a baby," says Lexie. "She's three years old." She leans forward and stretches her arms out to her sister. Vivian squirms off their mother's lap, crawls over the gear shift, into the back seat and onto Lexie's knee.

Released from its motor, the car hurtles down the steep hill. Their father's rule for himself is that every bit of speed they gain going down must be available to take them over the rises between, and all the way up the last hill. His rule for himself is that only the steering wheel may be used to control their flight. He may not put his foot on the brake, no matter what.

He pilots them around the curve at the bottom of the first hill. The car lurches and swings; in the back seat, Lexie and Graham slide heavily to the left. Their mother screams. Vivian looks up at her big sister. Lexie places her finger on her own lips, and smiles at her sister. "Whee-ee," she whispers, in Vivian's ear. There comes a slight rise in the road, a rise that slows them slightly, then a steep straight descent, a series of hilly curves at the bottom.

The car lunges at the descent, no longer a car but a wild creature they cling to, a creature that feels as if it's flying. Lexie holds Vivian tighter with her left arm; with her right, she clutches the door handle. They have left their ordinary lives. The fields of wheat and corn, the cattle and sheep and horses, the barns and long straight garden rows—all slide by like jet streams, out there in the world they left when the motor switched off and the car jerked free and anything became possible.

Going up the last high hill, they lose speed. At the top, their father switches the key that returns them to their lives. Lexie and Graham uncurl stiff white fingers from the door handles. Their mother stares out the window as if she's not part of the family.

Their father does this every Friday afternoon as they set out on their journey. His name for it is coasting. "Coasting saves gas," he says, as he turns the key, and the wild creature they've been clinging to turns back into a sky-blue Austin.

Their father knows the curve in the road that is halfway to their destination, and it's not until they reach that point that their mother unwraps supper and gives each of them their share—salmon sandwiches on white bread, lemonade containing pulp and round seeds that have unexpected sharp points protruding from their roundness, an apple cut in four, its flesh brown. Two home-made oatmeal raisin cookies.

Graham is on his knees, rocking back and forth. "What's the matter with you?" says Lexie, just before they reach the halfway mark.

Graham edges over, puts his face beside Vivian's and whispers into Lexie's ear, "I have to pee."

"Tell dad."

"I have to urinate. I have to urinate badly," says Graham loudly. Since the day they first began to talk, their father has taught them not to say the word pee. The word pee is vulgar and unworthy of them, he says. Belly is another word that's common. Stomach also is unworthy. They must say abdomen. Lexie knows that their father intends that his children will stand at the head of every class, as he did, that they will advance without pause towards The Future, a high class place where the words pee and stomach are unknown.

Their father stops the car on the gravel shoulder. The ditch is a slanting tangle of weeds for which Lexie knows the words. Toothwort. Chickweed. Shepherd's Heart. Graham starts down the steep bank. A large greenish frog springs almost into his face, its sticky-rubbery body banging into his neck instead. Her little brother gives a startled shriek, loses his balance, and slides into the ditch. When he emerges, business done, his shoes drip black muck and his pants are grass-stained.

Their father gets out of the car. He takes Graham's shoes and socks, and wraps them carefully in the pages of an old Family Herald, puts them in the trunk. Lexie knows that he is showing his children the right way to look after their possessions. She watches her father's careful hands and feels the urge to jump out of the car and into the deepest part of the ditch, splashing her clothes and ruining her white sneakers. When their father gets a new shirt and tie for Christmas, he puts them into a drawer in their packages and continues to wear his old shirts and ties. Their mother explains this behavior by saying that their father was marked by the depression. Lexie has seen the depression. It's a sharp dip in the farm lane. If their mother is driving, their father always warns her to "slow down for the depression." Every time they jolt through it, Lexie puzzles over its "marking" of her father. Now he takes his white hanky from his pocket and wipes the damp from between Graham's toes. Lexie understands that this is so his son won't catch a cold that might cause him to miss school and fall behind the others.

Once every crumb of supper has been consumed, the journey becomes long. Graham squirms and asks every few minutes whether they'll soon be there. He and Lexie argue under their breath over the small pieces of cookie left in the bag. Neither of them argues with Vivian—Vivian is Lexie's favourite member of the family, and she is Graham's favourite too. In the days when Vivian was a crying baby, Lexie walked the floor with her for hours. She never tired of the warm, snuggly bundle Vivy made in her arms. Her little sister has fallen asleep now, against her chest, and Lexie shushes Graham with a glare.

On this road, their father knows every farmhouse, every barn, every field of cattle, every crop of wheat or hay or corn or timothy, every curve, every maple and spruce and poplar, every bridge, every swamp, every creek, every river, every stone. Near their destination, he knows the history of every family on every farm. He has taken them on this journey twice a week since they were born, every Friday afternoon and every Sunday evening.

The house they're headed for in the country is the house where their father grew up. It has eleven rooms. Something lives behind the bedroom walls; busy feet can be heard day and night.

The house and the farm are a secret. It belongs to their father and their father's only living relative, Ephram. When people in the city ask Lexie and Graham where they go every weekend and every summer, their father has taught them to say that they are going to visit a relative, never that they are going to the farm and certainly not "their farm."

Their father drives the car across the stone bridge that spans the creek. He slides the Austin into creeper gear, and the car grinds halfway up the hill. They turn right, into the long lane. The farm house is situated halfway up the highest hill in the county, the only level spot on the entire one hundred acres. To their right as they drive in the lane, the field slopes into a deep valley. A creek runs through its bottomlands. To their left, the land rises to the peak of the high hill.

Their father drives past the farmhouse, on their left, and into the large open space between house and barn. He parks the car, and explodes out of it. When he comes to the fence that encloses the yard, he puts his left hand on the fence post and leaps, swinging his body over and landing lightly on the other side. He runs up the slope to greet Ephram. Before the rest of them have even stepped from the Austin, he's back, taking suitcases and boxes from the trunk, carrying the first load up to the house.

Their father always shifts into high gear the minute they arrive. He has Friday evening and Saturday until dark to accomplish all the tasks that must be done. A week's work to cram into twenty-four hours. Ephram is too old to do much around the place. Their father will not allow himself to work on Sunday, the Sabbath. Only essential work may be done on the Lord's day. Feeding the cattle, for instance. No fencing, no coating of wooden posts with creosote, no scything, no cleaning out of stables, no fertilizing or spraying of apple trees, no burning of tent caterpillars from the crooks of the trees at the Other Place, no taking of farm equipment to town to have it fixed, no visits from the vet to attend to the cattle. Their mother has explained that this is not because their father is more religious than the next person, but because their father worshipped his mother, and this was his mother's rule.

The sun is slanting through the lacey-green maple trees of the bush, creating long shadows across the outer yard. The air smells intensely of lilac, and something else. Lexie sees the long plot of newly-prepared earth on the level place west of the inner yard and identifies the smell as manure and newly-turned soil.

As far as Lexie can tell, her parents do not agree on anything. When they're in a fight, Lexie feels it inside herself. There's a place in her stomach, and a place in her throat. The places burn when the fights are going on. In between, they turn into hard lumps, sometimes big, sometimes so small that she barely feels them.

Lexie knows trouble is coming as soon as she smells the manured soil. All evening, she feels the lumps in her throat and stomach growing larger. Sure enough, that night, the old house in darkness, she hears her parents' voices behind the closed door of their bedroom at the back of the house, on the second floor. Her parents normally do all of their fighting in their little home in the city. They don't fight at the farm, because of Ephram.

Lexie gets out of bed and creeps down the long hall in her bare feet, crouches on the other side of their door. It's worse lying in bed hearing her mother's angry voice than it is knowing what's being said.

"I go 'til I drop," her mother is saying, "and it's never enough. No matter where I turn, there's always more to do. More cursed, stupid flies, more cursed cobwebs, more cursed, stinking rubber boots."

"I'd rather you didn't use those words, Irene," says Lexie's father.

Lexie knows which words he means. Cursed. Stinking. Unworthy words. Forbidden.

"Never mind your cursed, stinking words," says her mother. She sounds like the maddest person in the world. Lexie's stomach lurches. Her mother sounds as if she's spitting her words on the floor. As if she might bite Lexie's father. "I didn't want you to put in a garden here. You knew that. You had Tommy come over and do it when we weren't here."

"Irene, I told you I was putting in a garden. You can have tomatoes off the vine when you and the children are here in the summer. Half the garden will be tomatoes."

"Who's going to dig the garden? Who's going to weed and fertilize? Who's going to do the picking?"

"Irene, you know I'll do all that when I'm here weekends."

"You work yourself into the ground already. Who's going to preserve the cursed stinking tomatoes when all of them come in at once? A garden is more work—that's all it is to me. We already have a garden, in the city. Two is too many."

"Try to keep your voice down, Irene. You don't want Ephram to hear."

Lexie's mother raises her voice. "All our money goes to this place. We don't have a life in the city. We're never there. I'm sick of this constant back and forth, back and forth. Two houses to keep up. I don't know where I live. I don't have a real life anywhere. And you're working yourself into the grave."

"Irene, what would you do in the summers if we didn't have this place? You know how hot the city gets in the summer. The second floor of the house is stifling."

Lexie stands up and tiptoes back down the hall to her bedroom. Her mother never has an answer to this. She does like living at the farm in summer. She's a different mother here. She likes Ephram. She visits their Aunt Bea, right across the creek, their Grandma, their Aunt Anna, further along the same concession. She takes Lexie and Graham and Vivian on picnics to the lake, she makes a fire by the creek some evenings after supper and lets them roast wieners and marshmallows. Lexie knows that the bedroom door is about to fly open and her weeping mother will go to the spare room for the night.

Saturday is warm and bright, a perfect May day. After breakfast, Lexie walks out the long lane. Fluffy clouds scud high across the blue sky. All around her, the world is moving and twittering. She walks on one of the two bare tracks on either side of the gravel, smelling the damp earth, even the gravel itself. The sun feels warm on her head. The only proof that her parents' fight in the dark really happened is the way the lumps in her stomach feel. As if they're being pulled apart. It hurts.

She walks past the well and pussy willow swamp. On her left are the cedar trees and the elderberry bushes from whose bitter purple berries her mother will, later in the year, make pies. Lexie can hear the creek this morning, running high. She smells cedar and the muck of the swamp that's between the cedars that line the lane and the creek. In the glinting gaps between leaves, she sees the sharp-edged, green ribbons of coarse, thrusting swamp grass, the buttercups and marsh mallow.

She walks through the depression, puzzling as usual about its power to make her father put his new shirts and ties in a drawer until his old ones fall apart and her mother throws them out.

At the end of the lane is the mailbox, with Ephram's name on it. She raises the creaking door, breaking a spider's web in the process, and sees the weekly paper. On Saturday mornings she usually continues on to her Aunt Bea's and Uncle Tommy's. She hesitates. Her stomach gnaws at her. She takes out the paper and turns back. When her parents are in a fight, she needs to stay home. Almost as if she could hold things together by being there.

Lexie retraces her steps, climbs the rise at the east side of the old house. When she reaches the east kitchen window, she stops and leans into the glass, makes her hands into blinkers like

Uncle Tommy's horses wear, so she can see inside the kitchen.

Vivian has dragged her miniature, red table from the dining room, and is setting it with her child-sized dishes. The dishes are real glass, one blue-painted cornflower in the middle of each. Vivian is putting raisins on the plates. She pours milk into the toy cups without spilling it. Their mother and father are standing on either side of the table. Vivian points at the little red chairs. Her parents look as if they're protesting. Vivian continues to point and command until her parents sit down on the child-sized chairs, opposite one another.

Their father's knees are scrunched almost to his chin. He looks like a little kid. He's just washed his hair, as he does every Saturday morning. The blond strands are unruly; he hasn't yet tamed them with Brylcream. Vivian puts a doll's bib on their mother and on their father. As she pats their father's bib into place, his hair flops on either side of his head like corn silk, when you peel the green leaves off a corn cob. He looks like a girl. Vivian hands their parents forks and knives the size of her little finger. Their father tries repeatedly to spear a raisin with a plastic fork. It skids off the plate, off the table, and onto the floor.

Lexie wiggles out of her sneakers. Shifts her weight to her right foot and uses her left big toe to rub idly at an itchy place on her right calf. She likes being outside, looking in. She sees them; they don't see her. Vivy is the mother. Their father and their mother are the children, who have to obey. They look so ridiculous that Lexie giggles right out loud.

Vivy has their parents laughing now. They're shaking so hard that the table jerks and rattles. The milk spills. The raisins scatter. Even the mess doesn't stop them from laughing. Their father's face is the colour of a McIntosh apple in October. Tears of laughter pour from his eyes. Their mother is mopping her cheeks with her handkerchief. And blowing her nose. As Lexie watches, her mother bends double and laughs so hard that it seems as if she's crying.

Lexie looks at her little sister across their parents' helpless shoulders. You did this, she thinks. You are really something. You are like the magic person in the fairy tales. She bends, picks up her sneakers, and straightens. Feels her breath ride effortlessly in and out, her lumps reduced to harmless peas. All around her is the quick flitter of bird wings, the hum, the flick, the dart of busy lives taking up the work of spring.

She'll go to her Aunt Bea's after all.

ii.
Head-doors

LEXIE'S FATHER'S NOSTRILS ARE AS BUSY as a pair of hands or feet. They don't behave like anyone else's. They are the reason for Lexie's hatred of nostrils in general. And she hates the word nostrils almost as much as what it stands for.

In Lexie's opinion, this is a part of the human body that you are not supposed to notice. Nostrils should be still and unchanging. But in church, while the minister is preaching the sermon, Lexie's father's nostrils turn pink and quiver like a rabbit's nose. They get bigger, then smaller, bigger, then smaller. Her father leans over and whispers in her ear. "Not a note. He's got the whole sermon from memory." Tears stand in the entrance to his nostrils. Without moving her head, Lexie moves her eyes to see if anyone has noticed.

Lexie's family spends summers at the farm of Lexie's father's cousin Ephram. At Ephram's, her father comes in from the hot fields at noon. He picks up the tin dipper, fills it from the bucket of cold well water that stands in the back kitchen and drinks, his nostrils keeping time with his gulps. Lexie wants not to look, but she can't help it

In the notebook she received for her eleventh birthday, Lexie has begun to make a list of her father's rules. She has written "1. nostrils" at the top of the page.

When her father blows his nose on his handkerchief, his nostrils make a whining noise, like a mosquito in the bedroom at night. One evening, hearing this sound for the fourth time that day, Lexie decides to make up her own name for nostrils.

In her mind, at least, she will not have to hear the word. That very evening, she takes her father's forbidden straight pen from the drawer, dips the nib in his bottle of blue ink, crosses the word "nostrils" off the top of her list, and writes "head-doors."

The cluster of rules represented by the word "head-doors" have come from her father's ideas about the care necessary for this part of the body. It's because of Lexie's father's ideas about head-doors that her mother lets the Raleighman right into their city house. She keeps the door locked when the Avon lady knocks. She doesn't answer when the Encyclopaedia salesman taps and stands straight in white shirt and dark pants, his cowlick shiny with Brylcream. But she allows the Raleighman, in his shiny black suit, to puff up the steps of their house and in their front door twice a year. In his suitcase are compartments full of tins and small bottles. Lexie's mother looks everything over. Sometimes she even takes out a glass bottle of coloured liquid and holds it up to the light from the picture window. The Raleighman smiles and nods continuously, as Lexie's mother inspects his wares. Lexie's mother says, finally, that she'll take three tins of medicated ointment.

Their mother buys the ointment, then their father takes over. Every evening, once Lexie and her little brother Graham are in their pyjamas, their father comes upstairs and supervises the saying of prayers and the application of ointment.

The saying of prayers comes first. Now-I-lay-me-down-to-sleep. I-pray-thee-Lord-my-soul-to-keep. If-Isha-Die-before-I-wake, I-pray-thee-Lord-my-soul-to-take, says their father, at top speed, running the words together.

Next, the ointment. When Lexie wants to drive Graham crazy, she chases him all over the farm, listing the rules in a mocking voice. Make sure your index fingernail is well-trimmed so that you do not mar the surface of the ointment more than necessary. Remove a globule of ointment the size of the tip of your index finger. Put one globule in each head-door. Remove another globule from the tin and spread it in a thin layer over the surface of your nose and the lower part of your forehead. Apply the third globule in such a way that none is left over. Never leave the lid off the tin of medicated ointment and never open the medicated ointment at other times.

Their father demonstrates the correct application of the ointment. When he coats the outside of his nose, it becomes shiny and red, like Rudolph's. It shines with a groomed pride. In the light cast by her bedside lamp, Lexie can see the tiny holes in the surface of her father's nose, the holes called pores. Sometimes, at breakfast, there are still little clumps of ointment at the entrance to his head-doors. Lexie moves the box of cornflakes in order to blot out this ghastly sight.

Lexie does open the tin at other times. When the ointment is partly gone, she runs her fingers up and down the smooth hills and valleys in the tin. One day, Graham catches her at this and from then on, he can blackmail her; this is the end of her being able to chase him and scream the rules.

Nights, Lexie falls asleep with the prayer streaming inside her. The only confusing part is Isha Die. She lets the prayer run on and on, concludes that Isha Die must be Lord's wife. As Lexie wafts across the threshold of sleep, she feels a rush of Lord flatten the hairlets of her head-doors as He whooshes past to the medicated fields of the brain, there to curl up for the night in the arms of Isha Die.

The second item on Lexie's list is "2. envelopes."

Every payday, her father puts the exact the amount of money their mother will need for household expenses into a series of white envelopes that he has labelled by category: coal man, Fuller Brush man, Raleighman, groceries, music lessons, and so on. The rule is that money may be spent on the necessities of life and on lessons for Lexie and her brother Graham. The only exception to this is that Chiclets may be purchased once a month and Coca Cola for Christmas day. The envelopes are packed in the high cupboard over the fridge, in an upright row, between two heavy, lion-headed bookends that Lexie's parents received as a wedding present.

Lexie blames the envelope rules for the fact that she and her brother Graham don't get the allowance of twenty-five cents a month that the other kids receive, that they are not allowed their own packages of gum, that their father will never buy the television set that, one by one, the other families on the block are acquiring. Still, when she gets her shiny new tin, turns the lid round and round until it comes off, and sees the smooth unmarred surface of the ointment, she does feel her own head-doors twitch a tiny bit.

In order to stretch the gum treat, their father has a rule. He cuts the Chiclet in half and gives one half to each of his children. Lexie and Graham fight over the tiny crumbs of the sweet, white coating left on the cutting board.

One hot, humid summer day at Ephram's, Lexie and her little brother slide open the heavy doors of the barn as far as they can, turn sideways, and squeeze in to the upper floor. You can get into the upstairs of the barn from the ground, because the upstairs is partway up a hill. Inside, it's a dark cool cave; long thin rulers of sun slant through cracks in the boards that form the barn's wall. Within each ruler of sun, little dots of dust dance up and down. The barn's upstairs smells of hay and old pieces of rusted metal. A buggy and a democrat and a cutter clutter up the floor. Bales of hay are stacked by the walls.

Lexie sits on one bale of hay and makes her little brother help her pile two others in front of her for a desk. She lays a book from the farmhouse bookshelf—*Girl of the Limberlost*—on top of the bales, using it as a hard surface on which to write.

"Sit down on that bale, Graham. Pretend you're a student in my class. We're going to finish our list of dad's rules. Repeat whichever rules you can think of, and I'll write them down in any old order. I'll organize them after."

"Never go in sock feet," says Graham promptly, in their father's rule-reciting voice. "Never do nothing. Never wear new clothes until your old clothes are worn out. Save your elastics."

"Never turn in circles 'til you're dizzy," he continues. "Never say pee or belly or stomach. Never say shut up. Say please be quiet instead. Never say stupid."

"You're going too fast. Wait 'til I get them written."

When she's caught up, Lexie looks at her little brother thoughtfully. "Never eat between meals," she says. Once, she'd asked her father about the five Spy apples he ate every evening at nine o'clock, before he touched his toes one hundred times. "Isn't that eating between meals?"

Her father had hesitated. "I can see why you might ask that," he acknowledged, "but I consider it a meal. My bedtime meal."

"Never go in circles," says Graham.

"You said that one already. Honour your father and your mother," says Lexie. "Never ever give up. Never seal a letter until you're at the mailbox. Never pay the asking price."

"Watch out when a horse lays back its ears," says Graham. "Don't swear."

"You may say doggone it or blue blazes if you feel like swearing," adds Lexie. If something really bad happens, you may say Judas!"

"Always say may," says Graham. "Not can."

"Only when you're asking permission," says Lexie. "Otherwise can is okay. You're going too fast again. Raise your hand when you want to speak."

Graham raises his hand. Lexie writes. Even when she's finished, she waits until Graham's right arm is so tired that he must lay it down and put his left in the air instead.

"Yes, Graham," she says.

"Never marry a Mick."

For a long time, Lexie and Graham thought that a Mick was a kind of dog, because Ephram's dog's name was Micky.

"Why does Dad tell us not to marry a Mick?" Graham had asked his sister one winter evening, at home in the city, as they were putting away the farm animals they'd been playing with.

"Does he think we'd marry a dog?"

"Search me. You know he's loco." Lexie made her index finger circle her ear and shrugged in the direction of the kitchen, where their father was at the table doing paper work.

One day, in the schoolyard, it became clear to Lexie that a Mick was a Catholic. She told Graham. That night at supper, Graham said to their father. "What would you do if I married a Mick?"

Blue fire shot from their father's eyes to his son's. "Cut you off without a penny."

Graham looked across the table at Lexie. Lexie shrugged. Their father never had a penny, so this didn't seem a problem.

"Never drink coffee or tea or soft drinks or spirits," recites Graham. A ruler of sun slants down and cuts across his neck, making his face seem separate from his body.

"Never say hate," says Lexie. Once, she'd asked their father what they could say in place of hate.

"Say, 'I can do without it,'" he'd replied. "Or better still, 'I can take it or leave it.'"

"What if it's a person that you hate?"

"Never hate a person," said their father. "Understand that the person you hate is not evil. He or she is…limited."

Their father won't allow them to say hate, but he does hate certain things, on this Graham and Lexie are agreed. Their father hates peanut butter and carrots. He hates them because that's all he had to eat the year he lived in a boarding house in order to finish high school.

The previous Thanksgiving, Lexie and Graham had made a plan, and had tested their father at dinner. "Would you like a carrot?" said Graham, passing the carrots to their father.

"No, thank you."

"Why not?" said Lexie, to her father.

"I can take them or leave them."

"If you can take them or leave them, why don't you take one?"

"No thanks."

"But you never take one. If you could really 'take them or leave them,' you'd take one sometimes."

"No-thank-you-very-much!" said her father emphatically. He said it the way he said the prayer. Running the words together. He said the blessings like that too, in one breath.

Lexie knows that their father believes that if she and Graham follow the rules, they will succeed in life. She knows that their father sees his children, living in The Future, with money and good jobs and the admiration of ordinary people, limited people, who are still in the present wearing sock feet, saying belly instead of abdomen, and going in circles until they are so dizzy the ground rises up and smacks them on the side of the head.

Lexie straightens and picks up the notebook, pencil, and *Girl of the Limberlost*. "Class dismissed. Tomorrow, when the bell rings, we'll work on subdividing the list and putting it in order."

"Don't read fiction," says Graham. "It's a waste of time. And we forgot another one."

"Which one?"

"Always line the inside of your nostrils with medicated ointment."

"Don't say nostril."

"Why not?"

"Just don't."

"Nostril, nostril, nostril," says Graham. He follows his sister through the space between the heavy barn doors, chases her down the hill, into the farmhouse and up the back stairs, shouting "nostril, nostril, nostril."

Lexie slams her bedroom door in her brother's face. She walks over to the wavy mirror on her dresser and looks in. Sun-bleached hair, sun-burnt nose, freckled face. She frowns and wrinkles her nose. Then she does something that has become a habit with her. Tilts her head backwards to look.

It's late afternoon now, the sun coming in the west window of her bedroom. She can see the sheen of golden hairs inside her head-doors, and beyond that, the darkness. She knows that this dark unlit passage leads to the brain. Medicated ointment must be food for the brain, she reasons, just as the manure her father spreads on his and Ephram's fields is food for the soil. She knows that her father hopes that she and Graham will grow up to have superior brain power. She thinks idly of Lord, lolling with Isha in the medicated fields of the brain, then of her father's head-doors, how they don't behave like anyone else's.

She tilts her head further back. A ruler of sun strikes the mirror, lighting up her head-doors in a new way, and she sees something that she has never noticed in her many inspections. Her own head-doors are shaped exactly like her father's.

iii.
Her Mysteries

HOUSE
They have two houses, a small clean city house that keeps everything out and a big old farm house that lets everything in.

In the city house, not a crumb survives. They can see their faces in the polished furniture.

Into the farm house come burrs, wisps of straw, bits of grass, windfall apples, tin cans hung with worms, caterpillars, kittens, rain, stones, wild phlox, buttercups, daisies, acorns, empty birds' nests, bats, mice, flies, the smell of the barn.

The city house is a dollhouse. Lexie feels as if each room has one wall open, as if her mother can reach into any room and rearrange the family. In the city house, her mother is always home. When Lexie gets up in the morning and goes to the bathroom, she finds her bed made and her clothes tidied when she returns to her room. When she's at school, her mother walks through the open wall of her bedroom and grazes it with her nose, finding her washing, her diary, and her schoolwork.

The phone is in the living room, attached by a short cord to the wall. There are no chairs close enough to sit in when talking. When one of them is on the phone, the whole family can hear the conversation. When Lexie talks on the phone, her words belong not to her but to her mother.

The farm house has eleven rooms, not counting the attic or the basement. It has two stairways to the second floor—the broad front staircase, with its smooth steps made of cherry wood and its rounded banister, and the narrow back staircase made of cheap wood.

The attic and the basement do not belong to the family; they have other inhabitants. The attic belongs to the bats. Their dirt covers the attic floor. At dusk they come alive and crawl through small cracks to the outdoors, where they dip and swerve at high speed through the air surrounding the house. Sometimes a bat flits into a second floor bedroom.

The basement floor is made of cold, hard-packed dirt. There are stacks of wood with loose bark, and a shelf that swings. Down there live the scurrying insects and the scampering mice. At night, the mice come up into the kitchen.

Secret

The old house and the farm it's on are a secret. It belongs to their father and to their father's only living relative. When people in the city ask where Lexie's family goes every weekend and every summer, their father has taught them to say "to Ephram's," never to "the farm," and certainly never to "their farm." Farm is a word they must not utter. If they say the word farm by mistake, their father corrects them: "Ephram's." Sometimes, even their mother forgets and says the word farm. Their father corrects her too.

Lexie and her brother Graham don't know why Ephram's is a secret. Their sister Vivian is too young to wonder why.

Ephram

Ephram comes with the farm. Summers, he lives there. When winter begins, Ephram gets on the train and rides all the way to Texas, to live with his sister, who has a pecan tree in her back yard. There is no such thing as snow in that land.

If Lexie walks around the wood stove in the farm house kitchen, there it suddenly is—the door to Ephram's bedroom. A green vine grows over the outside of Ephram's window, making his room a dark, greenish cave. Afternoons, Lexie can see the outline of Ephram on the bed—a long, dark bump. In the dim, green light, she can't see his face.

Ephram has white hair and no teeth. He comes down to the creek only on the hottest days. When Ephram chews, his nose touches his chin. When they have corn on the cob, he has to take a knife and scrape the corn off onto his plate. The last two fingers on both of his hands are stuck in the closed position. Ephram is bent, and he walks slowly. His dresser is so close to the bed that he can't open his drawers all the way. The table on the other side of the bed holds his pipe, an ashtray, his jackknife, a tin of tobacco, matches, a lighter.

Their dad loves Ephram insanely, as much as he loves tomatoes. Ephram is their dad's only living relative. Ephram and their dad inherited the farm together.

Because of Ephram, their life at the farm is different from their life in the city. Their mother and father are too embarrassed to fight in front of Ephram. If they have a fight at the farm, it has to be a quiet one, upstairs, behind their closed bedroom door.

Their father's eyes are different when he looks at Ephram. The blue fire that's always there when he speaks to Lexie and Graham disappears. Instead, his eyes look like their mother's lamps. Her mother got these lamps as a wedding present. When she turns them on there's a soft glow. She always does her hair and puts on her lipstick with the lamps on. When Lexie looks at her mother's face in the mirror at these times, it looks prettier than usual, softer. This is how her father looks when he speaks to Ephram. Like someone has turned on one of these lamps inside his eyes.

Lexie wants to ask her mother whether their father loves Ephram more than he loves his children, but she knows her mother will boil over if she asks this question.

Ephram has a bad heart. He coughs and coughs and coughs until he's making little wheezing gasps and his face is purple-blue. Then he makes a quick sign with his hand. This means that Lexie or Graham must run to his bedroom and get the bottle of cough medicine from under his bed. The glass bottle is tall, with pale liquid contents. On the paper label, Lexie reads the word Seagram's.

Orange Man

Every summer in July, on this one day, Lexie's father and Ephram have baths in the back kitchen, using water heated on the big wood stove. They shave in the back kitchen too, taking turns squinting into the wavy, scarred mirror that makes your face like a monster's face. They take white shirts out of the deep dark closet in the kitchen that goes way back under the stairs. Lexie's mother irons the shirts.

Their preparations are different from Sunday morning preparations for church. The motions and the costumes are the same. But there's an expression on both of their faces that isn't there any other day of the year, and on this morning they don't hear what anyone says to them. Ephram stages around the kitchen. (Stages is the word Lexie's mother uses to describe Ephram when, later that day, she goes across the creek to see Aunt Bea.) On this one morning, Ephram is like a train. If you get in his way, you'll be reamed right out of this life. It's like the excitement of Christmas, with something deadly mixed in. "What's the matter with Ephram?" Graham asks Lexie, one year.

"Search me," says Lexie, with a shrug.

Before noon, a man named Lott Scott drives in the long farm lane. Her father and Ephram go off with him and don't come home until long after dark.

"Where are they going?" Lexie asks her mother.

"Ephram is an Orange Man." When Lexie keeps standing there with large question marks in her eyes, her mother elaborates. "It's the Glorious Twelfth."

Lexie knows from the way her mother snaps out "Glorious Twelfth" that more questions will not be welcome.

Later, she asks Aunt Bea the question. Aunt Bea stops washing dishes and looks out the pantry window. The soapsuds slide slowly down the plate she holds in her hands. Her hands are bright red from the dishwater. There are tiny beads of sweat among the dark hairs of her moustache. "Ephram is an Orange Man," she says.

Doors

They always enter the farmhouse through the back door. They treat the back door in all respects as the front door. It is years before Lexie even realizes that the door she always thought was the front door is the back door.

It takes a good yank to get the back door open, and it scrapes over the stone floor of the porch with a loud bark. The small porch smells of stacked wood, rubber boots, turpentine, grease, and fly spray.

Their secret house has a front door upstairs as well as downstairs. The upstairs front door is never used. It opens into nowhere, into air. They are forbidden to go near it.

Once, Lexie did go near. It was early morning, just before the sun came up. She'd awakened having to use her chamber pot. It wasn't there, under her bed, so she went down the hall and used her mother's. Coming back, her steps slowed. She stopped at the door, edged forward till her nose almost touched the screen, because the familiar valley and the hill beyond had disappeared. The sky was streaked with gold and purple. Where the valley had been, a filmy mist was rising, taking on tinges of pink and gold from the sky.

As she watched, some of the streaks in the sky got bright around the edges, then turned to gold. Lexie thought that she might be seeing the land of the fairies. Or maybe she was seeing heaven.

Rose

The rose bush grows up the stone wall at the front of the farmhouse. It is pink, its petals silken-slick under Lexie's fingers, the scent when she puts her nose right into a blossom almost too wonderful to be borne. The scent says: there are things in this world you know nothing about—you—Alexia Elizabeth Kerr, eleven years old—things so wonderful that you can't imagine them, things so deeply ecstatic that they are a thousand times better than the fairyland you saw out the door that opens into nowhere. Lexie knows the word ecstatic from reading *Anne of Green Gables* and she knows it doesn't mean happy; it's something better than that.

The scent of the pink silken rose tells her that there exist things that her two lives are not going to give her one clue how to find. Her two lives—this life at Ephram's and her life in the city.

Lexie can bear to put her nose in the rose and feel ecstasy only occasionally. The scent gives her a wish so strong it turns into a longing. The longing makes an ache that takes all day to go away. Once, when she sticks her nose into one of the pink roses, a bee pops out and whines angrily past her eye. It seems to be a warning. Don't do this too often.

Doubles

They have two fathers. In the city, their father is dry and crisp. His blond hair is slicked darkly to his head with Brylcream. To the office he wears suits and ties and rimless glasses. Evenings, he places crumbling pieces of foam between his glasses and his nose because after a day at the office, his glasses cut into his skin. In the city, their father smells of ink and paper and shaving lotion.

At the farm, their father is Jack be nimble, Jack be quick, like the nursery rhyme. He works in the fields until his face is broiling red; even his scalp is red beneath his blond hair. He smells of the fields and the barn. There's a paste of dirt and sweat on his face when he enters the back kitchen and picks up the tin dipper and drinks and drinks and drinks, like their Uncle Tommy's horses. He can drink all the water that's in the pail and send Lexie to the well for more.

While he drinks, his nostrils get larger. Lexie tries not to look when this happens, but something won't let her turn her eyes away until she's seen this ghastly thing.

Their father has two mothers. The one they used to visit had black circles around her eyes and running sores the size of quarters on her body, on account of lying in the hospital bed for so many years. This mother is dead. The other mother is a secret. Lexie's mother says she can't know about the secret until she's grown up.

There are two Lexies. At the farm, she's quick and smart. She can leap like a mountain goat, or even fly. She can take on the form of the wind or a field mouse or an egg snug under down and dried grass. She can disappear. Here, she's the leader. Graham and her first cousin Ruth are her lackeys.

In the city, she's clumsy and lacks essential knowledge. At school, she watches the others, stays quiet. She never knows what the other kids are talking about; her family has no TV at home; they're never in the city on weekends. Lexie is never picked to be the leader. She's the last picked for the teams.

At the farm, her mother is two mothers: one mother when their father is at the farm and one when he isn't. Their father has only the first two weeks of July for vacation. The rest of the summer he's at the office, in the city. When their father is not at the farm, their mother sits and has coffee with Ephram, laughing at his stories of the West. She goes to visit her sister Beatrice, across the valley, and her sister Anna, half a mile along the hilly, gravel road, and her mother and brother, a little further on. She sweeps and roots out, but not as often.

When their father is at the farm, their mother is mad. She waits until he comes in from the fields, then—once they get electricity downstairs at the farm—she gets the vacuum out of the kitchen closet and runs the brush up and down and across the downstairs windows. Or she scrubs around his feet with short, jerking swipes, cleaning up the bits of straw, dried shreds of manure, dead insects, mice droppings, cat hairs, dog hairs.

In the city, their mother is two mothers as well. Inside the dollhouse, she's the boss. She gives orders, gets mad, fights with their father in the bedroom or kitchen. Outside the house, she's a mouse. She wears a little smile to the store, to church, and in front of the neighbours. Her mother is afraid of the people at church, afraid of the neighbours. She thinks city people are "well bred," wise in city ways, secretly looking down at her, a country bumpkin.

Most of the time, Lexie's mother stays in the house and the yard. They never have company except when one of their relatives comes down from the country. The inside of their house is not good enough to be seen by city people.

Her father is two fathers in the city too. At the office her dad is the boss. At Christmas and on his birthday, he gets cards from the people who work for him. The cards have little letters on them, thanking him for his helpfulness, his patience—people telling him they could never do their jobs without him. Lexie wants to ask her mother about these letters. The letters say the opposite of what their mother says about their father. Lexie knows her mother would boil over if she asked.

At home, their father is like Aunt Bea's hen—the one with hardly any feathers on its rump. Aunt Bea says this hen is the lowest in the pecking order. Their father is the last one to get his bath. He gets the worst jobs—doing the supper dishes, going to the basement for preserves, washing the car in winter, carrying their tricycles and bicycles up and down from the basement every day, digging the garden, weeding it. He has no say in anything.

At five minutes to nine in the evening, their father goes to the kitchen and touches his toes one hundred times. He's an up and down blur, like the handle of a pump gone crazy. Then he gets down on the floor and does one hundred pushups without stopping or letting his knees touch the floor.

After that, their father goes down the basement stairs and into the fruit cellar where there is a bushel of spy apples. He picks these apples every Thanksgiving from the old trees at Ephram's and he has them stored, for a small amount of money, at a Meatkeeper's in the city, getting a bushel out of storage whenever he runs out. He returns from the basement with six large, spy apples.

Standing at the kitchen sink, he cuts each apple into eight pieces. He turns around and offers the apple on the knifepoint to his children. Lexie and Graham usually refuse the apples because they taste like meat and because they have scabs on their skins and the occasional worm in their flesh. One evening, Lexie counts as their father eats. Forty-eight pieces of apple. Lexie's mother is never in the kitchen for this performance, so it passes in silence but for the sound of their father's chewing. A word comes into Lexie's head as she listens to her father chew. Mastication. She feels her neck and her cheeks turn red.

When no one is around, she looks up the word in the dictionary. To grind or crush food with the teeth—that's all it means.

Bats

Lexie has read about bats in the *Books of Knowledge*, volume one. The picture of the bat with open wings takes up a whole page. It's the wings she stares at the longest—huge, leathery, with human veins, like those on her grandmother's hand. The arms are the most horrifying. The bat's arms are in prison inside the wings, as if caught in a spider's web. The bat in this picture looks as if it's crucified, forever hanging in its own wings, like the picture of Christ on the cross at Sunday school.

On the next page, Lexie reads that an evil spirit can take the shape of a bat; even the Devil himself can do this—come right into your body while you're asleep. It doesn't say how the bat gets in, but Lexie knows. First it winds itself in your hair, kicking and fluttering, then, invisibly, the evil spirit comes out of the bat's mouth and into your ear, and right into your body.

The bats fly only at night. In the day, they stay in the attic. Lexie was in the attic once, before she knew the bats lived there. At the other end of the long upstairs hall is a room full of extra furniture, and boxes—a storage room. At the end of this room is a locked door. Only her father has the key. On that day, her father unlocked the door and she followed him up a flight of narrow stairs with two twists. They came into a large room with rough bare boards and a window at either end. The sun was coming in one of the windows. There were large trunks and suitcases and stacks of boxes everywhere. You could taste dust on your tongue. Her father directed her to look out the window at the other end of the attic. She was up so high and could see so far that she felt as if she were seeing the whole world.

"Look up there," said her father, pointing at the rafters. Lexie looked. It took her a long time to know what she was seeing. Rows and rows of upside down bats. She shrieked. Ran down the twisting stairs, screaming, through the storage room, down the narrow back stairs, around the bend near the bottom where her mother stood with her eyes popping out and her hands white with flour—*what's the matter, what's the matter*—through the door of the back kitchen, through the porch, into the yard, around to the front of the house, over the fence, down the path through the field, across the creek, up the lane, bursting into Aunt Bea's kitchen, throwing herself into her arms, sobbing, as Aunt Bea, not knowing what was the matter, held her and patted her hair.

It's a horror beyond bearing that one of these creatures sometimes flits through her bedroom at night when she's asleep and defenseless, unable even to know enough to go under the covers. She's tried sleeping under the covers, but after a while the air doesn't seem like air anymore and she's gasping for breath.

Books

In one of the downstairs front rooms is an organ that works only if they pump the pedals hard with both legs as they play. There's a bookcase in this room. Five books: *Swiss Family Robinson, The Chautauqua Girls At Home, Lone Bull's Mistake, Girl of the Limberlost, Anne of Green Gables.*

Every summer, Lexie reads these books over and over. She reads each of these books hundreds of times. From them she learns words that become her words. Of the five books in the organ room, Lexie reads most often *Girl of the Limberlost*. Elnora Comstock lives with her mother at the edge of the Limberlost, a large wild tract of bush and swamp. Elnora was born to a life of drudgery—farm chores and housework. Her mother doesn't love her. A little way into the Limberlost, just off the main trail, Elnora has made a room for herself inside a clump of bushes. In the room she keeps a large padlocked wooden box. Inside is a mirror, a butterfly apparatus, books, and other odds and ends. Elnora calls the box her case. When Elnora goes to school, she is shunned and teased because of her country clothes and her ignorance of what the city kids are talking about.

Elnora's nearest neighbours are Wesley and Margaret Sinton. Margaret is Elnora's second mother. Margaret's two little girls died of diptheria, so she gives all her mother-love to Elnora.

Lexie pretends that she is Elnora Comstock. Aunt Bea is Margaret, her second mother. When Lexie is shunned and teased at school, she pretends that Elnora is right beside her.

Pecker

Lexie and Graham and their cousin Ruth, Aunt Bea's daughter, sit on the log that fords the big creek and bake in the sun before they go in swimming. They lower themselves onto the big flat stone one at a time. There's a pecking order. Lexie, Ruth, Graham. Lexie keeps her running shoes on. There are leeches in this water. She's as scared of leeches as she is of flies and bats.

The water is warm and golden brown. A needle alights on the board near her hand. It has a bright blue body. Ephram calls them dragonflies, but she and Graham call them needles, copying Ruth, who lives on the farm year round and knows more about such things than they do. There are minnows and chub and stonefish in the water. Trout. Ephram has seen an otter down here, early in the morning, when he fishes. He's seen a muskrat and a great blue heron.

Lexie scrapes brown stuff off the flat stone with her feet, so that it's clean and not slippery. Only then does she take off her running shoes and set them on the log.

One hot summer day, Ephram comes slowly down the hill to the creek. Lexie stands on the flat stone and watches him. He's through the fence and coming along the squishy path. He doesn't avoid it by using the big stones, just lets his boots get mucky. He's wearing his old yellow bathing suit and his boots. His legs have knobs and bumps and purple streaks and splotches. A mottled blue tube hangs half way to his knees.

"What's that?" Lexie says to Ruth.

"What?"

"Hanging down his leg."

Ruth pulls herself up to the log and gawks. "It's his *pecker*," she hisses. She grabs Lexie's elbow hard. "It's his pecker." She throws herself off the stone in a frenzy of giggles. Lexie and Graham dive off the flat stone in quick succession. They dog-paddle downstream, kicking extra hard with their feet. They lie on their backs and kick so hard that the water rises into the air like a fountain and rocks against the creek banks. They squeal and shriek and belly flop and thrash.

Ephram is crossing the board across the little creek, coming to the big log. He drops his blue towel on the grass beside Lexie's striped red towel. The thing is still there, hanging down.

"It's like the dong on the bull," Ruth hisses into Lexie's ear.

"Come on," Lexie screeches at Graham and Ruth.

She paddles past the willow into the sunny, shallow part of

the creek, where they never go. The stones scrape her belly. She's half floating, half crawling, scraping her knees and her hands on the stones.

Ephram sits down on the flat stone, creek water to his neck. Not for long. Five or ten minutes. Once he's cooled off, he climbs out, over the stones, and plods back up the hill. He pays no attention to Lexie, Graham and Ruth.

Enemas

Lexie's mother tells Lexie and Graham that they have to have an enema. Their mother sets the tallest white chamber pot that's like a pail in the storage room that leads to the attic. She tells Lexie that when she has to go, that's what she should use. She takes her daughter into the middle bedroom and makes her lie face down on the bed with her pants down. She puts a tube into the hole in Lexie's bare bum, squeezes a large round bulb. Lexie feels the seas of the world rush up inside her, headed for what she breathes with, threatening to drown her from within. She runs for her life to the chamber pot, releases a dramatic rush of brown river.

Her mother hovers in the hall. When Lexie comes out of the storage room, her mother looks like someone who's had a gold star placed beside her name on the teacher's chart.

Her mother says she has to sterilize her apparatus, then it'll be Graham's turn. She catches Graham that once, but ever after, Graham is like the cat who sees the cat cage or the suitcase or hears the rattle of car keys, and knows he is about to be taken to the vet. Even in their small city house, Graham is able to hide so well that their mother can't find him, and must put her equipment away and turn to another task.

Eyes

There's a fire in their dad's eyes. His eyes can kill or command or mesmerize. Shards of blue ice, swords of blue fire. Blazing beacons that must be answered, followed, obeyed.

Their mother's eyes are like the odd marble among the clear marbles they keep in a faded-pink, corduroy bag in the toy box in the city. The odd marble is green and brown and yellow, with black specks here and there.

The creek is an eye. An eye that never blinks. Not the whole creek, just the swimming hole beside the log where they cross, where the willows overhang. The creek bulges there, and the willow hides the far end of the bulge, so its shape looks round. You can see the round creek eye better from the door that opens into nowhere, better yet from the top of the hill behind the house. The eye gleams and shines, as if tears were wetting its surface. If you look into this eye, you can see the trees and the sky.

The swimming hole is the eye of the farm. That's what Lexie thinks. It watches all their comings and goings. It's different from her mother's eyes. Her mother's eyes watch, and the next thing you know, her mouth is talking or her hands are doing. The eye of the farm watches and says nothing. It might ripple, or gleam, or change colour, but it's silent about what it sees.

The eye of the farm understands. It makes a note of everything it sees and stores it somewhere under the water among the stones and the crayfish. It's never shocked and it never forgets.

Their mother's eyes see everything, just like the eyes of the shiny new houses on their city street. Even at recess time, their mother's eyes are looking over the silver fence, watching to see whether they have friends or whether they're off by themselves moping, whether they're chosen first or last or not at all for the baseball team.

One Sunday morning this very summer, when the whole family was at the country church, the minister described Lexie's mother. This shocked Lexie out of her church daydream.

The tiny church is only a five minute drive along the dusty gravel road. Lexie can see corn growing in the field outside when she looks through the window. Usually, in church, she's thinking about her hat. White straw with a wide brim, a white ribbon and a blue flower. Or about her dress, the same shade of blue as the flower on her hat, lace down the front and around the collar. Or she's looking at her white shoes with the two buckles, or at her white gloves with the tiny pearl buttons.

On this Sunday, the minister announces a Psalm, then starts to read something that makes Lexie forget her hat and tremble in a place below her rib cage. *Whither shall I go from thy spirit? or whither shall I flee from thy presence? If I ascend up into heaven, thou art there: if I make my bed in hell, behold, thou art there. If I take the wings of the morning, and dwell in the uttermost parts of the sea; Even there shall thy hand lead me, and thy right hand shall hold me. If I say, Surely the darkness shall cover me, even the night shall be light about me.*

That afternoon, back in her farm bedroom, Lexie copies the words from the order of service onto one of the curling pages in her little notebook. She changes what needs changing: *Whither shall I flee from thy presence? If I go to my bedroom, thou art there. If I go to the bathroom, thou art there, outside the door. If I go to the schoolyard, even there do thy eyes find me. If I go to sleep in the dark in the dark and pull up the covers, thou creepest in with a flashlight, searching around the hole in my bum for pinworms. If thou foundest this notebook, thou wouldst read it. When I talk on the phone, thou listeneth.*

Lexie hides the notebook in a drawer, under her clean underwear.

Vivian

Vivian is the favourite of every single person in the family. Lexie was seven-and-a-half years old when her baby sister was born. Every time their mother put Vivian down, after feeding her, Vivian would cry.

"Just leave her," their mother always said. "I have more to do than spoil a new baby."

Lexie never left her. She picked up her little sister and walked the floor with her. She loved the feel of Vivy's soft, damp cheek against her own, the gums with no teeth that sucked on her little finger when she put it in the baby's mouth. The round spot on Vivy's head where Lexie could see her heart beating. She pretended she was Vivy's mother.

Whenever their mother bakes, Vivian stands on the chair. She knows what goes into the muffins and the applesauce. She asks their mother questions like: "Do you want the measuring cup? Do you want the measuring spoons? May I grease the pan?" Their mother never boils over at Vivy's questions.

Sometimes Lexie watches them. Her mother's black hair and Vivian's blond hair curl the same way. The bone at the back of their necks sticks out exactly the same. Their shoulders have the same slant.

Once, when Vivian and their mother were rolling the dough for curly cues, Ephram looked at Lexie and winked: "Your mother and Vivian are cut from the same cloth."

Graham

Aunt Anna says that Graham is a sturdy boy, a handsome boy. Graham's skin is the colour of the toffee that Lexie looks at longingly in the city corner store. Graham's hair is the colour of maple syrup in a glass jar. Lexie wishes she looked the way Graham looks. But she doesn't wish she was a boy. She likes getting dressed up in her blue dress for church, making paper clothes for her paper dolls, pretending she's Vivy's mother. She wishes she looked like Graham, that's all. Graham is maple and honey and toffee, while she is freckles and red peeling sunburn and questions that make her mother boil over.

Her mother never turns on Graham, never spits out the words at him. She never scolds him for not doing his chores. Lexie wants to get Graham in trouble.

Hiding Place

Lexie pretends that the bush to the west of the barn is the Limberlost. Halfway along the path through the bush, you turn and go down the hill to the creek. At the bottom of the hill are half-fallen evergreens. Other wild young trees grow there in a crowded clump, and when she lifts the right branches, there's a sort of room, made by nature. Inside is a log, a carpet of brown crumbling leaves and dead needles. A short slide down—the creek.

There's a seat she has scooped out here, where she sits, her back against a tree. The floor of her hidden, outdoor room slants downhill, and the bottom third of the space is the creek, running through the lowest area of her room, an overhang of evergreen boughs, their lowest tips almost touching the water. Vivian is the only person Lexie ever brings to her hidden room.

Lexie goes to her room often. She kneels before her case and opens it so that she can see the contents, then settles with pencil and notebook.

She needs to think about the mysteries of her life.

The mysteries: House Secret Ephram Orange man Doors Rose Doubles Bats Books Pecker Enemas Eyes Vivian Graham. Father father father. Mother mother mother.

iv.
Fullness of Time

LEXIE RUNS DOWN THE BACK STAIRS of the farmhouse and into the kitchen to stand beside her mother at the counter. Her mother is pulling pin feathers from the rear end of a chicken. Lexie shrinks from the naked goose-bump skin and the faint odor of little dead body that no one ever believes she can smell. Her mother always says that if she can smell that she must have the snifter of a hound dog.

Lexie looks at her mother's efficient damp hands, the bits of feather that cling to them. A question has been in her mind for days.

"Blighter!" Her mother spits the word, as she twists a pin feather and the flesh of the chicken tears.

Lexie moves a step closer. "Mom, I've been wondering. Why are we on earth? What's the meaning of life?"

The August day is hot and humid. Her mother sets down the chicken and shakes a straggle of black hair away from her damp forehead. Her greeney-brown eyes look at her daughter as if she has just stepped off Mars. Her mother's eyes, their disbelieving stare, make Lexie remember that her white, china chamber pot is still beneath her upstairs bed, unemptied. Sure enough, her mother's stare turns into a question about the chamber pot and ends up as a listing of her daughter's faults. Lexie is saucy, selfish and sneaky. She's a show off. And lazy.

"Now go outside and make yourself scarce," her mother finishes, stamping her foot for emphasis.

Lexie slams through the screen door and sticks her feet into torn sneakers. She never knows when her mother will boil over. The scoldings spatter her skin and leave it smarting.

Scuffing her sneakers along the damp grass, Lexie wanders into the west yard between house and barn, where the horses are standing together, under the old maple. The skin along their withers twitches and bunches, and their manes and tails pass ceaselessly over the clumps of flies that seethe around their eyes and along their haunches. One of the mares blows from soft oval nostrils. The rasping chirr of the cicadas ebbs and flows from the maples that surround the outer yard.

She climbs the rise to the knoll in front of the house, from which she can see across the valley to her Aunt Bea's. Her father stands on this knoll when he wants to tell Aunt Bea something. He yodels so loudly that Aunt Bea hears him in her kitchen, where the radio is always on. (Here, the radio is on only for the news and for In Memoriam, the program that announces who is dead.) They have phones, but Aunt Beatrice is on the Bethel line and they are on the Rilling line. To phone Aunt Bea would be Long Distance, and therefore out of the question.

A cow bawls and her Uncle Tommy's voice comes, high and hectoring. "Get on outta that, yuh crazy old fool." Lexie knows he's bunching the cow's tail up hard against her rump, shoving her out the stable door. The back kitchen door bangs—her aunt setting out the blue plate that holds bacon rinds for the barn cats.

Lexie goes down the hill and across the creek to visit her aunt so often that her mother says, "You're going to wear out your welcome." Once, her mother said, "You're over there so much, Bea's almost your second mother." Often, Lexie argues with her mother. But not about this. She likes the idea that Aunt Bea is her second mother.

Still smarting from the scolding, Lexie decides to go to Aunt Bea's this very minute, though she knows her chores are undone. She climbs the fence that borders the front field. The long grass on both sides of the path is up to her chin. At the bottom of the hill, a rail fence. She can just squeeze through the space between fence and post if she turns sideways and holds her breath. The path here is soggy but she jumps from one big stone to the next and avoids the muck.

As she crosses the log over the creek, she looks down into the golden-brown water. On the bottom, the stonefish are silent shadows. On the other side of the creek is another rail fence; this one keeps the cattle from going on the road. She climbs up and swings her leg over the top rail, still slippery with morning dew, and stops to eat raspberries growing wild in the ditch. Gigantic mosquitoes hang in the deep shade. They begin to light on her brown arms. She shakes them off and runs up the gravel lane, past the barn, past the old pump, and the swing.

Aunt Bea's inside back porch smells of manure and dog, with a hint of hard-packed dirt cellar floor mixed in. Nutty is lying full length on the cement of the inside porch. He raises his head slightly and his tail thumps once as she comes in. In fall and winter, the porch smells of apples too.

Aunt Bea is sitting at the kitchen table. On the blue-checked oil cloth is a bowl of raspberries. Lexie's aunt is fat, her mother is thin. Her aunt has curly brown hair and a line of friendly brown whiskers between her nose and her mouth. Her mother's skin is smooth and clear there, though Lexie sees the occasional black dot on the skin along her mother's upper lip. Her aunt wears house-dresses, short white socks and tough-looking brown shoes that tie. Her mother wears slacks and shorts, sleeveless tops, sandals. Her mother is "citified." Lexie has heard her father say that. Lexie's family lives on the farm only in the summer, and on weekends and holidays. The rest of the time, they live in their little house in the city. Aunt Bea's family lives on the farm all the time.

Lexie asks Aunt Bea the questions.

Her aunt straightens, wipes her hands on her apron, and plants them on her hips. She laughs. "Well, Lexie, you do beat all. Sit down and have a scone; then you can help me with the berries." Her aunt breaks a scone in two, lathers it with butter, hands half to her niece and takes half for herself. She brings the scone partway to her mouth, making a delicate pausing gesture, her little finger separated from the others and curved in a refined way. Aunt Bea has manners.

The phone rings, two longs and a short. "That's Mary's ring," her aunt says. "I have to listen-in. Hush now, Lexie, there's a lamb."

Aunt Bea goes to sit on the stool by the phone. She picks up the receiver, says nothing. Listening in on the party line is something all the farm ladies do. Lexie's mother calls it eavesdropping. When Aunt Bea finally gets off the phone, she does the whole conversation for you. First she talks in the one person's voice, then the other. When she's finished, she hugs herself and laughs and rocks back and forth. Lexie has never seen her mother listen-in.

Today, Aunt Bea doesn't act out the conversation. She returns to the table, sits down and picks up her scone. "We're in this world because the good Lord put us here, Alexia. We don't know why." Her aunt lifts a forearm and wipes the sweat from her temples. "We'll know in the fullness of time."

Lexie takes another bite of scone, tastes the butter and the fluffy white interior, chews the one raisin contained in this mouthful. Her mother says Aunt Bea is ungenerous with her raisins.

"Can you finish these berries for me, Lexie? I need to attend to the dough. Just pick out the bad ones, there's a lamb." Her aunt slaps the dough down on the kitchen table, punches it, pushes it, folds it, slaps it down again.

"The fullness of time." Repeating her aunt's phrase over and over, in her head, Lexie picks out the bad berries, eats the best ones, puts the rest into the cut glass bowl. She likes to work with her aunt. Aunt Bea is slow, like her. She doesn't get her midday dishes done 'til mid-afternoon. Lexie's mother can peel five potatoes while Lexie peels one. Sometimes her mother snatches her potatoes and finishes the job herself. Her mother can finish washing the dishes, then more than half of Lexie's drying. Sometimes her mother gets mad and says Lexie is worse than no help at all. Once, she said, "You're no child of mine."

Above Aunt Bea's dinner table is a long sticky spool, with dozens and dozens of flies stuck to its length. Lexie has heard her mother say to her father that she can't believe that Bea keeps that filthy, fly-swarmed spool right above the table and doesn't seem even to see it. This morning, as Lexie sits at the table picking over Aunt Bea's berries, she notices that one of the flies on the spool above is still alive. She keeps her eye on its almost invisible struggle to lift off, knowing it will fail. She wants to see the exact moment when the fly passes from life to death.

"Tommy'll be about ready to feed the pigs," her Aunt Bea says, looking at the clock. "If you hurry, you might catch him." Aunt Bea knows that Lexie's favourite thing is watching her Uncle Tommy feed the pigs.

Lexie runs to the barn, pounding her feet and raising the dust. As she enters the dark interior, she can make out Uncle Tommy, bent over, lifting two heavy pails. His arms are turned almost inside out from their weight.

When the pigs hear Lexie's uncle, and smell the chop, they put up such a frantic racket, squealing and screeching, that you can't hear anything else. Lexie covers her ears with her hands, but she likes the way the pigs scream. Her uncle drops the chop into the trough, followed by the water, then releases the board that lets the pigs at their dinner. The racket stops instantly. This is Lexie's favourite part. The screeching is so loud, so desperate, that you think it's something that would have to last forever. Then it stops. Completely. Dead silence, every time. Maybe there are other things that seem as if they have to be forever, but could be stopped this easily, if only you knew how.

This morning, in the silence after the squealing, she and her uncle hear the Austin shake and rattle, then stall on the steep driveway. "That'll be your mother, over for the eggs," says her uncle. They hear the crunch of tires on gravel that means her mother has the clutch down and is backing the stalled car back down the hill. Then the sound of the car whining up the hill in creeper gear.

Lexie waits until her mother is in the house before returning to the low cement porch by the kitchen where the orange barn cat is nursing her kittens in the sun. She lies down on her side on the warm cement beside the mother cat and watches the kittens open and close their small claws against their mother's fur. She hears her name and realizes that her mother and her aunt are talking about her. Her mother says something she can't hear. She holds her breath, the better to hear her aunt's reply: "Lexie puts me in mind of Vinny McSweeney. You can't predict her either. She's not your usual. But don't forget, Irene, everybody loves her."

Lexie keeps holding her breath. She wants to make space for her aunt's words to go inside, where she can keep them. She feels the hot sun on her hair, feels the words move inwards. When they're firmly lodged behind her ribs, she lets herself roll off the cement stoop, jumps to her feet and gallops to the opposite side of the house and into her aunt's garden. The day is lighter and greener than it was earlier this morning.

Aunt Bea's garden stretches from one end of the yard to the other, its paths made of hard-packed earth. The corn and the raspberry bushes are so high that Lexie is almost hidden when she follows a side path to the carrot bed. She crouches, looking for the tallest, sturdiest stem. The trick is to grasp the stem where it joins the earth, so it doesn't break before you get the carrot out. The one she chooses today comes out easily. She takes a tin pail from beside the separator and runs to the outdoor pump, lifting her feet off the ground and hanging on the handle to make it come all the way down. When her pail contains enough water, she plunges her hands in, swishes and rubs the orange root to remove the dirt. She breaks off the carrot's whiskers, then sits down on the pump stand to eat, while she waits for her mother. Held secure by the bone wall of her ribs are Aunt Bea's words: "But don't forget, Irene, everybody loves her."

As she chews the sweet root, she pictures the fullness of time billowing towards her. It raises a dust like the dust that rises behind her Uncle Tommy's stone boat, when the horses pull it across the brown field in spring. The dust is dramatic and glorious. It makes everything around it disappear—her uncle, the two horses, the rumpled field, the pale sky. From inside the dust appears The Good Lord. His white raiment is miraculously clean and shining. He steps forward, ready to tell her, Alexia Elizabeth Kerr, the meaning of life.

V.
Flies

AUNT BEA STANDS THERE, in the hot sun, watching Lexie and her mother. She looks like Bella, the most friendly of the Hereford cows, the patient way she bears the sun. Lexie thinks of a phrase from her favourite book, *Girl of the Limberlost*. The dumb endurance of the beasts. That's the look her Aunt Bea has. She'd never dream of frantically shooing flies. She could ride in a car full of flies, have them crawling all over her, and do nothing more than shrug them off every now and then. Lexie longs to be like her Aunt Bea, free of the misery caused by flies.

There's no shade in Aunt Bea's driveway, so Lexie's mother has left the car windows rolled to the bottom. Without having to be told, Lexie opens both back doors of the Austin to their widest point and rolls up the back windows. Her mother does the same in front. Lexie gets into the back seat, her mother into the front, and both of them go into a frenzy of fly-shooing, their arms and even their legs flailing, their bodies lunging from one side of the car to the other. The two of them look like a pair of windmills gone crazy. When only a few flies are left in the small car, they slam the doors shut in unison.

Lexie's mother starts the car and Lexie crawls over the gear shift from the back seat into the front. They wave goodbye to Aunt Bea. As soon as the car has a little speed, Lexie rolls down her window and her mother does the same. They work at shooing the few flies that remain out the open windows. The ride home to Ephram's will take less than five minutes. A large bluebottle fly bangs against Lexie's mother's cheek, then buzzes angrily on the inside glass of the windshield. The car lurches and her mother swats the air. "Blighter!"

Lexie and her mother are the same in how much they hate flies. Especially the upstairs farmhouse flies that her mother calls cluster flies. Lexie's mother is in a war with all flies but especially those. Lexie is her mother's spy and ally in this war. The upstairs farmhouse flies are fat and half-stupid; often they're on their backs waving their legs, unable to sit up. When they fly, it's a heavy, blundering flying; their wings seem as if they can't support their bodies. Often they bang into Lexie's face, or her hair. They seem in their clumsy way to be not going about their own business, as the outdoor flies do, but aiming for her, Lexie; they seem to want to crawl across her fair, freckled skin, deep into her thick blond hair, to bed down and buzz, to crawl over her scalp, to swarm and seethe around her ears, perhaps even right inside her ears while she is asleep, into her mouth and down her throat, around her eyes, where they'll cluster in the corners as they do on the eyes of the horses and the cattle. They might even crawl up her nose while she's asleep, up her nose and into her brain, where they could lay their eggs and hatch in the same crevices where her thoughts and feelings are being born, and turn her into a crazy person who has to be locked in the insane asylum in Goderich, only a twenty-minute drive away.

Right after breakfast, right after lunch, and again before bed, Lexie's mother fastens a long extension cord on the old vacuum and plugs it in downstairs, there being no electricity upstairs. She hauls the vacuum up the back steps, runs the small brush fiercely up and down and across the windows of each of the five bedrooms, sucking flies by the dozens, by the hundreds, into the tube. She sprays the windows of all the bedrooms several times a day with Raid. She comes running upstairs with the red fly swatter or the Raid container whenever Lexie calls down to tell her that more flies are in the windows. Aunt Bea's swatter has tiny shreds of fly wings and fly blood sticking to it but their own swatter is smooth and clean, because Lexie's mother scrubs it and sprays it after every use.

The Austin groans up the steep rise beside the farmhouse. Her mother parks the car at the fence in the shade of the Melba tree. Here at Ephram's, where they live in the summers, they can leave the car windows shut, because the car is in the shade. Lexie follows her mother up the little hill to the small enclosed back porch. Her mother keeps the porch door shut when it's this hot. She keeps the porch sprayed so a million flies won't get into the back kitchen every time somebody opens the inside door. The back kitchen is cool. Lexie's mother closes the heavy inside door firmly, takes the carton of eggs to the kitchen. Lexie lifts the tin dipper off its nail, dips it into the pail of cold water that's on the long narrow bench by the back door, and drinks deeply.

That night, Lexie wakens in the dark. She hears a muffled buzz, so close it seems to be inside her ear. She screams for her mother, screams as if the floor were cracking open and a monster rising from the darkness to take her away. Her mother's feet rush down the long upstairs hall to her bedroom. Her shadow leaps on the wall, huge and jagged. She sets the coal oil lamp on Lexie's bedside table. She searches the length of the bed, strips the covers and sheets one by one. Finally, she lifts up Lexie's pillow. There, on its back, lies a huge, half-dead fly. It pedals the air weakly with its legs. Lexie screams till her face is hot and her eyes straining to pop. She screams the horror of having this fly under her pillow while she lay asleep, unable to save herself.

Her screams have wakened the whole household. Graham is standing in the bedroom doorway. Their father appears behind Graham, Vivy in his arms. Graham steps forward. His face is white, his eyes big.

"I'm going to leave and never come back," their mother

says, when she sees their father. "I can't stand this any longer."

Lexie throws herself against her mother's legs and bawls her protest at this new horror. Graham adds his cries to hers. His chin trembles and two streams of snot roll from his nose.

Their father comes right into the room. Vivy is screaming almost as loudly as Lexie now. "Not in front of the children, Mommy."

Their mother raises her voice. "I'm beyond caring what the children hear. I go 'til I drop, but it's never enough. No matter where I turn, there's more to do." She kicks the vacuum. "More cursed, stupid flies, more cursed, stinking rubber boots. Rain coming in and ruining the wallpaper. Mice in the kitchen, bats in the attic. I'm fed to the teeth." Their mother grabs Vivian from their father and puts her face right up to his. "And don't 'Mommy' me. One of these days, you'll come home and find me gone."

The next morning when Lexie wakes up, the sun is right in her bed, instead of being a small patch on the floor by the window. She can smell coffee and fried trout. She hears the clang of pails across the valley at her Aunt Bea's, the bawling of cattle, the barking dog. When she goes downstairs in her pajamas, her mother and Ephram are drinking coffee and chatting in the kitchen, the sun a wide golden stripe across the floor. Her father and Graham aren't around. Vivian is on the floor with the sun, playing with the orange and tiger kitten that has four white paws.

Everything seems normal. Look as she may, Lexie can see no trace of the night's horror, no slowly spreading circle, not even a few wavelets nibbling at the day world's shore. The horror is in the night. The day knows nothing about it.

vi.
The Accident

THE PATH TO THE OUTHOUSE has been worn smooth by their bare feet. It winds through a grove of spruce. Under the trees is a coating of brown needles, a scattering of cones. A thick gum that turns your skin black and sticky oozes from the bark of these trees.

The outhouse door is always wide open. It's trapped in the earth. The grass has grown up around it and the soil and roots have taken it over.

Lexie looks at her little brother. He's lost the fight for the small hole this morning, as usual, and his bum is hanging over the large hole, the one at the far end, so that he's facing the light that comes in through the open door of the outhouse, and she can see clearly the colour of his eyes. The same as their mother's—cow plaster-brown and dragonfly-green, all mixed up. Her brother shifts slightly on the wooden seat. If just one of his hands lost its grip, his body would fold in half and slide into the darkness.

Lexie has no idea that this is the last morning Graham's eyes will look their familiar selves. This August day has begun like any other. They ate breakfast; their mother sent them here, to the outhouse.

Their mother decorates the outhouse with a new coat of wallpaper every summer. Every day, she scrubs the wood around the holes with cleanser. She dumps soft, gray ashes from the wood stove into the holes. Still, Lexie can smell the outhouse. A smothered, dull smell that might grow up to be a stink.

Graham says he should get the smaller hole because he's not as big as Lexie. The large hole is so big that both of them are afraid they'll lose their grip on the worn gray board and slip through the hole into the dark world they try not to look at when they climb aboard. Lexie says Graham's not as big, but his bum is bigger. Even though she's three years older, girls' bums are smaller than boys' bums, she tells him.

As they sit on the holes, side by side, they gaze at the huge hill that's behind the farmhouse and the outhouse. Above and behind it, the sky curves like a cow's belly. On top of the hill, Lexie has a nest. Up there in the long grass is the only place she really feels away from the scrutiny of her mother's eyes.

Every morning when they return from the outhouse, their mother says the same thing. "Did both of you do a B.M.?"

Every morning, they reply in the same way. "Yes."

This morning, they watch the wind stir the white heads of the wild carrot. They sit until they have a red line where the edge of the outhouse hole presses into their flesh. If they stay long enough, the kitchen table will be cleared and the dishes done. When Lexie gives the word, she and Graham will slide down from the wooden seat, pull up their shorts, and retrace their steps through the pines and into the farmhouse kitchen.

She's about to give the word when Graham turns to her and says he thinks they might go to hell.

"Why?"

"We tell Mommy a lie every day."

"Listen, Graham, Mommy's stupid. She sends us here, to do this, as if we could make happen. But it's something that just happens by itself, when it wants to. We're only kids, but even we know that. Mommy's dumb. What can we do but lie to her? God understands that."

"Oh," says Graham.

"Do you want to have to sit here all day, 'til your B.M. happens by itself?"

"No."

"Then don't be bringing up hell."

Later that morning, Lexie climbs by herself to the top of the hill behind the house. The cicadas are a shrill ebb and flow against her ears, a swarm of tiny flies dances around her head. Her heart thumps in her chest and in her ears, the day hotter than she'd thought when she began the climb.

She hangs her head like Queen, her uncle's workhorse, and slows to a plod. At the top, she flops sideways in the long grass. She's often seen Queen lie like this on a hot day, her dappled gray belly rising and falling. Lexie rolls onto her back and lets her eyes wander the blue. Up here, in the humming, chiming morning, no one but the hawks in the sky can see her.

When she sits up, she sees Graham through the curtain of tall grass. Way down there, staggering across the farmhouse yard. Playing the game of turning himself round and round 'til he's dizzy. Their dad is at work in the city, but if he were here, Graham wouldn't be doing this. Going in circles is forbidden. Her dad has never said why, but Lexie knows. You might stay that way for life, unable to walk a straight line, staggering from place to place like a crazy galoot, always in danger that the earth would rise up and smack you hard on the ear.

Graham's skin is tanned the colour of toffee. Lexie's Aunt Bea says that Graham is a beautiful boy, a sturdy, healthy boy, like her own son Petey. Graham's hair is the colour of maple syrup when their mother holds the glass jar up in front of the window. Everybody says Graham looks like their mother and Lexie looks like their father—blond hair and red, peeling sunburn. Freckles. Graham's toffee skin never burns or peels.

Still watching her brother, she stretches her leg and prods a dried cow plaster with her foot. It disintegrates onto her running shoe. She doesn't think Graham is a beautiful boy. He's a brat. He runs to their mother and cries over every little thing. He tattles. Their mother turns on Lexie and blames her. She wants Graham to get in trouble for a change. She wants her mother to call him a clumsy, bumbling fool, a careless oaf. A simpleton. A plan is forming itself in her head. She sits still and lets it blossom.

A gust of hot wind lifts her bangs. She jumps to her feet and turns herself into the roan calf. Sideways, she galumphs and half-slides down the steep hill, kicking up her hooves to avoid the fresh cow plasters.

"I saw what you were doing," she shouts at her brother, as soon as she's close enough to make him hear. "You'll be in big trouble if I tell dad when he comes up on Friday night."

Once the supper dishes are done, and they've watched *Front Page Challenge* on Ephram's black-and-white TV, Lexie and Graham go for the milk. They make this journey every evening, but tonight something is different. Tonight, after supper, before putting the butter away, Lexie scraped some of it from the plate onto a page she's ripped out of a *Family Herald* magazine. The paper is scrunched in her hand.

Graham is just ahead of her. In the field to their left, the white cattle are dark shapes against the slanting orange light that comes through the trees of the bush west of the barn. She can smell the creek from here, the stirring of slightly cooler air that comes from its surface.

As she and Graham cross the log bridge, a frog honks. Below, water striders jerk on the surface of the water. She smells the black muck along the creek banks, the wild mint. Between creek and road is the rail fence, clammy wet against their bare legs as they climb over.

Up the gravel hill to their uncle's barn. They stop outside the stable door. Willie the bull is tethered just inside. At the first sound of Graham, Willie jerks on his short metal chain. Graham pushes open the door, and Lexie sees one red eye. She and Graham stay so far back from the bull that their left arms brush against the rough, cool, cobwebbed stone of the barn's wall. Willie is the husband of every cow on this farm and the father of every calf. This is the reason for the blue-murder look in his red eye.

The dark corners and beams of the stable are hung with nests of swifts and spiders' silk. She's seen them in the daytime. She and Graham pass behind Willie, then King and Queen, Uncle Tommy's workhorses. They pass the pigpen, its sharp smell, so fierce tonight that they start to run. They climb over an empty stall and land where the cows are tethered, chewing their cuds and waiting their turn.

Their uncle is on a milking stool, his head butted into Bella's belly. His hand slides hard down her teats, and the milk makes a loud steady ping against the side of the tin pail. Graham crouches in the gutter just out of reach of the cow's back legs.

Stay here, she tells her brother; I'm going to the house for a minute.

She disappears into the darkness of the barn, slips past Willie and out the door. Her heart crashes into her ears and her stomach flops. Instead of going to the house, she half runs, half slides down the gravel lane. Over the damp rail fence and onto the log bridge. It's almost dark now. In the middle of the log, where the creek is deepest, she sits down, one leg on either side of the gray board, and spreads the butter, rubs it in with the paper until the area is greasy and slippery. She shoves the paper into her pocket and hurries back up the hill to the barn.

When they emerge from the stable, Graham is carrying the warm sealer of milk intended for their porridge the next morning. The milk has a bluish tinge and it tastes watery. Lexie doesn't like it.

The moon is almost full. Their feet on the gravel make crunches that are almost impossible to hear because of the crickets' loud, chirring song. Ephram says the crickets are a sure sign fall is coming. Lexie holds the warm sealer for Graham as he climbs over the rail fence, then gives it back to him. She can feel the thump of her heart. Graham walks ahead of her over the log bridge. When he reaches the buttered place, he slips, takes a long, staggering step, screams, and falls in with a thudding splash. He falls near the edge, where the water is shallow, where the big stones are. The sound of glass shattering. Her brother screams again.

Almost immediately, her mother is in the side yard, up the hill at the farmhouse, and her aunt, on this side, is in her yard, both of them calling down, asking what's going on.

Graham is on all fours in the shallow water at the creek's edge, choking, crying loudly. "Graham fell into the creek," Lexie shouts, trying to make her voice heard over her brother's.

"I'll go, Irene," her aunt calls. "I'm closer."

There's a frantic quality to Graham's screams. He turns his head, looking for his sister, and by the light of the moon, Lexie sees a wash of darkness on his face. Her brother tries again to climb over the slippery stones onto shore. Lexie's heart pounds so loudly that she can barely hear anything else. She scrambles to the creek edge and pulls a handful of muck, crawls to the centre of the flat log and spreads it on the buttered place, scrubs it with the heels of her hands to remove the grease and is barely off when Aunt Bea arrives, calling Graham's name. Moving quickly down the hill on their side of the creek is her mother's dark shape.

Lexie crouches on one of the smooth boulders, her arms wrapped around her body. Through Graham's choking screaming sobs, she hears her aunt's voice. "It's his eye, Irene. We have to take him to the hospital. Tommy's in the barn. I'll get him to bring the truck."

Lexie stares at the silver path the moon makes on the creek where the water flows through the open field on its way to the bush. Here, beneath the willows, the eye of the creek is secretive and dark. Silent.

It's a long wait, with Ephram, before anyone comes home. Lexie is upstairs getting ready for bed when she finally hears the Austin on the gravel of the lane, and as the car turns into the west yard, the lights come through her bedroom window. Then darkness, and a minute later, the back screen door opening and shutting.

She tiptoes to the landing of the back stairs from where she can hear what her mother is saying to Ephram, in the kitchen. It's not Graham's eye exactly, it's the skin just above his eye, below his eyebrow. He's been taken in the ambulance to the big city hospital where a plastic surgeon will fix it. Their father is there already. He'll have scars, but he'll still be able to see.

Lexie's legs feel as if they might not hold her up. She imagines going down the last three steps, to the kitchen, sitting at the table. She imagines her mother hitching one of the wooden chairs close to hers. Her mother's greeney-brown eyes looking straight into hers, her voice: "Lexie, Graham says he doesn't know how he fell in. What happened? You didn't push him, did you?"

"Of course not, Mom. What do you take me for?"

She knows what her mother's reply would be: "Well, what happened? The broken glass cut Graham around his eye."

"I don't know."

"You should have been watching him. I count on you to do that. He's only seven and a half years old."

Crouched on the landing, Lexie feels as if she might cry. She intended only for her brother to fall into the creek, to be shocked and wet, to get in trouble for being a clumsy oaf and wasting the milk. She never dreamed he'd have to go to the hospital in the city. She imagines her mother's eyes looking inside her and seeing the black lie. She tiptoes back up the stairs, avoiding the places that creak. Folds the clothes strewn on the floor, places them neatly on a chair. Gets into bed and curls into a burr.

Much later, she hears her mother coming up the front stairs and down the hall to her bedroom. A familiar smell of Jergens lotion as her mother comes in and bends over the bed.

She feels her mother's hand smooth the damp bangs off her forehead. Her touch is gentle. A hard dam that was in Lexie's throat breaks. She clenches her muscles until her mother leaves the room, then feels the scald of tears on her cheeks and neck. When she thought up the plan, it had seemed a little bad, but harmless. She opens her eyes. In the darkness, she sees Graham's face as it looked this morning in the outhouse. How will it look when he comes home from the hospital?

A thin twist of cool air from the creek makes its way through her bedroom window and crosses the room to where she lies. It hesitates by the side of her bed, then reaches out cold fingers and moves them along her neck and face, coming to rest on her forehead, just above her left eye.

vii.
Blossom

IN THE BASEMENT OF THEIR CITY HOUSE is a wringer washer. Lexie has begged her mother to allow her to operate it, and today her mother has given in. Lexie leans her belly against the hot thumping body of the machine, pleased that even her useless dead-end finger of an appendix is getting all shook up. She fiddles with her blond pigtails and looks at her freckles in the dim basement mirror over the laundry tub. Her mother is telling stories of children who were not careful. Children whose finger (hand, arm) went through the wringer.

Lexie wants to know more. Why did they let their hand get too close, was the hand flat forever, did it feel like getting born, did the hand have to be cut off, did these careless children scream the kind of scream that brought neighbours running from blocks away, was the ambulance called, was the ambulance pulled by a horse like the milkman's cart, would the ambulance be delayed by the horse arching its tail to release hot buns so strong your nose hairs lay down and died?

Lexie's mother knows nothing. All she can describe is the moment of carelessness, the instant when the human hand strayed too close and was seized.

Suddenly, her mother hauls off and whacks the white metal. Lexie springs back, her heart lolloping against her throat. The wringer flies apart. Its helpless insides are displayed before her. "If ever the wringer takes your finger, God forbid, hit that spot with your free hand," says her mother, snapping the wringer together, and disappearing up the basement stairs.

The two black cylinders of the wringer move toward one another. Lexie fishes with the smooth stick in the dirty rinse water, as she has seen her mother do, pulls up a bulgy, water-swollen pair of jeans, a ballooning navy-checked shirt. She feeds them to the wringer. They are sucked in, streaming water; they emerge on the other side reamed into flat stork shapes. To feed the smaller items, such as socks, Lexie must put her fingers closer to the moving cylinders. She wonders if it was really carelessness, in the children who got caught by the wringer. The more socks she feeds, the closer she moves her fingers, until they are pushing the socks right up to the moving crack. The more often she does it, the more certain she becomes that the children deliberately moved their fingers closer and closer. The longer she stands there, feeding socks, the more afraid of herself she becomes.

She's relieved to hear her mother's voice, calling her upstairs.

In the kitchen, her mother hands her the cold, plastic-encased rectangle of white margarine. Lexie has to squeeze the orange eye of dye throughout the hard block until it becomes an even yellow, and looks like butter. She hates this job. Her fingers ache and get cold as they squeeze and push the dye.

Supper is silent. Lexie's parents aren't speaking. When her mother clears the table of leftover salmon loaf, mashed potatoes and tinned peas, she clatters the knives and forks loudly against the plates. As she sets down Lexie's bowl of tapioca pudding, she says, "Don't blat that mark of yours all over the neighbourhood."

That afternoon after school, Lexie had waved her spelling test under her mother's nose. Fifty out of fifty. As well, a letter from the principal announcing a series of spelling bees—school, city, district: Provincial Champion Speller. Lexie's mother had said nothing, but her mouth turned down when she read the letter. She has worked hard to slap her children down and round them off; she wants them to blend in, not stick out. "Who do you think you are, anyway?" she once said, when Lexie taped a perfect test to her bedroom mirror. "The Queen of Sheba?"

Lexie pokes at the pudding with her spoon. "Ugh. Fishes' eyes and glue. I hate tapioca pudding."

Her mother jumps from her chair so quickly that she knocks it to the floor. "I'm sick and tired of your remarks." Her gaze travels the table. "I'm fed up with all of you. I spend the whole day washing and ironing your clothes, shopping for food, cooking your dinners. I'm nothing but a slave. And all I get is sauce and back talk." Her mother bangs into the table and causes Lexie's brother's milk to slop over. She hurries down the short hall and slams her bedroom door. The house is so small that Lexie's parents' bedroom is only five steps from the kitchen. Three-year-old Vivian tiptoes after their mother.

Graham says he doesn't want his fishes' eyes either. Their father says nothing. He eats his own pudding, then Graham's, then Lexie's.

While their house was being built, they went regularly to look at it. On their first visit, to the foundation, Lexie had felt her heart shrink and become hard. It sank below her waist and hung there, bumping her belly button from within. She said it out loud. "This hole is so small. Will our new house be this small?"

"Once the house is built, Lexie, it won't seem small," said her father. He was holding a leather-bound box. A Brownie camera received by Lexie's mother as a gift when she was twelve. Lexie's father had often explained that this was 1930, when a camera was an unimaginable treasure.

Her father took a picture of Lexie and her mother looking into the hole. He handed the camera to Lexie so that he could turn his back on the sharp November wind, take out the white hanky Lexie's mother washed and ironed every week, and blow his nose. "Don't drop Mommy's camera into the hole," he cautioned.

Lexie leaned over to look into the foundation and dropped the brown, leather-cased camera into the hole. She didn't do this on purpose. It just happened. A hard swing from the hanging heart of her disappointment.

Her father and mother turned on her. In their eyes and on their foreheads, she read that she was a bad girl.

Lexie's father carries the empty bowls to the kitchen sink. He's so thorough in his eating that there isn't even one fishes' eye stuck to the inside of a bowl. He cleans the table, then reaches into the bottom drawer of the kitchen buffet and with grand, crackling gestures unfolds the lists. Their father is the opposite of their mother. He works hard to make his children stick out above the multitudes. He works especially hard on Lexie, his firstborn. The lists contain long words that are difficult to spell. On the right hand side of the page is the meaning of each word and a sentence that includes it. "Mr. Brown moved his family to new accommodation when he got a raise." Lexie's father picks a word, and Lexie must spell it, at top speed. When she makes a mistake, her father corrects her and moves on to the next word. Later, he re-tests Lexie on the misspelled words. Lexie's mother absents herself every night while this drill is going on. If she has to come to the kitchen for something, her movements are jerky, her mouth pressed tight.

Lexie's father has eyes that can command or cast a spell or wither. They contain slivers of blue ice. Fire, too. Blue fire. Her father fastens his blue eyes on Lexie and she understands without him saying a word that it's her destiny to become Provincial Champion Speller.

The house turns out to be a dollhouse, just as Lexie predicted. Her mother shines and polishes until the surfaces of the furniture hurt Lexie's eyes and make fun of her face with their angled, sliding reflections. Her mother is always home; her eyes see everything. While Lexie is at school, her mother grazes her room. At recess, her mother's eyes find Lexie and Graham in the schoolyard.

Tonight, as her father smoothes out the lists, Lexie hears her mother sobbing in the bedroom, then blowing her nose and murmuring to four year old Vivian.

Lexie spells "accommodation" with two c's and one m. Her father gets her to chant the word five times, breaking it into clumps: Acc-omm-od-at-ion. After this, he washes the dishes, as usual, and while Lexie dries, he drills her on the multiplication table, making up rhymes so she will remember. Twelve times twelve is one hundred and forty-four. Shut your mouth and say no more. Six times eight is forty-eight. Eat your meat and clean your plate.

Finished with the multiplication tables, her father has her spell "accommodation" once more. He follows his daughter outside, to supervise her hanging of the yellow-striped dish towel on the clothesline. As she places the second peg on the damp material, he says, "Ahh ... Alexia, as far as I'm concerned, it would be ... acceptable for you to reveal your spelling mark, if a grownup asks how you're doing in school."

Lexie shoves her feet into her sneakers and runs from her father's words. She knows that he wants to be the puffed-up father of the best student in the class. Behind the row of new houses are hills of soil. The hills belong to Lexie and the other children who have moved here. Evenings, they run and jump up and down and around the hills, wearing paths smooth, creating hideouts and way-stations and lookouts. The side of the hills that is hidden from the parents is where the roughest jostling and sliding and barefoot leaping into space goes on. Lexie pretends she's a mountain goat.

Beyond the hidden side of the hills is a field of long grass. It's so tall that when Lexie walks through it she's a swaying and a flash of colour only. She can lie down in the grass and disappear.

For the rest of the evening, she runs and digs tunnels on the side of the hills that is hidden from the parents. As she runs and jumps, she hears the chant in her head: "Acc-omm-od-at-ion."

All that spring, her father drills her. As the skipping ropes circle and circle for the dancing feet outside in the long, bright evenings and the hopscotch stones flip from square to square, Lexie memorizes the exceptions to "i before e except after c," repeats that accommodation has two "c's" and two "m's," that allotment has one "t" and allotted two. Stared at by the intensely yellow margarine, she notes the one "r" in occur, the two "r's" in occurred and occurrence, learns that memos has no "e," and medicine two "i's." By the time the week of the Spelling Bee arrives, Lexie contains rows of rules and columns of silent, obedient words. Her father tells her she's invincible.

On the sweltering first Friday of June, the contestants sit in a row on the stage of the school auditorium. Facing them are the students from kindergarten to grade eight. Lexie looks at the staring eyes and feels a strange sensation. The columns of words, tilting, running together. Her father has taken a half day of his annual two week vacation from the office; he's in the front row, beside the vice principal. His eyes blaze as brightly as the sun in a July sky. Lexie avoids them, as best she can. If she looked directly into them, she might go blind.

The principal calls her name second. Alexia Kerr. His voice seems to be coming from far away, although he's in front of her. As she attempts to stand, her shining chair of varnished walnut sticks to the sticky pink flesh of her legs, stretches the flesh away from her muscles, releases it at last with a reluctant rip and a clunk. On smarting legs, she straightens to receive her first word.

"Blossom," says the principal. "Roses blossom in June."

A sensation that's becoming familiar, a doom walk over a trembling floor that she can't stop herself from taking. "B-l-o-s-o-m," she spells.

The red creeps up her neck and onto her face and ears. It stays there and burns her for the whole time it takes the principal to eliminate the other contestants one by one. She does not look at her father or meet the other staring eyes. She twists her hands in her lap and silently spells the words with which the principal tests each contestant. She gets every single one right. At last, the principal crowns Gordon Youngblud the winner who will proceed to the next level of the contest. Lexie has beaten Gordon Youngblud in every class spelling bee this year.

Bulldozers come to the street. They take away the caves and the hiding places. They flatten the hills of dirt into rectangles for seeding as back yards. A machine cuts the long grass behind the hills and makes it into a schoolyard. A silver steel fence is erected between Lexie's back yard and the school property.

Now, instead of bounding up and over a mountain and rippling through long grass, Lexie leaves her house by walking down the straight, bright street. She knows the mothers' eyes are upon her. The mothers in the small, new houses know what time the fathers come out of the houses in their white shirts, which children go to the Protestant school behind the new silver fence and which children go to the Catholic school in an older part of town, where tall trees shade the sidewalks. If a family has a visit from the minister, the doctor, or the teacher, the mothers' eyes know. If a family gets a new appliance or a mother gets a new outfit, they know.

Lexie walks along the straight, white sidewalk in the bright light. She holds her shoulders firm and takes tiny breaths. Everything that might attract attention she rounds off and pushes in. She makes sure that the eyes see nothing to report.

viii.
Beyond Aunt Bea's Garden

THE OTHER PLACE IS SO HIGH that Lexie feels as if they're traveling to another land. Lunch over, they're on their way to pick the blackberries. Their mother puts the Austin in creeper and they grind up and up and up the gravel hill, the car straining and groaning, a billowing of white dust behind them. It's as if the car is alive, and this job is too much for it. Lexie holds her breath and tries to make herself lighter; her brother Graham crunches his legs and his arms against his body. At the top of the hill, their mother stops the car and wipes her face with a hanky, as if she and not the Austin had pulled them up. Their father's cousin, Ephram, takes off his hat and wipes his forehead with the back of his hand.

The Other Place is the name their father has given to this land a quarter mile from Ephram's. There are no houses or barns up here; it seems a wilder country. Their mother parks the car under a tall elm tree beside the deserted gravel road and the four of them set off along the hilly, dirt track towards the bush. All around Lexie as she walks is the whole seething, rasping, heat-dazed symphony of August. The sun beams its force into her head and presses down on her shoulders and neck, grasshoppers shoot in every direction, some batting against her face, sparrows make quick trips from one thorn tree to another, cicadas saw against her eardrums, orange butterflies flitter across her path. Years later, she will look back on this day and watch herself, eleven years old, walking that dirt track. Innocent of what is going to happen.

Just when she thinks that the hot plodding trek in her long pants and long sleeves will last forever, the path curves and dips sharply. In front of them is a live electric fence; they hear the telltale tick. Her father keeps cattle here, at The Other Place; they are out of sight on this hot afternoon. Lexie's mother sits down and beckons to the rest of them to do the same. She's wearing the straw hat that has hung on a peg in the back kitchen for as long as Lexie can remember. The sun makes little speckles on her face. Their mother takes off the hat and lies down, then all four of them, including Ephram, get on their backs and squirm carefully under the fence.

In the bush, the symphony comes to a sudden stop. It's shady and quiet and almost cool in here. The trunks of the trees are huge and the sun is in the leaves at the tops of the trees, not down here; only a few long golden swords slice through and reach the ground. Graham takes their mother's hand. Lexie has told her little brother stories about the foxes and wolves in this bush, the children they've dragged to their den and mangled, then eaten. When Graham said he didn't believe her, Lexie marched him to their parents' bedroom and placed her hand on the Bible that lay on the nightstand. She looked into her brother's eyes and said, "I swear in the name of the Father and the Son and the Holy Ghost that every word I have told you about The Other Place is true."

Graham said he still didn't believe her but his lower lip quivered.

Lexie has tried to be nicer to her brother since he came home from the hospital with a red scar right underneath his eyebrow. Every time she looks at it, she's reminded that she caused it to be there. But despite herself, she's still mean. She's never mean to her sister. They've left Vivian behind, today, with Aunt Bea. Lexie pleaded with her mother, promised to look after Vivy, to carry her all the way across The Other Place if need be, but her mother said there were too many dangers on this expedition to bring along a three-year-old child.

They walk in single file through the bush, their mother leading, Graham still holding their mother's hand. Next comes Ephram, then Lexie. They follow the shady path until they arrive at the top of the high banks.

Lexie tiptoes to the edge. The river is far, far below. The banks drop away from Lexie's feet. They go straight down, overgrown with thick vegetation and scrubby trees. If she stands still and turns her ear sideways, she can hear the river.

Her mother motions her away and starts along the path that follows the top of the high banks. Lexie stays where she is, listening, forming in her mind the words to describe this journey to Vivian when they get back home. Secretly, she thinks of her little sister as her child. Vivy waits at the window every day for Lexie to get home from school. Sometimes Graham takes Vivian to the barn and lets her watch while he currycombs his horse. He shows her where the barn cat has hidden the new kittens. When her brother takes Vivy away, Lexie feels a simmering in her stomach and a hard place at the back of her throat. She wants her little sister all for herself.

She hears Graham now, whining about something, and runs to catch up. Her brother is more of a baby than her sister. The path begins to slope gradually downwards. In places, the gnarled tops of tree roots reach across their way. To Lexie, they look like massive arms, there to trip the unwary. Gradually, the trees become further apart. Their mother calls that they're almost here. They emerge into hot sun, at the level of the river. Now Lexie can hear the rush of the water without even straining her ears.

For what seems like hours, then, they pick blackberries in the afternoon heat. Mosquitoes whine out of the shade and veer away from the smell of the repellent their mother greased them with before they left the back kitchen. Little claws on the bushes tear at Lexie's long sleeves and leave tiny blood speckles across the backs of her hands.

Their mother fills her honey pail first. She goes and picks

beside Graham, helps him to fill his pail, scolds Lexie when she sees her sneak a berry to her mouth. Sweat runs into Lexie's eyes. She's conscious of the white knobs she's leaving behind on the bushes, conscious of her purple fingers. Their mother is wearing a torn, white shirt of their father's, with pale, blue, up and down stripes. Lexie notices a berry stain on the front, near the top button.

Under their clothes are their bathing suits. When they've finished picking, their mother sets the pails in the shade of a stone pile and covers the tops with tea towels held down by large rocks, then leads them along the swampy path to the river.

They're so hot they can't wait to get into the water; even Ephram can't wait. With their feet, they rub away the slippery brown silt that covers the rock bottom, and sit down in the warm, brown, lazy water. It comes up to Lexie's shoulders and up to Graham's mouth. The water smells of summertime. A horsefly torments Graham, but leaves her alone. Lexie sits there in water up to her shoulders until the skin on her hands shrivels. She stays in longer than anybody. She pretends Vivian is there, beside her, in the water, wet to her ponytail. Next summer, she'll teach Vivy to dog paddle. She does the dead man's float on her stomach, letting her long hair spread on the surface, feeling the current carry her slowly downstream. She opens her eyes underwater. A yellowish-brown, murky world. Minnows wiggle by. She stays in until they call her out for peanut butter sandwiches and lemonade. Their mother has built a small fire, and with his jackknife Ephram has whittled the willow sticks with which they toast marshmallows. Lexie pulls off the hard golden shells with her fingers and shoves the gooey melt into her mouth. She eats as fast as she can, devouring twice as many marshmallows as Graham.

After the picnic, she's groggy. Contented, except for her shriveled hands. The warm stickiness of the day wraps its arms around her. Their mother is in a good mood.

Lexie has no idea that she has just lived the last afternoon of her childhood.

Aunt Bea hurries out of the house as they drive up her hilly lane. Before the car even stops, Lexie sees that something is wrong. Her aunt's face is white. Her hair net is torn and hanging to one side.

Lexie's mother opens the car door and gets out. Aunt Bea takes hold of her sister's arms. "Irene, I don't know how to tell you. We ... Vivy is missing. We can't, we haven't ... been able to find her."

Lexie's mother's face turns the same colour as Aunt Bea's. She moves her mouth but no words come out.

"She's been missing for half an hour, Irene. Maybe a little more. She was on the front step with the black and white kitten. I went into the bathroom for a few minutes. When I come out, she was gone. I searched the yard. You know there's a fence all around this place."

Their mother looks like a statue.

"Tom is ... down at the creek. I've been phoning the neighbours. Irene, I'll never forgive myself. I..."

Their mother's lips give silent jumps and twitches, like a horse's skin when a fly is bothering it. Without a word, Ephram turns and heads for the creek. His shoulders look like the setting-off-to-war shoulders Lexie has seen on a soldier in a book.

She looks over at Graham, then opens the back door of the car and stands on the sharp stones of the laneway. Her legs feel like someone else's legs. Graham crawls out her door and stands beside her.

Their mother lets go of Aunt Bea. Aunt Bea takes hold of the open car door; her fingers look like the chubby fingers of a little girl. Their mother runs for the house. Her straw hat falls off.

"Where's she going?" says Graham. "Does she see Vivian?"

Lexie stares. Her mother does look as if she's seen her daughter and is running towards her. She veers around the house and comes to a sudden halt in the front yard just before it begins to slope downwards, the spot where Aunt Bea stands when she wants to call across the creek to tell them something.

"Vivian," their mother yells. "Viv-eeee-aaaaan."

"Viv-eeee-aaaaan," comes the mocking echo from across the valley. Then silence. The bark of a neighbour's hound dog.

"Viv-eeeeeeeeee," their mother yells again. It's not a yell this time. The sound makes Lexie's skin prickle all over. It's the sound a wild animal makes, in the bush at night. Graham moves closer; she can smell the river in his hair.

Their mother waits. She turns her head sideways, to listen. The echo comes again. Then nothing. No answer.

Lexie remembers a sentence from her favourite book, a book she's read maybe a hundred times. *Girl of the Limberlost*. She knows the exact words. *The only thing on earth of which Elnora knew herself afraid was her mother; when with wild eyes and ears deaf to childish pleading, she sometimes lost control of herself in the night and visited the pool where her husband had sunk before her, calling his name in unearthly tones and begging of the swamp to give back its dead.*

This is when Lexie knows that Vivian is really lost. The way their mother is yelling—if you were anywhere, you'd have to answer.

Just last week, Lexie's mother and Aunt Bea were retelling familiar stories about their aunts and uncles and cousins. Auntie Gert, whose dress caught fire and who was burned to death right in front of her six children. Their cousin Nell. How Nell's mother had died, having her. How Nell's father had been drowned in the river six months later, leaving Nell an orphan. Cousin Josephine, who everybody thought was barren. Who unexpectedly at forty gave birth to a longed for baby girl. How the child had drowned in a rain trough outside the stable just before she turned two.

"The Lord works in mysterious ways," Aunt Bea had said. She always said that after these old stories had been retold. Lexie, listening, had thought: nothing like that ever happens to us. Now something has.

Lexie imagines no Vivian at the window when she gets home from school. No Vivian to read to. No Vivian to take to her secret places on the farm. Her legs feel as if they won't hold her up; she moves closer to Graham and leans against the car and it comes to her in a sickening rush that without Vivy there will be no meaning in her life. No happiness. She lets herself down onto the sharp gravel, her head against the warm metal of the car door. A sickly-sweet liquid rises in her throat. Marshmallow. A minute passes. Maybe an hour.

All of them hear the phone. Aunt Bea's ring. Lexie has never seen Aunt Bea run, but she runs now, into the house.

Right away, almost, she's back outside, her arms in the air, running towards their mother. "They've got her, Irene, she's safe, she's safe, she's at Anna's. Lord be praised, they've got her."

Their mother sinks onto the grass. She laughs and laughs and laughs. She leans her head back and howls. The echoes come back, jumbled and crazy.

Graham looks at Lexie. "Is Mommy laughing or crying?"

Aunt Bea's face is wet. Their mother is on her knees in the grass. She looks up at their aunt. "I thought she was at the bottom of the creek, Bea."

Aunt Anna has brought Vivian home to Aunt Bea's. Aunt Bea has carried kitchen chairs outside and placed them on the grass beside the garden. A big red sun is on the horizon. The round ball of it seems to fill the whole sky. "Another fair day tomorrow," Ephram says, when this kind of sun appears at the end of a day.

Vivy is on their mother's lap. The slanting orange rays come across Aunt Bea's orchard and her garden—the long rows of raspberries, potatoes, corn, radishes, carrots, lettuce, tomatoes—and finally across them, on their circle of chairs.

Aunt Anna tells the story. She heard the dog barking and went to the door of the back kitchen. There was Vivian, her face red as a raspberry, blond curls dark with sweat. She beamed. "My got out," she said. "I runned all the way."

"The little tyke," says Aunt Anna. "That's a good half mile from your place, Bea. It's a miracle she didn't get lost."

"I runned all the way," says Vivian, looking up at their mother, who puts her face down in Vivian's damp hair.

Aunt Bea says, "How be I bring out that brick of maple walnut ice cream I was saving for the men. Lexie, come and help, there's a lamb."

In the kitchen, Aunt Bea cuts the hard, cold brick with the bread knife. Lexie carries out the plates one by one, a square of pale beige ice cream sliding on the white, china surface, a spoon teetering on the edge.

They eat their ice cream in silence. Lexie smells sweet peas and hay and grass and manure. She smells the Melba apples that have fallen and split open in the orchard grass on the other side of Aunt Bea's garden. She chews the bitter pieces of walnut in her ice cream and suddenly is no longer quite steady on her chair. A thought, a surety, has come to her that will make all the days of her life before this different from all the days that follow.

Some day my mother and father and Aunt Bea and Uncle Tommy and Ephram and Aunt Anna will be dead. All of them. Only Graham and Vivian and I will be left. Somebody else is going to live here. When I'm old, I'll come back to Aunt Bea's and everybody will be gone.

She looks at the friendly brown hairs above Aunt Bea's lips. At the little bump on Aunt Anna's nose. Her mother's bare ankles with one red place that she keeps reaching down to scratch. Aunt Bea's white ankle socks, how they've slid beneath the bones on her shins almost into her brown shoes. Her mother and her aunts are like the trees that have always stood here beside the pump. How can it be true that one day they'll be gone forever? The momentous thing fills her, pushes at her from the inside. She feels as if she might burst.

    Each spoonful of cold ice cream that slides down her throat makes her shiver a little, her bathing suit still damp under her clothes. The big red sun has slipped below the horizon now. Beyond Aunt Bea's garden, the whole sky is on fire.

PART II

Soft country air on our burnt red faces. Crickets, frogs, the crunch of tires on gravel, an occasional stone pinging against metal. Dark shadows, the black sky, a moon one night away from full. Smell of the Sanasateen.

No one says a word. This is Kerr country.
    —"The Sun is Out, Albeit Cruel"

ix.
Europe on Five Dollars a Day

WHEN MY SISTER VIVIAN WAS SEVENTEEN, I received a letter from my mother. In those days we would not have considered using Long Distance for a conversation that might last more than three minutes. I was married and living in Toronto; I had been out of the nest for almost a decade. The letter began with my mother telling me she was having difficulty raising my sister to be *the girl God would have her be.*

I was familiar with this phrase. *As a Canadian Girl in Training, it is my purpose to cherish health, seek truth, know God, and serve others, and thus with His help become the girl God would have me be.* We had recited this every Monday evening in the United Church basement, at the beginning of each Canadian Girl in Training meeting. For five years, I had dutifully attended these meetings, wearing my white middy blouse with navy sailor collar. Vivian, almost eight years younger, had inherited my uniform but not my staying power. She dropped out after three months.

In the letter, my mother informed me that at the beginning of the summer, her sister (my Aunt Bea), had taken her aside and told her that the Concession was ringing with talk about Vivian. The party line buzzing. Vivian had been sighted climbing a silo in her bikini, her body gleaming with tanning oil, hands slippery on the rungs. She was "inebriated." Not only that. Vivian had been seen traveling the gravel roads with boys in fast cars.

My mother's handwriting became smaller and darker on page three of the letter. In early July, Vivian had started going out with Vernon Stackhouse. My parents had been worried, but thought that it surely would not last. But one week ago, Vivian had accepted a ring from Vern. "Your sister is engaged to be married to her *first cousin.*" My mother had underlined the last two words of this sentence with a black crayon. There were shreds of black wax stuck to the paper and in the envelope.

At the end of the letter was a postscript written by my father. "As you know, Alexia, your sister and Vernon are cousins. The products of such unions are not always scholarship material."

I was twenty-five that summer, and until the moment of reading this letter, I had automatically taken the opposite point of view from my parents' on all matters. For instance, my mother had taught me to wash out the feet of my stockings every night without fail. As soon as I moved away from home, I began to wear my stockings day after day until I figured they were dirty enough to throw in the load of wash I occasionally trundled out to the Laundromat. My mother had taught me to eat nutritious meals. Therefore I stopped at Loblaws each day on my way home from my job teaching high school and bought a Sara Lee cake for dinner. When she was twelve years old, my mother had placed her hand upon the Holy Bible and pledged never in her life to drink alcohol. Therefore I drank a beer every night with my Sara Lee cake.

Part of me wanted to sit down at the teak table in the dining room of the Toronto apartment I shared with my new husband, Zack, and reply that Vivian should marry the person she wanted to marry, not the person my parents approved of. Yet my stomach lurched as I re-read the letter. My heart beat faster when I came to the words underlined with black crayon. The truth was that, like my parents, I had imagined a bright future for Vivian. As a little girl, she'd been able to learn whatever I chose to teach her. She mastered typing when she was six. By the time she was seven, she could repeat the entire "Rhyme of the Ancient Mariner" by heart. I got my license when I was sixteen and she was eight. I put her on my lap and let her drive the lane to the back field. She learned how to steer, how to shift gears. Her legs weren't long enough to reach the pedals. I taught her how to swim, how to cross the river where you couldn't be seen from the house.

As a young child, I knew that you couldn't live with your parents forever, that you had to leave, and you did that by finding a person to marry. I wanted that person to be Vivian. I explained this to her when she was very small. Her blue eyes never left my face. She nodded and took my hand when I finished talking.

I paced the floor of my Toronto apartment for several minutes, then sat down and read the letter again. A solution presented itself. Like the knowledgeable older sisters of the novels I had grown up on, I would take my unwisely-betrothed younger sibling Abroad. Once Vivian had been exposed to civilized European society, she would understand that a hot, fly-infested, hand-hewn cabin in the backwoods of Huron County, Ontario was not where she wanted to spend her life.

Zack and I had been talking about a trip to Europe during my next summer's vacation from my teaching job, but I'd had a worry that had given me pause. A year before, during Zack's and my honeymoon to the east coast of Canada, I'd experienced a strange illness. My mother and I often fought, yet once I was away from her, I'd developed a hollow gut, a feeling of impending doom, a craving for her so strong that it felt like a matter of life and death. Spells of imagining that she had died, the realization that my life would be meaningless without her. The further we got from home, the worse this condition became. A hard knot formed in my stomach; I began waking early with panicked dreams that my mother had died.

I told Zack that we had to go home; the honeymoon was over. Once we were back in Toronto, I insisted on making the three hour drive to the farm in Huron County.

My parents welcomed Zack and me. They showed us the photographs of our wedding, which had just come back. Yet, before the afternoon had passed, my mother and I were in a fight, me screaming that she was a provincial ignoramus, she shrieking that I was full of myself. "Who do you think you are?" she howled, running up the back stairs and slamming her bedroom door.

"I hope you die and rot in *hell*," I howled back, taking the front stairs two at a time and slamming my door with a force that surpassed hers.

While this went on, my husband of less than two weeks and my father sat outside in the August humidity under the mock orange tree. My new husband was tall and scissor-thin, thirty-one years old, a philosophy graduate who had not yet been able to find a job, and had been living with his mother when I met him. I'd been drawn to him by the devotion with which he foiled his mother's every wish. My father and his new son-in-law brushed away flies and discussed the recent sinking of multiple containers of nerve gas in the Gulf Stream by the Americans. I crouched at the upstairs farmhouse window in the stupefying heat and looked down at them. They were seemingly oblivious to the nerve gas that had just been released within the house.

Physically, I felt fine. The strange illness had disappeared.

Now, sitting at my new teak table, gazing at the pale Toronto sky, I realized that taking Vivian to Europe for seven weeks would solve two problems. It would not only break her connection to Vernon Stackhouse, it would mean that I would have my own flesh and blood with me every minute of the trip and wouldn't get homesick.

I pushed my chair back from the teak table and stood up quickly, gathering the pages of my mother's letter and replacing it in the envelope. My father, I was certain, would pay Vivian's expenses for a trip to Europe. The specter of a descendant who was not scholarship material would be even more excruciating than the act of withdrawing money from his savings account.

This is how it happened that in July of 1971, Zack, Vivian and I arrived in London, England. We found the populace prone beneath a broiling sun, for we were at the beginning of the most intense heat wave the country had experienced in a century. In jeweled parks, on benches, in tiny front yards, on the bright green lawns surrounding public buildings, there lay row upon row of the whitest people we had ever seen. Their skin was the white of creatures who had spent their lives clinging to the damp underside of forest vegetation. Zack and Vivian and I could not bear five minutes of this fierce sun, but these people were splayed beneath it nearly naked.

In February, I had sent Zack to the Public Library to get *Europe on Five Dollars a Day, 1971*. From the section on accommodation, I chose the cheapest lodging in London, Amsterdam and Paris, and purchased thin blue airmail paper on which to write and book our rooms.

The section of general advice in the guidebook recommended that a person travel light. There might not be anyone to help with your luggage. Your suitcase should be something you could "carry a good distance unaided." When the time to pack arrived, I decided to take only the short dress and the underwear I had on. For deviations in weather, I included a navy sweater and tights. The tights matched the navy stripes of my red, white and navy dress. A sleeveless nightgown. As suggested in *Europe on Five Dollars a Day*, I would wash my underwear every night, and my dress, which was made of quick-drying nylon, once a week. Everything I needed for a month in Europe fit into my oversized, shiny-red, vinyl purse. I advised Zack and Vivian to model themselves after my example.

When we arrived in London, we discovered that our accommodation was two long bus rides distant from the downtown.

When we finally got there, we told the landlady that we were going straight to bed.

"Nor, nor, nor!" she said. "If you sleep now, you'll never get on our time. Go downtown and start your sightseeing."

We obeyed her. Two bus rides, even more interminable than before, landed us back downtown. With the roar of London setting our bones a-hum, we found at last a restaurant in our price range. We were served a dish of white, mucilaginous rice, chicken skin, and chicken tendon. We pushed this around our plates, rode the two buses again, and fainted onto the beds. It was nine p.m., the end of our first day abroad.

We slept until four the next afternoon, English time. Every day that we were in England, we slept until four, setting forth on our sightseeing just as Londoners were returning from work. We arrived back for bed at four in the mornings.

On our first two days in London, we shouldered through the crowded streets, the big city din jumbling our thoughts. The English were foreigners, I realized with surprise, their speech difficult to understand. These were the people from whom Wolfe the dauntless hero had sprung; I'd expected them to be like us. "Look to the *right* before you cross," I instructed my seventeen-year-old sister, every time we approached a street.

We spent hours attempting to locate the restaurants I'd copied from the Budget section of *Europe on Five Dollars a Day*. There was little time to see the sights that would broaden Vivian's mind and allow her to understand that Vernon Stackhouse was a new world hick. Not only that, many of the sights I had on my list were closed by the time we'd located and eaten our evening breakfasts of fatty bacon.

On our first day, we made the arduous climb to the top of St. Paul's cathedral. Up there was an outdoor roof with a railing that came only to our knees. Zack looked down and turned the colour of an alabaster lamb. Vivian said it was a tea-whistlin' sight. She said she wished Vern were here to see it.

On our second day, we picked our way across the green sward of Hyde Park, stepping carefully to avoid the thousands of preternaturally-white bodies. The sun slanted through the trees and the heat we endured as we crossed the patches between the long shadows was fierce. Vivian said this park reminded her of the river flats behind Vern's cabin. She said she wished she could take a dip right now. I said crossly that there were no people lying in Vern's field so how could Hyde Park remind her of the river flats.

Once the sun had set over the great city on that second day, we had our usual search for a restaurant, for it was time for lunch. When we had at last located the place and settled ourselves at the table, Zack and I began a conversation that was typical of us.

"It may not be possible," I said to Zack, "to say absolutely that a certain absolute is absolute, but surely it is possible to say that any given absolute is relatively more absolute than another." I paused as three dishes of tapioca pudding were set before us. "If you think there are no absolutes, that means a comic book is as good as Shakespeare."

"It is simply a matter of who is reading the comic book and who is reading Shakespeare," said Zack. "Some people will think the comic book is better, some will say Shakespeare. One is not *intrinsically* better than the other."

"Zack, anybody who thinks a comic book is better than Shakespeare has not been educated to know what great literature is and what it is not."

"Who knows, Lexie? Who is qualified to do the educating? *Who* defines what's better? It's all relative. Everything is relative."

Vivian looked first at Zack, then at me. Points of fire glittered in her blue eyes. "If I have to listen to another argument like this, I am going to dog paddle back to Newfoundland," she said. "We will have *not one more word* about absolutes on this trip."

I was startled from my thicket of self-preoccupation long enough to take a real look at my little sister. Until this moment, she'd been an appendage of myself. At an instinctual level, I'd been aware of her long hair, the same honey-gold as mine, her nose, the nostrils triangular-shaped like our mother's, her light-filled blue eyes the colour of our father's, her full lips, like our Aunt Bea's. Our father's slender figure, his small bones. Long fingers, shaped like mine. When I came close to her in the humidity, I inhaled the scent of honey softening in a clay bowl on a sunny sill, just as I had when I carried her around as a baby and brushed the top of her head with my nose.

Vivian's command had the power of a medieval king's. This was the end of Zack's and my incessant "philosophical" discussions. As I attempted to swallow the sticky portion of pudding, I realized that I didn't know my sister anymore. I'd been living away from home since I was seventeen, the age she was now. She'd been a little girl of nine when I left.

I pushed away my bowl. "This is a revolting mess of fishes' eyes and glue," I announced. "I can't get it down. You don't have to finish yours, Vivian."

With one gesture, my sister swept her long blond hair off her neck and twisted it into a knot on top of her head. "This dessert reminds me of Vern's mother's tapioca pudding," she said. "It puts me right back there. She often makes this." She reached for my bowl and picked up her spoon. "I'll polish off what you've left here."

I looked at my sister again, and received my first glimmer that the hidden mission of our trip abroad might not be as easily accomplished as I'd thought.

Sometime later that evening, I experienced a sharp, stabbing pain in my gut and a gurgling that was audible to Zack and Vivian. This was the beginning of a bug that would repeatedly rush the juice of my young life into the sewers of London. After our first two days in London, the time that remained to us, each day, once we finished looking for restaurants, was spent looking for a loo. Zack and Vivian were employed fulltime finding the nearest lavatory, while I swooned against the handiest wall with clenched sphincter, enduring pangs that exerted the force of labour contractions.

Vivian's education would have to wait until we got to Holland.

Our lodgings in Amsterdam were in a tall, narrow house on a canal that stank. To get to our third floor quarters, we ascended a narrow, twisting staircase with ceilings so low that Zack had to bend double. I took the stairs first, silently thanking the author of *Europe On Five Dollars A Day* that I was encumbered only by my large, red purse. Zack and Vivian had not followed my example. They swore and sweated up the stairs behind me, their large, heavy suitcases knocking and scraping at every turn.

There were no "quarters" on the third floor. There was only one room, containing one double and one single bed. Zack and Vivian collapsed, and I clattered back down the stairs to look for the landlord.

Mr. Van Den Bovenkamp was in the kitchen. He was dressed in a shabby black suit, which gave off a fainter version of the canal smell, and his shoulders were permanently bowed, as if he had spent his life climbing his low-ceilinged stairs. I pointed out that I had written, airmail, to book two rooms.

"We have given you the large room on the third floor, Miss," said Mr. Van den Bovenkamp. "You are only three."

"But we wanted two rooms."

"You are only three," said Mr. Van den Bovenkamp, turning his attention back to the potion he was stirring on the stove.

"Did you get me my own room?" said Vivian, when I returned. "By the way, the water that comes out of the taps smells like the canal." She was sitting on the narrow bed, painting her toenails crimson.

"We are only three," I shrugged. "You have to be five or so, I guess, before they give you a second room in Europe."

"I'm getting a little tired of the sound of you two humping as soon as you think I'm asleep," said Vivian, blowing on her toenails. "Try to keep it down, wouldja?"

I gave Zack a stricken look. At twenty-five, I would no more speak of sex, even to my husband, than my mother would have spoken about menstruation to me. "Vivian, for goodness sakes, we don't ... we didn't. I've been, I've had, you know, the trots." My face was the colour of a broiled English nose.

"Oh, you don't have to get all red," said Vivian. "I'm just kidding. Come on, let's go. Let's explore. Let's rent a bicycle. Let's go to the red light district. Let's do *something*!"

The next morning, Mr. Van den Bovenkamp served us three identical breakfasts consisting of one hard-boiled egg, which was neither runny nor dry but perfectly in between, two square pieces of toast, one spoonful of raspberry jam, and a pitcher of something that Zack thought was coffee, I thought was hot milk, and Vivian thought was canal run-off. On each flowered plate, the jam was placed beside the same yellow petal and the toast was lined up by the same stem.

After breakfast, we went to the bike rental shop. A leaflet of instructions was pressed into my hand as we exited the door with our bicycles. After riding one block, I made Zack and Vivian stop while I read the instructions loudly in Vivian's general direction:

If you rent it for more then one day, never let your bike by Night on the street. That is much to dangerous, because many bikes are stolen, most by Night.

Remember, any car is much bigger as you and you live only one time, not twice. Please don't forget it.

Sure do you know that in Amsterdam, like many other World-Towns, most Car-drivers are crazy. Always let them go first, also if he had to wait for you. The next Day you can read in the News-paper by with Accident he was killed.

"Very funny," said Vivian, swinging her leg over her bike in insouciant fashion and pedaling away. Zack and I followed. After lunch at a small hotel not far from Amsterdam, we settled into lawn chairs in the sunny garden, dark beers in hand. The beer was making me pleasantly woozy. I suggested staying there and having another. "Good idea," said Zack.

"No way," said Vivian. "We're going to get our money's worth of Holland. Get your arses back on these bikes."

I sat up, remembering that the whole purpose of the trip was to broaden Vivian's horizons, to make her see Vernon Stackhouse for the yokel he was, to whet her appetite for the finer things of life. I hauled myself out of the chair.

Zack ordered another beer. "No way am I riding this bicycle any further," he said.

"You'll have to ride it back to the rental place."

"Exactly."

Vivian was already on her bike. I mounted mine and followed her along the deserted country road. As we pedaled, I realized that this was the first time in my life that I had encountered true flatness. I felt like a giantess riding across a child's quaint, make-believe world, a windmill here, the odd bird there. The landscape was so flat that all of life seemed to be in front and around you, to be seen at a glance, plain and interminable. There was no mystery. I thought about the country road that led to Vern's cabin, the curves and gentle swells of it, the trees, the pleasant uncertainty about what might be over the next hillock. I looked at my slim sister riding ahead of me, the swirl of blond hair that reached her waist, the burning arc the sun described across her crown. A weight settled onto my shoulders. Holland was a failure, I realized. In no way was it going to serve my ends.

My rear end was exquisitely sore. I was further hampered by the odd posture that my clothing forced me into on the bicycle; I had to fold the short skirt of my dress tight to my body and crunch the extra material under me on the seat so that the Dutch would not see the one pair of underpants I had brought to their flat, joyless country.

When we returned, Zack was still in his chair in the garden behind the little hotel, head lolling back, mouth slack, long scissor legs up on the small wooden table. I roused him. In slow, single file we rode back into Amsterdam. Remember, I told my husband and sister, as we reached the stinking canal, *Any car is much bigger as her.*

In Paris, we immediately encountered the famous French arrogance we'd been warned about. "We reserved two rooms here," I ventured, on our first evening, when at last we had found our hotel.

"*Parlez français*," said the proprietress. Her face had been ravaged by an undefined sorrow, or perhaps by imprudent exposure to the sun on a Mediterranean beach. Each eyelash was encased in black mascara and her eyebrows had been plucked into an arch that announced no tolerance for the gauche and the unchic.

The three of us looked at one another. "It'll have to be you, Lexie," said Vivian, with the by now familiar gesture of winding her long blond hair into a topknot and stabbing it with a pin.

L'ordre est venu de Berlin de ne plus enseigner que l'Allemagne, I recited. Put on the spot, it was the only high school French I could think of.

The proprietress stared at me with an anger that approached apoplexy.

I came to my senses. *Nous avons des réservations pour deux chambres ici.*

We were marched to one room. It contained one double and one single bed. I turned to Vivian. "What can I say?" I mimed the grimace of the proprietress and fell backwards onto the bed. "We are only tree!"

Our hotel was on a street of little shops. In the tiny courtyard, a small table and two chairs. Next to the hotel, a groceteria. Its front window was large and unscreened. A passerby could pick out an avocado and a pear, a few snails oozing from their spiral shells, then lean into the dark interior to press a coin into the shopkeeper's palm. In the back yard were penned rabbits and geese. The chickens were at large, and occasionally wandered around to the front. The shopkeeper would as readily seize one of these creatures and dispatch it to the next world with his axe as he would hold forth to his customers in rapid-fire French. The axe stood at all times near the counter, congealed blood and the occasional feather on its blade.

This was not so different from Huron County.

By breakfast time, the wide sill of the front window of the groceteria was piled with freshly baked loaves and baguettes. Every morning, when the sun reached the sill, an orange and white cat mounded itself among the unwrapped loaves, its pink nose and whiskers twitching. Dozens of flies explored every crevice and crack of the golden crusts.

"God!" said Vivian, tossing her long hair. "At least in Huron County, we wrap our bread in plastic and hang those long spools of sticky paper in the bakeshop to catch the flies."

About the time the cat appeared each morning, Zack took up his post at the small table in the courtyard of the hotel. There he spent the hot sunny mornings, swatting the flies that landed on his table. Ants bore the corpses away. I heard Zack tell Vivian that one small ant could manage the body of the largest of flies. He was sure the ants of Canada were not so capable.

"Formidable," agreed Vivian. "Now let's get this show on the road, eh!"

Zack did not get the show on the road. Once the entire yard was in sun, he retreated to the cool dark bedroom, where he swatted the bottom of a wine bottle with his shoe. This was his method of removing a cork. Each swat dislodged the cork a fraction of a centimeter. By the time it was four o'clock, and part of the courtyard was again in shade, Zack had the bottle open. He would order coffee and swig from his own bottle of wine when the concierge was inside.

"It's highway robbery, what they charge for a bottle," he said. "I'll drink my own."

On the third day, I realized that this was how my husband intended to spend the majority of his time in Paris. The idea that I had married an intellectual who preferred debating important concepts to the mundane activities of life was receiving blow after blow. And I was beginning to feel like the bottom of the wine bottle.

I took Vivian on the metro. We visited the Eiffel tower, Notre Dame Cathedral, the Louvre, Versailles. I looked and looked, stared until my eyes throbbed. My best friend back home had been to Paris three times, had told me of the atmosphere, the culture, the beauty, how the very cobblestones were soaked in history.

All I could see were buildings, paintings, furniture, parks. They were without meaning. History, art, culture—whatever schooling I'd had had gone in one ear and out the other. I didn't know what I was seeing; therefore I could not see it. Nor could I help Vivian to see it.

Late one afternoon, near the end of our third day in Paris, the three of us were again on one of our long searches for a budget restaurant that was on the list I'd composed. The broiling weather had followed us from London to Amsterdam to Paris. We were lost. Vivian wanted to forget about the restaurant on my list and go into the nearest café and have a cold drink and a French pastry. I said that we were on a budget and we had to stick to it. Not only that, eating between meals would spoil our dinner.

Vivian stopped so suddenly that I ran into her. She whirled to face me. Her nose, so exactly like our mother's, became red. Her eyes sparked off nails of blue light. "I'm sick of your budget restaurants," she said. Red flooded her entire face. "You're a dictator. I'm sick of dragging around through boring old buildings. I'm sick of looking at you in the same dress, sick of seeing your wet bra and underpants dripping from the towel rack at bedtime, and sick of you boasting about how easy it is to carry your hideous red purse." Vivian's eyes squirted tears. "If you want to know the truth, I'd give anything to be home with Vern right now, swimming in the river. I'm bored to death. I hate it here. I wish I'd never come."

Heat coursed through me—onto my skin, up my neck and onto my face. My ears pounded so loudly I could barely hear myself speak. "How dare you!" I choked. "You're lucky we even invited you. You're a baby. You're a spoiled brat. I'm sick of you tagging along and, if you want to know the truth, I'm sick of having you in our marital bedroom at night."

"I can't help it that you booked us one room," screeched Vivian.

"I can't help it that I booked two rooms and they keep giving us one," I screeched back. "Having you along is like having an immature child that I'm responsible for."

Then we were pulling one another's long hair and digging our nails into one another's arms. "I hate you, Alexia," Vivian screamed. "I hate you, I *hate* you." She broke from my grasp. "I never want to see you again." She turned away and ran in the direction from which we'd come.

Out of the corner of my eye, I saw the look on the face of a white-haired woman dressed in black who was taking a small terrier for a walk under the row of plane trees in the adjacent park. The look went beyond aversion; it was as if every one of her sensibilities had been scraped and deranged.

Tears mingled with the sweat that dribbled down my temples and my legs gave way. I sank onto the curb and looked up at Zack. "What if we never *do* see her again," I bawled. "Oh, I never thought our trip would be like this. What will mom and dad say if something happens to Vivian? Oh, God, I just want to die."

Zack sat down beside me on the curb. He took off his tinted glasses and rubbed his eyes. He stroked his blond, Frank Zappa moustache. "She has a point about the dress," he said, finally. "Why don't you go buy yourself something chic." He pronounced the word chick. "I bet that big salary you make teaching high school is burning a hole in your pocket."

On our return to Canada, our parents picked us up at the Toronto airport and drove us not to the farm, but to their small city home, which was closer to Toronto than the farm. Vivian was animated. For the entire hour and a half drive she talked, leaning forward from the middle of the back seat to direct her words first to our mother then to our father. She made everything into a funny story—the food, the accommodations, the sights I dragged her to see, the heat, even the fight. Sprawled to her right, head back, mouth open, long legs folded into a cramped position in the small space, Zack was asleep. To her left, I was wide-awake, silent, my mind a jumble of thoughts.

When we arrived, I plodded into the house and carried the shiny, red purse upstairs to Vivian's and my old bedroom. The heat increased with each step; the little room at the top of the stairs was stifling, and the mere act of removing from my red purse the sweater and tights I had had no occasion to wear caused me to become wet with sweat. I heard a car door slam and looked out the window. Vern's red Ford Mustang.

Vern stepped from the car. He'd grown a scruffy black beard during our absence. Tall, rough, swarthy—a woodcutter from a fairy tale. I heard the back door of the house slam, then Vivian came running into the side yard. She leapt forward, flung herself into Vern's arms. Her long blond hair mingled with his ragged black locks. The two of them looked as if they were stuck together so firmly they'd never come apart.

Small fists of blood pummeled my ear drums.

I remained at the window, looking down at the pattern of blond and black formed by their commingled hair until the two of them sauntered out of sight around the corner of the house, arms around one another's waist.

A bitter burr of failure slowly formed and lodged itself in my throat.

X.
Her Mark on Men

VIVIAN IS DETERMINED TO BE MARRIED outside, at the farm. Our mother immediately sees a problem. The farm is situated halfway up a high hill. From the front porch of the farmhouse, you look into a deep valley; behind the house is the upper third of the hill. The only level place on the farm is the side lawn, in front of the outdoor privy. We wouldn't be smack up against it. A grove of tall pines surrounds the little gray shack. Nevertheless, our mother is distressed at the thought of wedding guests sitting in front of an outhouse.

Our mother has always gone to great lengths to conceal the fact that this little building is the place where we conduct unsavoury business. When she loses to Vivian over the location of the wedding, she intensifies these efforts. The outhouse fight ends with her martyred picking out of wallpaper patterned by blue cornflowers from tag end rolls at the general store in the village. She brushes on glue from a tray she tilts on top of a nearby stump and she papers the interior walls. She whitewashes the seats and pours ashes into the holes, morning and night. She hangs a spool of sticky paper from the outhouse ceiling to catch the flies that grow fat on our wastes.

Our father has his own worries about this wedding. He allows that Vernon Stackhouse is a handsome fellow. But Vern habitually says, "I would have went." He says, "I come home early yesterday." He says "anyways." (This is before "anyways" got into the dictionary.) Our father feels that any child he has raised will be unable to go through life listening to her spouse make these grammatical errors. Not only that, Vivian and Vern being cousins, our father has fears about his descendants. "It is possible," says our father, "that cousins may produce issue who are not the sharpest knives in the drawer."

In the last days before the wedding, our parents get down on their hands and knees and manicure the level area in front of the outhouse. They soak it and pull out tough twitch grass by the handful. Our mother sits on the ground and feels with her fingers for the roots of the creeping Charlie, painstakingly removing it strand by strand. In our mother's mind, dirt, weeds, waste products, disorder of any kind is closely connected to sin and shame.

The wedding day is a shirt-sticker, as they say in Huron County. Forty or so guests assemble and sit down on the hard-backed chairs that have been borrowed from the church. The chairs teeter from one leg to another on the patchy grass of the baked August soil. Ironically, it was my husband Zack who was the casualty of our trip to Europe with Vivian. The intended casualty of the trip is now my sister's groom. I sit in the front row, hand in hand with my new boyfriend David, who teaches history at the same high school in Toronto where I teach English.

I'm wearing a polyester turquoise pantsuit printed with large, dark-red roses, and feeling as if I'm at the periphery of Vivian's wedding. I long to be standing up with my sister, to be her one and only bridesmaid. I have no business to be feeling this way, I know. Sitting on my hard chair in the second row, I imagine what my mother would say if she knew what was in my head: keep those shameful feelings to yourself.

The bridesmaids are Vivian's friends from high school and university. I've hardly seen my sister in the two years that have passed since our trip to Europe. I've been living in Toronto, going through the hell of marriage break up. Vivian has been studying hard at university, working for the credits she needs to get into medical school.

Vivian has placed a portable record player on the floor of the kitchen, and has left the side door slightly ajar. At a signal, Billy, a fifteen year old nephew of the groom, will drop the needle for Wedding Day at Troldhaugen, a dramatic, upbeat composition by Edvard Grieg that Vivian learned to play on the piano as a child.

Vivian's bridesmaids are wearing full-length, low-cut, fuchsia gowns. The dresses are identical, but the breasts that give them their fall and flow are a startling and wide-ranging education in the variety of the human female form. They range from a pair of pointed wonders that come at you like a zeppelin to a set of dugs that I swear are smaller than the pectoral muscles above them. Vivian wears a long white dress with full skirt and train. On her head, a tiara to which a dramatic white veil is attached.

Vivian's long white train drags in the henbane, as she approaches the manicured area of grass. Billy drops the needle and the first flourish of Wedding Day at Troldhaugen begins, scratchy and hollow-sounding. Vivian walks toward her groom, picking her way in the space between the rows of chairs. My father is beside her, wearing a blue summer suit, his hair pasted to his head with Brylcream. A cow on the other side of the rail fence sticks her runny nose in the air and bawls loudly. She produces a plopping rain of patties just as the minister launches on his words to the assembled guests. The aroma of cow dung mixes with the perfume of purple phlox.

"And I was worried about the outhouse," says our mother afterwards.

Out of Vivian's hearing, our father restates his opinion that no child raised by him will be able to go through life listening to her spouse make egregious errors in grammar. He says he doesn't give the couple five years.

He isn't out by much. During the years of her first marriage, Vivian puts in four years of medical school. In her fifth year, for the last rotation of her internship, and still wearing her hair in one thick blond braid, she returns to the hospital in Rilling—a small town twelve miles from the farm. There she meets Werner Krause.

Werner is a doctor twenty years Vivian's senior. Soon, whenever Werner goes home for lunch, Vivian is lying flat on the back seat of his Mercedes, covered from crown to toe by a blanket. Shortly after that, Werner's girlfriend returns to the old country and Vivian divorces Vern. She buys a family practice that's available not far from Rilling.

None of us is at Vivian's second wedding. It happens in Germany. There are not even photographs for us to look at. The brief ceremony takes place in Munich in front of a Justice of the Peace, or its German equivalent, and the words of the ceremony are, of course, in German. Vivian tells me years later that she didn't understand a word and never really felt married.

From Werner, Vivian learns how to set up her own medical practice, how to spend money, drink, and throw parties, how to travel in style, and just how mutable love can be. One day, when they've been together for six years, she comes home unexpectedly at noon and picks up the phone in the study to make a hair appointment. She overhears Werner and the female half of their best couple-friends discussing how best to tell "Vivian" that they are lovers.

"No need to bother," Vivian croaks into the mouthpiece. She slams down the phone, runs to her car, and squeals away. Werner jumps into his Mercedes and squeals after her. In the next ten minutes, they endanger as many lives as they have jointly saved in the small town of Rilling that is their home.

I'm happy to see Vivian and Werner break up. I've more than once, over the preceding year, come across Vivian crying; most recently, she said that she thought Werner didn't love her anymore. During their first year together, Werner was visibly enchanted by his young bride and he made an effort to be hospitable to us, her family, but when the novelty wore off, he sank gradually into a state of sour introversion that I believe was probably his habitual mien. He seemed fonder of his single-malt Scotch than of his young wife. Krause, louse, in my opinion.

Once they split up, Vivian buys, furnishes, and moves into her own house on the Sanasateen River, on the edge of Rilling. Almost instantly, her social life takes off and the parties she throws eclipse those of her ex. It turns out that she has an inborn talent for creating social events where the guests feel both entertained and at home. The couple-friends in Vivian and Werner's circle are loyal to Vivian. Except, of course, for the couple with the traitorous female half.

It's around this time—after Werner, before Mike—that I remember Vivian getting dressed up in a carmine dress with a deeply vee'd back. I'm there one evening in December when she's getting ready for the annual hospital Christmas party. Black stockings with tiny sequins that flash when she walks, and heels so high that she teeters as she puts on her lipstick. I lounge against the doorway of her boudoir watching her final preparations. She stands back from the mirror, then leans forward to apply another coat of dark-red lipstick to those full lips of hers.

"You won't be able to kiss anyone if you don't blot your lips," I say. "They're sticky-thick with the stuff."

Vivian swivels around and poses with one hand on her hip. "I leave my lips unblotted on purpose, Lexie. I like to leave my mark on men. There's hardly a man in this town that hasn't worn my lips at one time or another."

At the hospital party, Vivian gets drunk. I hear the story later. A colleague dares her to put her dress on backwards. She goes to the washroom and returns, exposed to her navel by the vee. Except that her long hair provides a swaying, beckoning curtain that conceals as much as it reveals.

That story goes the rounds, of course. Small town lips buzz.

Molars stew in their own spew. Jaws need soldering.

Vivian causes a stir every couple of months. She doesn't care how much she makes the grapevine vibrate. She's a good doctor, and everybody knows it. It's this that gives her the confidence to live as she pleases.

I look on from a distance, most of my information about Vivian coming to me through my mother, to whom I write a long letter every week, and who writes back with news of the family, gleaned from her weekends on the farm in Huron county, for she still, at that time, goes to the farm with my father most weekends. My mother writes that Vivian is so busy that she hesitates to bother her. We do not phone. Long Distance is something all of us reserve for passing on the word of a death or a serious illness.

By now, I have two young daughters. Teaching fulltime feels like more than I can handle, yet part-time work is not allowed. I make it to the farm only on the occasional long weekend, and at Christmas. My life is a blurred round of tasks. I exist only as mother and teacher. Sometimes I think of Vivian—her long blond hair, champagne in hand, red dress on backwards, long legs flashing sequins as she walks. Our worlds are so different that I've almost lost awareness of how much I miss her.

xi.
The Discovery of the New World

THE FIRST TIME I SAW PASCALE CHAUTEMPS, I thought that there could not exist a human being who looked more like a horse. A purebred filly—the lines, the breeding, the thin ankles, the huge brown eyes set wide, shining like dark suns, the high cheekbones, the shape of her face, tapering into small mouth and chin, the long mane of coarse, curly dark hair, braided and coiled in a shining bun. Pascale would win the Preakness by several lengths, I thought, cross the finish line and toss that fine Gallic head at a field lost in her dust.

My sister Vivian and I had believed that my brother Graham would never marry, for he ate, slept, breathed and talked horses. That Pascale looked like a horse explained the inexplicable. But when Graham met Pascale, on a two week trip to Paris, I guess he never stopped to ask himself whether this was a woman to take a back seat to a horse.

When Pascale arrived in Canada, Graham was waiting at the airport on the wavy, steaming asphalt. His neck was crooked backwards, his wide eyes burned into the hot blue sky. The authorities moved him inside to stand with the others behind a glass wall. Ontario, that September day, sweltered in a humidity that was like Rangoon's. Pascale had expected cold. She was wearing a three-piece pinstriped suit of fine wool.

Pascale removed her jacket. A white blouse gleamed behind the dark silk of her vest. My brother suggested a picnic. It would be fifteen years before I learned what happened then.

They went to a corner grocery store. Pascale bought tomatoes and my brother bought corn. Pascale wondered why her husband-to-be didn't eat the tomatoes. She didn't know that he had a horror of them that amounted almost to a phobia. When he was a small boy, I had crushed a ripe tomato in my hand and told him that the gushing pulp was blood, the seeds globules of pus, then chased him with my red, tomato-streaming hands, hissing "pus, pus, pus."

Graham roasted the corn in foil on the park barbecue. He put the cob to his lips and gnawed, his nose coming up for air now and again, shining yellow kernels stuck to the isthmus of skin between his nostrils. Pascale stared. In France, corn on the cob was food for the pigs.

Crossing the field to return to the car after the picnic, they saw a snake swallowing a frog. The snake was writhing mightily and they could clearly see the outline of the frog's body against the tightly-stretched skin. Never having seen such a thing in Paris, Pascale crouched to watch. The frog was going in backwards. A breech death, thought Pascale, and was frustrated because she did not know how to say this in English. The frog's head was still out in the world; its eyes were open, bright, expectant. It looked up at Pascale. My brother turned the colour of the dry marsh grass at their feet.

Pascale and my brother were married at Toronto City Hall a week later. None of the family knew about the wedding until it was over. That day, my brother took an extra half hour for lunch from his job at one of Canada's five big banks. After the brief ceremony, he took Pascale to Burger King.

On December 24th, my brother brought Pascale to Christmas Eve dinner at my parents' small city home. We ate at the kitchen table.

My mother set a carved turkey, dressing, mashed potatoes, gravy, coleslaw, cranberries, jellied salad, pickles, white rolls, and a carton of milk on the table. Every bit of space was taken up, so that the rolls had to sit on my mother's dinner plate and the carton of milk on my father's. Without warning, my father screwed up his face. Running the words together, he recited, in the voice of an automaton: "God is gracious, God is good. Let us thank Him, for our food." That was the signal for all of us to reach out and use the tablespoons that were sticking out of the bowls to dump helpings onto our plates. The package of rolls and carton of milk were passed around, then set on the floor by my father's chair.

Everyone ate in silence. In less than ten minutes, the food was gone. While Pascale was still chewing her small helpings, my father cleared the table at top speed and ran water for the dishes. He washed them in the kitchen sink four feet from the table, while my mother put out homemade apple pie and a carton of vanilla ice-cream.

A week later, my brother held a party for his bride. He invited his relatives, the country folk of East Wawanosh, in Huron County, the location of the farm where we had spent every weekend and summer holidays, when growing up. Pascale was responsible for the food at this party.

She made delicate, open-face sandwiches and adorned them with anchovies. She prepared mounds of pâté and trays of cheese. The cheese smelled to the farmers like their rubber boots when they removed their feet after a day in the barn. They took one look at the sandwiches and grinned slyly at my brother. "What are these here things? Where are the lids?" Loaves of doughy white bread and jars of peanut butter and jam appeared. The same knife was used to slather jam and peanut butter onto the bread, then stuck back into the jar.

Both men and women, my brother and sister among them, drank Scotch straight from the bottle and got skunky-drunk. They went out and vomited in the snow.

In the morning, Pascale packed her trunk to return to France. My father sat her down and had a talk with her about the different ways folks have of behaving. He told her he'd seen the bottles behind the outhouse. He explained that he and his wife, to whom he referred as "Mommy," had signed a temperance pledge when they were twelve years old, promising never in their lives to let a drop of liquor pass their lips, and that they had kept their promise.

While he talked, Pascale imagined the smug faces of her parents, if she were to return home, and decided to suspend action for a while longer. During that while, she got pregnant.

Fifteen years later, Pascale is telling this story to my sister Vivian, her third husband Mike, and myself. Tendrils of Pascale's long dark hair escape into a kinky halo as she gesticulates from the head of the dining room table. Outside in the humid July evening, her five children and my two daughters are racing barefoot around the hilly farm yard, screaming and slapping at mosquitoes.

There had been a delay between main course and dinner this evening. My brother had therefore gone to ride the sit-down lawnmower that cuts the grass of the east field that stretches all the way to the road. He has scattered horse jumps around this field; the grass must be cropped close.

We have heard these stories of Pascale's before, but we have not heard them sitting together over wine, we have not heard them against the dogged drone of my brother on the lawnmower. When Pascale rises to her feet to mime my brother slobbering over the corn and swaying in the marsh grass, our screams are louder than the children's, outside. In certain moods, my mother would sit with us and abandon herself to the hilarity, but tonight she is scraping the remains of Pascale's *tomates provençales* and washing dishes loudly in the kitchen, so that she does not have to hear her son made a figure of fun by this foreigner.

One of the details Mike has not heard before is the wedding feast at Burger King. When Pascale tells this part, Mike loses control of his laugh. It rises two octaves in falsetto flight, beats with helpless disbelief against the aged wallpaper of the dining room ceiling, like summer moths against a screen door. Mike is a gourmet cook. Each of his meals is an occasion, a work of art. Cooking is at the heart of his being, as horses are at the heart of my brother's.

"Why did you take up with him, what did you see in him, back then in Paris when you first met?" we gasp, blowing our noses and wiping tears of laugher with tissues fetched hastily to the table.

"I'd wrecked my knee doing ballet. I was fed up with the big city, thinking about going to Australia. Along comes this guy with his English accent and his funny underwear. He could recite Baudelaire by heart." She shrugs and opens her dark eyes wide: "I mean, come on, guys. I had twenty-one years."

"He was exotic," says Vivian, "Our brother Graham was exotic." There is a silence as we think about Graham, the manure and straw stuck to his rubber boots, the faint smell of horse that accompanies him whenever he is here at the farm.

"Which of you was the snake and which the frog?" Mike asks. We laugh, then the screen door bangs and there is a spatter of sweaty feet across the kitchen floor and into the dining room. The owner of the smallest pair crawls into Pascale's lap. The others form a semicircle around her and, at a nod from my older daughter Julie, chant as one: "When do we get dessert?"

"There's cake and ice-cream. Come and I'll load your plates," says my mother from the kitchen. "Then you're to take them outside. I'm all cleaned up out here. I've got to stop in at Anna's yet tonight."

As she scoops ice-cream and lifts cake onto plates, the screen door opens again and my brother enters the kitchen in his boots. Pieces of dark, moist grass scatter from his cuffs onto the floor. "Yves," he shouts, at his eldest son, "watch what you're doing. You're dripping ice-cream."

"Do you want some?" my mother asks, lifting her forearm to wipe sweat from her forehead.

"Not at this hour. It'll soon be bedtime," my brother says.

This is a veiled rebuke for the delay in the appearance of dessert. Graham turns to peer into the dining-room where we're still sitting around the table. I look at him under the kitchen light, the dark red flush high on his cheekbones. Weekdays he lives with Pascale and the five children in a bedroom community twenty miles from Toronto, rises at five-thirty a.m. to commute to his office, arrives home fourteen hours later in the dark. Like his father before him, he lives for his weekends and vacations at the farm.

Now he speaks to his second son, the only one of the five to share his love of horses and farm. "Come on, Bernard, help me get Lucifer into the stall. We have to attend to his leg. Finish that in here and come on." My brother moves to the other side of the kitchen, and when our mother's back is turned, picks up a piece of cake from the counter and stuffs it into his mouth. He and Bernard go out the back door. A moment later, I hear them rolling the heavy lawnmower into the old shed beside the barn.

My mother comes to the dining-room door. "I'll be off now, kids. Just going to your Aunt Anna's. Things are pretty well set to rights in the kitchen, Pascale."

"Thanks so much Grandma Irene. Here, I'll carry your stuff out to the car for you." Pascale gets up and accompanies my mother outside. When she returns to the dining room she says, "Don't get up yet, okay? I have a special treat, just for the adults, once I get the kids in bed."

Pascale returns half an hour later. In this short interval, she has overseen baths, settled four of her children upstairs, and brewed a pot of amaretto cream coffee. She opens the glass doors of the built-in dining room cupboard and from behind the blue and white china vase that has sat on the top shelf for as long as I can remember, takes a small gold box. "I have the pictures back," she says, producing a yellow envelope from the sideboard, and bending over to light the white candles she has placed on the table.

"Oh, why didn't you tell us sooner? I've been dying to see them," says Vivian.

"There is a time and a place for everything," says Pascale with a smile, opening the gold box slowly to display four rich, dark truffles. "Fauchon. One for each of us. Flown across the ocean this week."

"I want you to tuck me in for the last time now," comes a faint cry from upstairs. It's the voice of the youngest, Annelise.

"Daddy will tuck you when he goes up to bed later. I'm busy with your aunts and uncle."

"I want you," comes the little voice. "Daddy smells like horse."

"I'll go," I say, pushing my chair back and getting to my feet. "Don't pour my coffee until I get back."

"I want Maman," says the child as I enter her room.

"But this is your lovely, sweet-smelling aunt, come to give you a great slobbery kiss," I tell her, smacking my lips and swooping at the bed.

Annelise giggles and attaches herself to my neck. "Get in bed with me Aunt Lexie."

"Just for a minute. They're waiting for me downstairs."

"Are you coming to the farm next weekend?" she asks.

"No, not for quite a while."

"Good."

"What do you mean, good, you slobbery snuggledy-bug-gums?" I tickle her into giggles. "Don't you like your aunt?"

"You always take my bedroom when you come."

"Your bedroom?" I look across the dark hall into the west room where I've slept since I was a child. "Is that where you sleep when I'm not here, mimine?"

She nods, her dark eyes glittering in the perfect heart of her face.

My head feels as if it needs defragging, as I realize that Annelise sees me as Gladys. Gladys was somehow connected to my father's cousin, Ephram, who inherited the farm jointly with my father, and lived on it for half of every year. An old woman with a deep voice, Gladys came from the United States to visit Ephram for a week every summer. The day before she came, each year, my mother would make me move all my belongings out of my bedroom and into the storage room at the top of the front stairs where the plaster was cracked, so that Gladys could sleep in my room which she referred to, inexplicably, as her room.

"Lexie, the coffee's getting cold, come on down!" Vivian calls from the foot of the front stairs.

"Coming."

I, the aunt who has displaced this little girl from the bedroom that once belonged to the little girl I was, look down at my brother's child, my head still topsy-turvy. I place the paws of her stuffed kitten on her cheeks. "Kitty can't get to sleep, Annelise. I want you to sing her all the songs you know. Ve-e-e-ry softly." I tiptoe from the room backwards, index finger to my lips.

On the way down the hall, I pass my brother's bedroom. Strands of broken harness crisscross the floor; heaps of horse magazines are scattered among the jeans and underwear.

Downstairs, the others are looking at the pictures taken during our visit to the farm a month ago for the 1992 township celebrations of the Discovery of the New World. In this part of the country there is no ambivalence about Columbus. He is seen as intrepid explorer, hero, bringer of civility to a savage continent. We watched fireworks, recitations, barbershop quartets, cloggers and square dancers. The photos show us in our costumes, riding in the Democrat, polished and hitched to Graham's best driving horse.

The others get up and go across the hall into the living room to watch the news on the small colour TV that Pascale has recently purchased against my brother's wishes. I remain at the table. There's one picture I want to see again.

As I sort through the pile, Graham and Bernard come in from the barn. Bernard goes in the direction of the TV, my brother stops at the dining room door.

"C'mere," I say. "What did you think of the pictures of the horses?"

He remains in the doorway. "They were okay. I'm going to bed."

"I have something for you."

"What is it?"

My truffle in its gold wrapper gleams with a dark, dense sensuality. I pick it up, place it in the centre of the white dessert plate and walk over to him in the doorway. "Pascale saved this for you," I lie, holding it out to him.

Graham hesitates. In the light from the white candles, the truffle glows with a richly civilized sheen, I offer the plate again, and my brother reaches out his hand and puts the candy whole into his mouth.

"Not bad," he says, retracing his steps across the kitchen. I hear water running in the back washroom, then the creak of his feet on the back stairs.

I return to the table. The picture I'm looking for is a family portrait, taken the night of the dance. As we got ourselves into our costumes, lined up for the one bathroom, and hunted for misplaced socks and bow ties, I heard my brother ask Mike to take a family picture of himself, Pascale, and the five children.

Here it is. Pascale is wearing a white eyelet dress with ruffles around the neck and flowered layers on the skirt. She is squarely in the centre of the photograph, her second son Bernard on her right. Bernard's dark eyes and hair are Pascale's. On their faces is an identical expression. Somewhere in an old history book I have seen figures lined up and gazing out at the viewer with just this look. The conquerors.

Pascale's first and third sons stand to her left, her two daughters in front. My brother is not in the family portrait.

I turn the picture this way and that in the candlelight. Perhaps he has blended into the dark green foliage behind the other figures. No. He is not there.

With the entranced stare of the fortune-teller searching the leaves in the bottom of the teacup, I gaze into this mystery. Through the screen of the inside front door, cool air from the creek drifts into the house like a wan spirit. The horses are grazing now by the fence on the other side of the lane. Through the door come gentle nickerings and the solid, steady rhythm of long grass being torn up and masticated.

I sit on, gazing at the picture until the figures blur and shimmer like the indistinct line of the horizon, back in the days when the earth was flat and the secret corners of the New World still wild under the shadows of the moving clouds.

xii.
The Sun is Out, Albeit Cruel

THE DAY PASCALE MAKES HER ANNOUNCEMENT, the whole family is together in Rilling, Ontario, for a parade.

I'm not thinking about Pascale when the float of old folks from the BONNIE BRAE NURSING HOME chugs by; my first thought is that when our mom sees it coming, she'll worry that our father is on it. Up there on display in the annihilating July sun, the old folks are so white they look as if they've been let out for recess from Hades. All of them are hunched and staring ahead with the look of a dog enduring a hose bath, except that it's sun coming at them with penetrating, pressure cooker force. Our father's not there of course.

Following the BONNIE BRAE wagon is a float of rubbery clowns lolloping up and down their small moving stage. The clowns are pink and genial, oozing sweat and flinging suckers to the crowds. HOME FOR THE TRAINABLE RETARDED, says the sign on the back of their wagon.

I'm on my bum on the curb, bare legs straight, straw hat my futile shield against the fierce sun. A horse wearing blue jeans shies back and high-steps sideways; its rider trains a water pistol on us. On one side of me is my sister, Vivian, on the other my sister-in-law, Pascale, her long, thick mane gone, her curly hair now short and spritzer-saucy. The three of us open our mouths and spread our arms. "More, more," we holler to the water pistol man.

Spoils are tossed our way. With my two kids and my five nieces and nephews, I plunge repeatedly onto hot asphalt, skinning my palms to snatch toffees and bubblegum, magic markers and pencils, suckers and ballpoints and black jawbreakers.

At the end of our row of family sit my husband David and my brother Graham. Graham has shaved his beard since I saw him last. He's shaking his head at me in disgust for fighting his kids for treats in the asphalt trenches. The newfound skin of his cheek and jaw looks like bark on the forest floor when you turn it over and the slugs scatter, when it still holds that damp film of stilly cool.

I lean against my sister: "Despite the heat, our brother doth give off a clammy air." The Royal Canadian Legion blares by, their float manned by a score of navy uniformed seniors standing straight as cedar fence posts. Faces under wool tams are puce poppies of pride and incipient stroke.

Again we topple together, knock heads in mock jackanapes clumsiness. We are on holiday. The sun is out, albeit cruel. We are in silly putty mode.

I remember the day Pascale discovered that Graham's surname, Kerr, was identical in sound to the word for surly dog. "It describe him perfectly," she said, a cruel beam in her brown eyes. That was soon after Yves was born. Yet she and Graham went on and on: Bernard—*merde*, another boy; Eliane—*enfin*, a daughter; Guy—yet another boy; Annelise—a last girl to look after *Maman* in her old age.

We Kerrs shook our heads at this folly. Why did they do it? Did they think big family meant big happy?

"Yes, and pigs might fly," Grandma Kerr was heard to say.

Sometimes, when we're by ourselves, my sister and I talk about Pascale. How beautiful she is, how French. How, when we're depressed, we can feel better as soon as she walks into the room. How much our father liked her before he got that he didn't know any of us anymore. How we can't imagine our family now without her.

Parade over, Pascale and I are on our way to the nursing home at the edge of town, to visit my father.

"Dettol, pee, shit, ennui." I chant the words to Pascale. "It's taken me years to identify it—the smell in Bonnie Brae. After I've been in to visit, it follows me home and wraps itself around my dreams." My sister-in-law nods.

"Your hair is great," I add, taking my eyes from the road to admire her again. "So chic, so French." We pull off the gravel road and stop in front of the new building that withers in a treeless field just outside Rilling. I let my forehead thump to the padded wheel of the car. "I hate to leave this air. Please go into his room ahead of me. Those few seconds before he sees us are the worst."

Even now, Pascale gives no sign that this day will be different from dozens of others we've spent together. She walks ahead and presses the buttons inside the doors of BONNIE BRAE. The heat in the hall is almost as torrid as on the sunny asphalt path outside. We head for my father's room.

Pascale enters first. My father is slumped in his wheelchair. Pascale zip-a-dee-doo-daws around the room, straightening and fluffing and animating. Take even a room like this, she can rev it up a few levels. Whereas I feel myself glub-glubbing in the dettol-pee quagmire before I'm even through the door.

But today, not even his daughter-in-law can rouse my father. He's slumped over, focused on his sleeve.

"Never mind about that, James," says Pascale to my father, rubbing his almost helpless hands with her warm ones, but as soon as he's left to himself, his right hand comes up to his left sleeve and works away. He's trying to grasp one of the coarse white flecks of wool that stand out from the weave of his sweater. We give up trying to get his attention, and the two of us sit on the end of the bed and chat.

Eventually, Pascale goes down the hall to find a local paper and I to use the washroom. Returning, I catch the moment when, after an hour of attempting to grip the fleck between his crippled thumb and index finger, my father succeeds in pulling it off. I survey the prize, which stands at attention for inspection on his finger, like the legionnaires.

This is the stuff of *The Guinness Book of Records,* is what comes into my head. Or the Commonwealth Games. (At the moment, they're having an unseemly public tiff over whether Disabled Athletes will be included in future.) *And this just in,* I imagine the announcer saying, *from BONNIE BRAE NURSING HOME in the hamlet of Rilling, Ontario. A man who has suffered an eighteen-year route by Parkinson's disease succeeded this afternoon in gripping and removing a fleck of wool from his sweater. James Kerr's daughter, interviewed before airtime, expressed hope that the fleck would be preserved in the Disabled Athletes' Hall of Fame, soon to be constructed in Victoria.*

Why don't we see headlines about these achievements? commented Ms. Kerr. *Here is where the real dramas are being enacted.*

"You have the silliest look on your face, Lexie." Pascale reappears in the doorway just as I'm handing the mike back to the reporter. "Come on, we have to get going."

I zoom in from never-never land, focus my eyes and stand up. "I was on TV," I tell her.

My father neither lifts his head nor looks at us as we kiss him goodbye and leave him to his sleeve. In my gut is the familiar twist of guilt and relief as the front door of BONNIE BRAE closes behind us.

Rilling is semi-circled by a wide deep apostrophe of water, the Sanasateen River. Across from the park, where it flows deepest and widest, is where my sister Vivian lives. One minute the Sanasateen holds the changing world of sky, the next, it repels reflection with its wrinkles, waves and ruffles. Vivian's back yard slopes down to the reeds, cattails, sedge, and rushes of the Sanasateen's banks. On the old cement bridge is a sign that would never have escaped the standardizing stamp of a city bureaucrat:

NO LEAPING, JUMPING, VAULTING, SPRINGING, PLUNGING, DIVING, OR CATAPULTING FROM THIS BRIDGE.

"I was so afraid they'd have your father up on that float," says my mother, when we stop by to pick her up, "that when I saw it coming my heart nearly stopped." She places her hand on her heart. "Imagine them putting Betty O'Hanlon and Violet Gray up there. They looked downright cranky."

"James was fully *occupé* in his own room, Grandma Kerr," says Pascale, as she moves the takeout box of empty coffee cups and helps my mother into the front seat for the short drive to my sister's.

As we glide along Rilling's back streets, I count one, two, three diminutive black men holding lanterns above glistening lawns of "Weed and Feed" green. The ornaments are highlighted by spikes of the merciless July sun.

"What are you gawking at, Lexie?" says my mother.

"Oh, everything and nothing—the look of a summer day in Rilling, Ontario."

"Well, keep your eyes on the road."

I stop the car in front of my sister's place, and the three of us slowly descend the slope towards Vivian who is ankle deep in the Sanasateen pulling on the anchor of her rowboat. Up the river a little way, the teens of Rilling are being catapulted from the cement bridge by their own uncontrollable energy; they're flying, really, aloft and omnipotent for a glorious instant against the burning blue sky. They land with a splash that rocks the Sanasateen against its banks.

Two of my mother's grandchildren are in the water—Eliane and Annelise. As we round the tangle of willow, we see them swimming away from us, across the river towards Rilling. Their sleek, receding heads look as if they belong to two otters. "It's a short cut to town," my sister says. "They didn't want to go around by the bridge."

"Ooo la la, that sun, he is hot!" exclaims Pascale, bending over to splash river water on her newly-bared neck.

"What have Eliane and Annelise got on?" says my mother, still watching her granddaughters' progress across the river.

"Their clothes—shorts and T-shirts," Vivian says. "Anyhow," she adds, splashing water on her face and stepping out of the river, "I have something to tell you. Hell Bent For Election is dead."

Hell Bent is Graham's best horse, the one he had such hopes for, the gelding with the white star out of Forked Lightning. "He had an accident in Linda Blair's stable," Vivian continues. "Graham had him there to have work done on his feet. Hell Bent got tangled in a rope and strangled. That's why Graham was clammy, as you put it, Lexie, at the parade. He found out just before he came."

"How could that happen?" says our mother.

Again Vivian shrugs. "Linda Blair couldn't understand it. She said a horse couldn't do that if it tried. She was really upset!" As Vivian speaks, I picture Linda Blair's bony face, imagine her bending forward to kiss the dead horse on his soft nose.

"So Graham's horses are suicidal now, I guess," says Pascale. Again I see the cruel beam in the brown eyes. Vivian gives her a mock slap. But as usual Pascale has made us laugh.

"Poor Graham," says Grandma Kerr.

Poor Graham indeed, I think, looking at my chic and feisty sister-in-law in her new hair. I'm only too aware that for a Chautemps, Kerr now may not mean Kerr forever. Still, I'm not prepared for this afternoon.

Kerrs—us, the family to which Pascale Chautemps has found herself joined in marriage. Chautemps—them, the clan of the *Haute Savoie* area of France which produced the woman named Pascale, the woman my brother met on a two-week vacation in France and brought to Canada and married, on the basis of that short acquaintance. Pascale, who has so enlivened and enriched our family of Kerrs. Pascale is fond of telling a certain story about her firstborn, Yves. The story is a good illustration of the difference between a Kerr and a Chautemps because, of Pascale and Graham's five children, four are Chautemps and only one, Yves, is a Kerr. I love Pascale's little story because it goes to the heart of the difference between our two clans.

On the day in question, Pascale is sitting on the front steps of her home west of Toronto, picking over raspberries. Around the corner of the suburban street comes her twelve year old son. At his mother's request, he's been walking Patsy, the family's Jack Russell terrier.

Yves approaches, his left hand holding the leash handle, the leash sliding behind him, an empty collar tumbling and skipping at its end. There is no dog.

Pascale stands up. She plants her right hand on her hip, with her left she shields her eyes from the sun. "Where is Patsy?" she hollers. (Patsy is her sixth child.) "Where's Patsy??" she yells again, though Yves is now turning in at the front sidewalk.

It takes this second shout from his mother for Yves to return to earth and focus his eyes. "Patsy?" he says.

"Yes, Patsy, *mon gar,* where she is?"

Yves turns around and looks at the empty collar.

"She's not here." He looks up at his mother. "I didn't know she wasn't here."

Pascale looks heavenward and crosses herself. "Yves!" she says, coming off the porch and putting her face a lemon's length from her son's, "how you can not know she gets away? It take a hell of a lot of wiggling and twisting for Patsy to get out of her collar!"

Yves produces a baffled shrug. Then there is a yip and a clip clipping of nails on cement as Patsy rounds the corner and trots purposefully towards her mother.

At this point the incident loses drama and settles into its place near the top of Pascale's extensive repertory of stories.

Yes, Yves is a Kerr, not a Chautemps, as Pascale often

points out. He is one of us: a slack-jawed, wool-gathering, belly-breather, his inner world so compelling that for long periods of time the outer ceases to exist. And Pascale, who is by nature as warming, as outgoing, as life-giving as the sun, has found herself in a swamp of introverts whose ways are as mystifying and as maddening as anything she has encountered.

On our way to the park across the river, by car, my mother gestures to the take-out box and says isn't it nice that they have a hole now in the plastic lid of a cup of coffee so you can drink it with a straw. Pascale says that the hole is not for a straw, it's to sip from. My mother says it's for a straw. I cross my eyes at Pascale and she rolls hers at me.

Across the bridge, we disembark and lock the car. We're going to buy tickets for the duck race. First duck to cross the finish line brings the ticket owner $500. Grandma Kerr safely out of earshot, Pascale grabs me by the elbow: "With Grandma Kerr for a mother, is it any wonder your brother ask me why I put on perfume to go play badminton when what I'm spraying on my neck is insect repellent!" She laughs, "Good Lord, Lexie. Hot coffee with a straw! Can you imagine?"

I take her arm. "Pascale, when will you realize that we Kerrs are baffled by the workings of the physical world? I know it's hard for a Chautemps to understand, but such things are mysteries to us! Remember the woman who made coffee from wiener water that was quietly minding its rank business on the back burner? I remind you that that woman is your mother-in-law!"

"Oh Lexie. I forget that one. That is a good one." She gives my arm a squeeze and we follow Vivian and my mother across the park. Their progress is slow. Living here, Vivian knows half the people at the duck race.

"Look, Lexie," Pascale is pointing at the bridge. There are no teenagers in sight now. Instead, a dump truck is edging towards the cement railing. The back of the truck tilts slowly upwards and, with the escalating thunder of an avalanche, five hundred yellow rubber duckies slide into the Sanasateen River.

Once the ducks are in the water, people again begin visiting with one another and lining up for cold drinks. Pascale and I find a shady spot under a willow and I spread my green, summer shawl for us to sit on.

It's then Pascale makes her announcement. When I raise my head, those bright, brown eyes are full upon me. "Well, Lexie, I think you have guessed," she says quietly.

"Guessed? No, what is it?"

"I'm getting out."

"What do you mean?"

"Separation. I'm leaving your brother."

"But Pascale, we've talked about this before, don't say it again, please. You know we can't imagine our family without you."

"Well, you will have to start imagining it."

She's said this before, but only in a rage. This afternoon, she is calm and there is a sadness at the centre of her bright, dark eyes. These words have not washed from her on a gush of emotion. They've been sorted and weighed and measured, they sit on a foundation that is not going to disappear.

I move closer and give her a hug. "Pascale, I know how it must seem, but try to understand. Graham loves horses, but he loves you too. In his own way."

She nods, staring now at the drifting yellow ducks. "I mean it, Lexie. I told your brother last night. It is not just the horses coming first, we have many more troubles. You know that."

"What did Graham say?"

"He refuse to discuss."

I look at over at my sister-in-law. Several speeches go through my head:

Pascale, your troubles aren't really Pascale/Graham troubles, they're Kerr/Chautemps troubles. But Kerrs need Chautemps. And Chautemps need Kerrs. It's hard for the sun to talk to the moon, it's hard even to see the moon when the sun is out. But where would we be without both? That speech is no good. It's Kerr talk.

Pascale, someday your duck will come in.

Ah oui, bien sûr, she'd say.

Pascale, without you, we Kerrs will drown in the dettol-pee quagmire.

Get a gill, she'd say.

"Pascale, can you imagine how the roof of a person's mouth would look after drinking coffee through a straw? All those little red, burnt circles—smarting like hell!"

She laughs. Throws back that elegant Chautemps head of hers and laughs. But that's only for now, and I know it. I look around the park. Though the sun is as fierce and as bright as ever, though a grand covey of yellow duckies floats serenely down the Sanasateen, I'm covered with hundreds of sharp little shiver prickles.

That night, after we've feasted on Vivian's barbecued chicken, baked potatoes, and strawberry shortcake, it ends up all Kerrs in our car for the twelve-mile ride out to the farm: Graham, Yves, my husband David, our daughters, me at the wheel. I drive slowly, windows down, high beams lighting a stretch of gravel road ahead. Soft country air on our burnt red faces. Crickets, frogs, the crunch of tires on gravel, an occasional stone pinging against metal. Dark shadows, the black sky, a moon one night away from full. Smell of the Sanasateen.

No one says a word. This is Kerr country.

When I coast down to the farmhouse fence and turn off the car, we sit for a moment, still under the spell of the night. Then the van with Pascale at the wheel rounds the stone wall, radio rocking, Patsy yipping, horn beeping, kids at every window.

"Hey, over there, are you every last one dead?" yells the driver. "Sitting like how-do-you-say zombies in the dark!"

PART III

Their lives, our lives, rippling down the years.
—"Our Mother and Dorothy Goodman"

xiii.
On Huron's Shore

Among the People, a child's first Teaching is of the Four Great Powers of the Medicine Wheel. To the North on the Medicine Wheel is found Wisdom ... The West is the Looks-Within Place, which speaks of the Introspective nature of man.

—Hyemeyohsts Storm

IF YOU BEGIN AT THE DENSELY-SETTLED SHORE of Lake Ontario and drive north-west for two and a half hours, you will find yourself in Lucknow. Lucknow, our sepoy town, says the sign. A sepoy is a native of India employed as a soldier by a European power. But India with its teeming crush of darkness, light, and every permutation of human existence between, seems as far from Lucknow as a dream at high noon. Lucknow is highway 86, lined on either side by an orderly series of run-down stores. One set of lights. Straight rows of Gladiolas and tall August corn at the back of the modest homes. If you walk down the main street of Lucknow at noon in August, life will seem no more than small change, perspiration easing onto the temple from beneath the straw hat, the price of eggs, dozens of six quart baskets of peaches and tomatoes.

One last hill as you pick up speed at the outskirts of the town. If you reach the top on a clear day, you might glimpse a strip of dark-blue on the horizon before you descend to a landscape as flat as in the days before Columbus. Here the factory sheds for the poultry and cattle are long and silver-white in the sun, *the barns painted green or red and proudly lettered. A. J. Halloran & Sons.*

Only once do you see any hint that this droning, heat-dazed landscape will ever give way to something else, and that is when one section of a green-leafed maple tree flashes a startling tangerine.

In the last field before the intersection of 86 with the blue water highway, you will see a sign: PREPARE TO MEET THY GOD.

This is how I imagine that a stranger might describe the journey from my city home to my dream cottage on the shore of Lake Huron. Not a stranger exactly, but someone with a more detached perspective than I have. Someone more knowing, more dispassionate.

Any time I drive this road to the lake now, memories are apt to spring at me like one of the frogs that used to frequent the ditches, and when I'm here, in these parts, I'm never without the knowledge that both of my parents are in their last flat stretch of life, like the road between Lucknow and the blue water highway.

It's not really *my* dream cottage. The place belongs to Ruby Gibson.

The phone booth in front of the Amberley general store is like Nebuchadnezzar's furnace on the June day that David and I drive north-west to look for a cottage that I will rent for two weeks in August in order to complete a project in solitude. As well, Amberley—a general store and a gas station—is only twenty miles from Rilling, where my sister Vivian lives and to which our parents have moved, so that my father can be in a nursing home in the town where he was born and where his daughter is a doctor. We find the cottage that hot day in June. The plan: that I complete the project and then have my mother and my aunt out to the cottage.

When you reach Amberley, at the intersection of 86 and the bluewater highway, drive straight through. The August sky, which until now has contained masses of white cumulus clouds, is clear ahead. Flat as before, the road continues for two miles to the brow of a steep hill.

There before you, painted in strips of midnight-blue, turquoise, teal-blue and aquamarine (by the God you have been warned to prepare to meet?) is one of the five great lakes of Canada. Huron. Descend the hill and turn left onto Amberley beach road. Drive to the gray board fence, turn right into the lane. In front of you is the dream cottage by the sea.

When I arrive by myself, in August, and turn in at the gray fence, Mrs. Ruby Gibson is coming toward me across the deep green length of yard. She's wearing a cream-beaded dress with shoes to match. Her hair is dyed a flat matte black that ages her face, her dark red lipstick has run slightly past the outline of her lips, her glittery eyes look me over with sharp interest. She is on her way to a wedding, she explains, then she will be staying with her brother for two weeks in Chatham. In her palm are pearl studs that she cannot get through the holes in her ears, it's been so long since she wore them. Would I?

I lean close and am invaded by the little-girl-sweetness of the powder that clings thickly-pink to her cheeks and ends with no nonsense abruptness at her jaw line. Under the sweetness I catch a faint whiff of something that smells like rotting molar. Trying not to breathe, I attempt to grasp an earlobe. Between my fingers, it's as plump and as slippery as the pope's nose of a chicken. The earring's spike will enter the hole, but will not reappear at the back, no doubt enjoying a wallow in the generous pad of flesh. I did not want to touch this woman in the first place, and now step away and suggest that she ask a wedding guest—perhaps a relative?—to help her, before the ceremony begins.

Walk across the long green yard. Above are elms, beeches, maples and spruce. As you approach the rear of the white cottage, you can see through the large back window to the wide front window, and beyond that, blue, a blue that is infinite and eternal. On the back patio, red and white impatiens set off clumps of hosta. Enter the door and walk the length of the cottage to the front. Step onto the stone patio and sit down in the white chair. Before you are sand and sea and sky. Wind and waves. The sun. That is all. No signs, no wires, no benches, no garbage pails, no garbage, no people.

You could be on the Aegean. You could be in the Azores. You could be in heaven, about to meet Thy God.

I have come here to write a letter to my father. A letter that will never be read by him, but one I urgently need to write, at this point in my life. I will walk the length of this beach morning and evening. Much of the rest of the time, I will dwell on my father.

If you enter the cold water, you will cross a band of pebbles, then come again to sandy bottom. By the time you have waded out to the place where the lake water is up to your chin, you will find it difficult to keep your feet on the bottom. They will tip up and you will float in the water as once you floated in the fluid of your mother's womb. When you return to the shallows, you will stagger as you clamber over the pebbles to dry sand, your body no longer supported by the water.

At the end of the two weeks with Huron, I have written the letter that I call *You My Father*:

You are slim and blond. Your blue eyes are pools of summer sky. Your arteries are clear, your blood pressure enviable. At seventy-one, it is likely that you have many years ahead of you.

You lived your life preparing for the future that is now, deferring enjoyment until the day you would at last be free of the job you did for forty-five years to support your family. You lived your life preparing for now, when you would farm full time, breeding your Charolais to a perfection of cattle beast.

Never did you deviate from your rules for good health: no salt, no tea, no coffee, no soft drinks, no alcohol, no tobacco, no eating between meals. Stretching exercises in the kitchen each evening at nine o'clock followed by five spy apples cut in quarters and consumed. Only on Christmas Day did you allow yourself to break these rules.

You exercised this self-discipline in order to be fit for the future.

When you were fifty-eight, an adversary appeared. For thirteen years it has been taking from you. Your herd of Charolais, built slowly over the years. The strength to lift your scythe. The endurance to make it to retirement with full pension at age sixty five. The competence to keep your records, do your income tax, communicate with your pen. Your remarkable memory. Your ability to turn over in bed. Your voice. Your driver's license. The ability to get to the end of a sentence, to read. Your interest in world affairs. The capacity to hold your urine and rid yourself of your feces.

"How are you doing?" I ask on a visit to your home.

"I shovelled the snow from the front and back sidewalks and the driveway too," you reply.

The drugs that allow you to move begin to take your ability to distinguish what is real from what is not.

The phone rings. My mother. "Were you here this evening?" she asks. I tell her I was not.

"I was out for an hour," she says, "and when I came back your dad said you'd been here. I didn't think you'd drive all the way over and stay only an hour."

Your wife looks after you. After long years her nest is no longer empty. There are vegetables to cut into tiny pieces, arms and legs to guide into clothing, baths to give, hair to wash, diapers to change, sheets to strip in the night, a voice calling her at midnight, two o'clock and four. She is seventy now. When she sits down, she falls asleep.

"Lots of evenings when I finally get him tucked in bed," she says, "I'm so tired that I think I can't do it anymore. Then I think about him in a Home. I know they couldn't cater to him the way I do. He'd be miserable wanting to be moved, you know how he gets, and no one coming to help him. I don't know. I can't do it, I can't not do it. So I just—do it—that's all."

"Him" is you—the man she fought in hand to hand combat over every inch of territory the two of you occupied for forty-five years of married life.

Yours was a powerful personality. All three of your children's lives have been shaped predominantly by you. You molded us to measure ourselves by our achievements rather than by who we are. You stressed productivity and competence. You valued the utilitarian over the creative. You showed us how to be hard on ourselves, how not to express our feelings. You taught us to work, to deny obstacles, to keep going, and never, ever, to give up or let go.

These are the traits that enabled you to survive abandonment and poverty in the Depression and you passed them on, intact, to us. I am gone from your house for twenty years before I realize you would not have dreamed that in other times they might become an ambiguous legacy.

Your youngest, my sister, is living out your ideal life. You went only to the end of high school; your career was as a medical underwriter. She is a medical doctor in the farming community where you grew up. She has divorced and taken back your name.

Your son works in business, as you did, for an employer with a reputation for being hard on its employees. Weekends he goes to the farm and works, as you worked. The farm is central to his life, as it was to yours. You had three children and wanted more; your son has five.

Your firstborn rides to work on an old bicycle, a plastic bag on her head when it rains. You jogged to work in your suit, in the days when no one jogged.

One Saturday last summer, I caught sight of myself staggering across the yard in the sun, arms turned inside out by the weight of the wheelbarrow they were pushing. I was moving clay from one end of the lot to the other. A week's housework waited for me inside. The clay won't grow much, no matter which end of the yard it's at. I took a hard look at that figure lurching along in the heat and finally recognized it. It was you.

In mid life, I find myself haunted by the shadow of your unlived possibilities, which are also mine.

Your adversary is relentless. You do not complain, you do not express despair. "I'm doing pretty well, considering how many years I've had this," you say.

You carry on. You cajole your wife into driving you to the farm. You deny, you struggle, you cut grass and fix fences though the effort leaves you drenched and shaking. Your last summer outdoors you cut grass with your spirit. No matter that the fields are peopled with phantasmagoria or that your every movement is monstrously choreic. You keep going.

A friend is with me at the farm one day that summer. She expresses awe at your willpower, incredulity at the strength of your denial. As she talks, I remember another time.

I am fourteen. You have not spoken to me for a month because I have broken one of your rules. Perhaps I said "stupid" or "shut up" or "belly," one of the many words forbidden by you. On this day we are alone in the house. You come to my bedroom and place your face close to mine: "Say you are sorry for what you have done."

I try to move around you and run from the house. Keeping your face inches from mine, you move with me, back and forth, blocking my way. You are agile, your reflexes fast. Screaming, lunging, this way, then that, I try to escape, as you move, right with me, your eyes holding mine, chanting, again and again, "Say you are sorry. Say you are sorry. Say you are sorry."

You will not give up. I will not give in. On and on we leap and turn, partners in this grotesque dance, until at last you hear your wife's car in the driveway and hurry from my room.

That night I write in my diary, "I hate you and live for the day when I will dance on your grave."

The time comes when there is no place for you to sleep because of all the phantasms already bedded down in your room. You are calling your wife repeatedly, wild-eyed, while she stands beside you in the kitchen.

The doctors say that drugs used to treat Parkinson's disease gradually lose their effectiveness and side effects become intolerable; it's time for a drug holiday. They put you in hospital for six weeks and gradually withdraw you from the long list of drugs you are on, attempting to discover which ones are causing the hallucinations and the confusion. They cautiously start over with a greatly reduced repertoire, trying to fine tune for the maximum mobility achievable without intolerable side effects.

My daughters and I visit you one Sunday. You reach up, wanting to hug me, something you've not done since I was a small child. You were given up at birth by your mother, abandoned as a boy by your adopted father. You don't risk rejection often. "I guess a person has to die of something," you whisper. I bend only far enough for you to touch my shoulders, then straighten.

Your attempted hug brings a scene from ten years before into my mind. An August dusk at the farm, phlox scenting the air, the first bats dipping and turning by the eaves. My youngest daughter is a baby. She's been screaming inconsolably for hours, as she often did. Now she's asleep at last in my arms. "You will be the death of me," I sigh into her hair.

From the shadows under the harvest apple tree where you are picking windfalls from the ground, you turn towards me: "She and her sister will be the most precious things in your life."

"Did you ever regret having us?" I ask.

"Never for one moment," comes your answer.

When your hallucinations are minimal, your confusion tolerable and your chorea eliminated, the doctors send you home. Though you are weak, your mind is clearer than before and we think you have improved. In fact, your adversary is about to show its face.

For gradually it becomes apparent that the disease has broken something in you that all of us thought was indestructible.

Throughout your life you dealt with adversity through physical movement. The bureaucracy and the office politics, the depression and the inability to sleep, the conflicts with your wife and children: the antidote to all of these was to go to the farm and work at the endless tasks supplied by a herd of cattle, one hundred acres, and an ancient twelve room house.

Once, at the nadir of my life, so desperate that I turned to you, I asked, "How do I go on?"

"Walk," you said. "Put one foot ahead of the other and walk. Walk and walk and walk until you are too tired to go any further."

Now you cannot walk. Only occasionally, stumblingly, with a cane, when someone starts you off, on a good day, or right after your medication.

A cycle has been at work in your life for many years. The power of your spirit was nourished by the movement of your body. The movement of your body was achieved by the power of your spirit. Now even your powerful spirit can no longer move your body. The cycle is broken and the nourishment to your spirit is cut off. Your spirit has died.

Your lifelong legendary zest for sweets is gone. Slowly, steadily you lose weight. The mask of your face is never touched by a smile.

I am eleven, Graham is eight. You and our mother have had a terrible fight. That weekend, our mother refuses to go to the farm with you. On the Sunday morning, she calls your two older children into the living room of your small city home. Graham and I. The three of us sit on the couch facing the floor-length green drapes that hang in the picture window. Our mother has just closed them, though it is daytime.

Graham is famous for these drapes. He picked them out, a child of three. The drapes have a repeating pattern of horses pulling a carriage along a winter road, evergreens in the background; they are modeled on a picture painted by Grandma Moses. Our mother often tells this story. Graham, so young, had the good taste to pick the work of this artist, who went blind and lived to be one hundred and did not start her career until age seventy-eight. I sulk and think to myself that Graham just liked the horses.

Our mother clears her throat and says she is going to tell us a secret about you. "Your father's mother," she says to us, "your grandmother, the person your father visited in the hospital, who had bed sores and black circles around her eyes—she was not your father's real mother. Your father's real mother was pregnant with him, but not married."

Our mother looks at Graham and me. We keep our poker faces steady.

"Your father's real mother was a sixteen year old girl. She gave him up for adoption. Your father is a bastard," our mother whispers. "Your father doesn't know who he is."

She leans closer to us. "No one must ever know."

No one must ever know.

Over the following months, I replay this scene over and over in my mind. I see the drape horses pulling the sleigh, the forest-green background, snow weighing down the green-needled branches, the slight chip in our mother's pointed tooth. I hear the thin rind of satisfaction that encases her words. He is a bastard. Your father doesn't know who he is.

I find myself compelled to search for something. I don't know what it is. The searching is almost against my will. It has to do with you, my father, who do not know who you are.

You have two places in our small house that are yours. The right side of the blond buffet in the kitchen. Here is where you place your papers. They are neatly stacked, one on top of the other. The pile is high. When no one is home, I carry the pile to the kitchen table. Look at every paper.

The other place is the top drawer of the tall dresser in the bedroom you share with our mother. Papers and letters are packed so tightly that it is difficult to take one out. Over a period of weeks, I remove the letters and papers one by one, and read them. I don't know what I'm looking for, but I do know that I never find it.

No one must ever know.

I am twelve years old. You are driving a carload of my schoolmates on an outing. These girls live on our street or go to the same church or have fathers that work at the office with you. They are telling stories, boasting, showing off snatches of their lives.

I have a story that can top them all. I turn around and look through the space between the front seats. "My father isn't my father," I announce. "My father is adopted."

There is immediate silence in the car.

"He doesn't know his real name," I continue, sliding a glance at your profile. "He doesn't know who he is."

With quick glances at the back of your immobile head, my school mates begin to argue that you are still my father.

"No," I insist. "He can't be my father."

You give no indication that you have heard me.

"I'm going to ask my dad," says Joan. Joan's father works

at the office with you. The girls begin to chatter about something else.

In the front seat, I take quick peeks at you, without turning my head. Your face is as still as the windshield. Your ears are bright red.

From then on, you do not speak to me. Even when I bring home an English test with 100% at the top, you turn your face away. You disappear me. Perhaps it is weeks that you do not speak to me. Perhaps it is months. Or years. Perhaps you never speak to me, or look at me, in quite the same way again.

Now one small, elderly woman with high blood pressure stands between you and the last thing you have left: staying in your own home rather than in an institution. Your disease may claim her as well. Exhaustion is changing the very contours of her face.

If this happens, your children will put you in a nursing home. You will spend your days among strangers who never knew you whole and have too many like you to look after.

No one, including you, will expect us to look after you at home. In your condition that's impossible, they'll say. You require twenty-four hour nursing care. You require the equipment of a licensed facility.

It's not impossible, of course. People used to do it all the time. There are many places in this world where they are still doing it. It is not impossible, but we will choose not to make the major rearrangements of our lives that would make it possible. We will choose rather to spend our lives earning money, pursuing our interests, and raising your grandchildren, far from the smell of suppositories and wet sheets in the night.

But today you are still living at home because your wife would rather die than put you in an institution. With great difficulty we persuade her to take a break. A ten day stay in a nursing home is arranged for you.

The others go to visit you. I do not. They are quick to excuse me.

My sister: "Oh, but you'd have to go as a daughter. I didn't go as a daughter. I went as a physician. How does this nursing home compare to others? Is the care he is receiving adequate or superior?"

My sister in law: "You go out to work every day. You're tired on the weekends."

My mother: "I'm not sure it makes much difference. A day later, I'm not sure he even knows you've been there."

But I know. I know that I, your firstborn, stayed home.

The Sunday afternoon of my intended visit you appear in my mind's eye just as I get into the car. I am walking to the end of a long corridor and find the room I am looking for. A small figure weighing one hundred and twelve pounds is standing alone in sock feet between the bed and the wall. It is you. One of your rules was never to wear sock feet.

I get out of the car and return to the house.

Now the winter solstice is here. The family has gathered at your younger daughter's home in Rilling, Ontario. Deep snow surrounds the house and buries the river. More snow is falling from a darkening sky. Around a table inside, the Lost Heir players wait while your younger daughter shuffles and deals the cards. The players make their bids.

Just outside the circle of light, you are frozen at an angle, unable to straighten or get up. An afghan protects you from the cold in a room blazing with Christmas merriment. Your mask is expressionless as the players shout and laugh and sweep the cards from the table. Only the spittle dribbling slowly from your hanging mouth tells me you are not a statue. You are enduring the moments until your wife will leave her grandchildren around the fire and take you home to bed.

Lost Heir is the only game you ever played. You were a risk taker, the talk of your kin for the outlandish moves you made.

When your risks paid off you laughed and laughed until your face was the crimson of the cranberry sauce you had eaten for dinner.

That evening, while our mother is putting you to bed, you whisper to her that it's time for you to go to the nursing home. That you don't mind. That you can see that she is going down.

Never do I look at you and see you only as you are. Always superimposed is what you were, what you might have been, had not your adversary come and stayed.

I try to see you only as you are today, locked in by your destiny. But always the other pictures come unbidden when I look at you.

I have read that if you look at the frog scalded in the hot tub, if you handle the dead bird, if you turn and face the dark shadow from which you flee, there can be a coming to terms. As the others play cards and visit, I watch you. Every day, as I drive to work or eat supper or lie in bed before sleeping, I imagine how it is for you. Acceptance does not come to me.

On Christmas Day, my sister's partner calls me to the kitchen table where you are sitting. Mike is a man after your own heart, a man you have trusted this fall to set your affairs in order just as you would have done yourself had you been able.

At your request, he has settled on your seven grandchildren seven insurance policies. As he explains the terms to me, I see a movement across the table. It's your hand, faltering towards the chocolate box. You succeed in putting a candy in your mouth. I don't absorb all the details of Mike's explanation, but it's clear that none of your grandchildren will have to subsist for a year on carrots and peanut butter, as you did in order to finish high school, no matter what becomes of their parents.

I look at you across the table. There are words I want to say. Something about wishing you had denied yourself less and lived your life more, even as I recognize that you journeyed the only way you knew to go. Then I see that this gift of your life's blood is one thing that's beyond the reach of your adversary, and that you have lived long enough to know that you are passing it on to your descendants. That this is what matters to you: making certain that your grandchildren will not endure the privation that kept you from the education you would have liked to have.

I cannot utter these thoughts. The words are locked inside. Instead I stand up, go around the table and give you a long, heartfelt hug. It is the first such hug I have been able to give you in my life.

Walk west along the shore. If you walk where the waves can lap your ankles, the wet sand will give under your feet. You will have to labour to keep going. If you walk above the reach of the waves, on dry sand, you will sink with each step and be in danger of burning your soles.

There is a narrow place between, where the sand is smooth and firm. You may walk in this space for a long time without feeling tired. It's easy to find the narrow path between the water and the sand because that is where you will see most of the footprints that have gone before.

On the seventh day of the second week, my solitude is broken. My mother and her sister Anna are driving out from Rilling to the cottage for lunch. I stay in the back room, tidying up and watching for them.

When they arrive, my mother parks the car, then they advance slowly across the dark green shade, white heads bowed, eyes helping their feet to pick their way across the still-wet grass.

I get to my feet and hold the door open. Not speaking because I'm still looking—so intently, so intensely, that the back of my mind muses, Will I be turned to salt, or to stone, for this looking? Will I lose them for this looking, as Eurydice was lost, and Eros?

Mother and aunt. Irene and Anna. Seventy-five years ago they were billed as the "Infant Wonders." Little sisters, dressed in identical plaid wool dresses, singing in harmony, performing in the church basements of East Wawanosh, driven to and from by horse and buggy, huddled under a buffalo robe in winter. Hired girls at fourteen, sleeping in beds with the children of the family, who sometimes had manure on their feet. Released from that life in their early twenties when factory jobs created by the war allowed them to save enough to get married.

Aunt Anna has brought potato salad and peach crumble. My mother has brought salmon sandwiches. "No wonder your name was once the Infant Wonders!" I say, accepting the offerings and the hugs. Aunt Anna laughs. "But infants no longer," she says, miming a grotesque limp as she enters the door.

Everyone says they look alike, but I don't think so. Aunt Anna has big breasts, and her expression is serene. It isn't an untried serenity; she's had a hard life. But Aunt Anna believes that the hard parts are pieces of a grand plan that will be revealed not too long from now, when the veil is lifted from her face. My mother frets, agonizes, believes in God one day, doesn't the next, flip flops from elation to despair.

They exclaim at the blue, as I take them to the front patio and settle them into the white chairs. The breeze is chilly, they say. I find an afghan of benign-blue, like the water and sky this morning, get my mother to hitch her chair closer to her sister's, tuck the blue blanket around the two of them, as once I tucked in Julie and Katie. The anxiety that for my mother precedes even such an outing as this is slipping away visibly, like dry sand down smooth glass. They begin to reminisce about their rare girlhood visits to this very beach, a mile or so down.

It seems as if the two weeks alone have given me clearer vision, better hearing. I continue to look at this pair who, by their dying, will pull me into a different world. How will it be without this generation of my family—sheltering, admiring, criticizing, standing ahead of me, between me and the finality of the unknowable? A large bug rattles by. Waves gurgle, lap, grate, and roar in the deeper hollows over the pebbles. It's inconceivable that soon these two will leave this world. It happens to everyone, but that makes it no less outrageous.

"This is how I imagine heaven," Aunt Anna says, her hand moving slightly on the blue blanket.

"I hope you see me beside you, just the way I am now," says my mother.

Aunt Anna laughs. "You bet I do," she says, and her hand moves from the blanket to take the hand of her sister.

When at last you become tired, sit and rest on Huron's shore. Look west at the flowing, curving, ever-changing line of water where it meets and makes its mark upon the land.

xiv.
Our Mother and Dorothy Goodman

IF YOU WALK DOWN THE MAIN STREET of Rilling, Ontario, on an August day at noon, life will seem slow and inconsequential. It will seem as if nothing happens here, as if nothing ever could happen. But surface is never the real story.

Our mother moved back to Rilling in her early seventies. She'd been raised nearby, and my sister had by now been a doctor for many years in the town. Our father had to go into the nursing home. It seemed the best arrangement.

The move had just been completed, and my sister and I were sitting in our mother's new apartment in the small town. It was time to list the house in the city where our parents had raised us and had lived for all of their married lives. This was my job. I explained to our mother that the realtor had suggested an Open House on the first Sunday after the listing went up.

My mother sat up straight. "You mean, where anybody can go in?"

"That's right; you've seen the signs for Open Houses—it's a common procedure."

"We're not doing that. The neighbours will get inside. They'll see everything that's wrong with the house."

Our mother had spent the best part of every week dusting, vacuuming and polishing the interior of our family home. "Mom, there's nothing wrong; it's the same inside as most of the houses on the street."

"Everything's wrong with it. All the nosy Parkers will go in. I won't have them sneering at how James and I lived." Our mother leaned her head back into the smooth taupe sheen of the sofa upholstery and pressed her fingers to her eyes. Her hair had been permed within an inch of its white, wiry life. I could see the back of it only in my mind's eye, the perm ending abruptly at the lower border of the occiput, the hair beneath that point tapered close, and left straight. It was a deplorable style. I had tried without success to wean her off it.

"Mother, they won't sneer."

She opened her eyes. "Oh yes they will. They've all got the very latest thing. The last word in kitchens and bathrooms. I won't have it."

I looked at Vivian. Her blond hair was showing white at the roots; she looked exhausted. She was in the rocking chair, pushing her right foot rhythmically against the beige carpet. She shook her head just enough to signal me to back off.

"Okay, Mom," I said. "We'll have the house seen by appointment only."

"I don't want anybody going in there."

Vivian got up and went over to the sofa. Our mother had slumped against the cushions again. Her eyes were closed and she wore a certain long-suffering look with which Vivian and I were on intimate terms. Vivian sat down and took our mother's thin, splotched hand. She spoke quietly. "Mom, you know people have to see the inside of a house before they buy it."

Our mother snatched her hand away and stood up. "I don't know anything of the kind." Two bright red spots appeared on her cheekbones. "I don't want to sell the house at all. Why can't you two just leave me alone." She walked to her bedroom and slammed the door. We heard sobs.

"Don't talk about it, Lexie," said my sister wearily. "Just go ahead and do it."

Our mother was on the ground floor of a four-plex. Vivian had made a good choice. The place seemed like a townhouse; there was even a front patio outside the full-length sliding glass doors.

It was a two hour drive, now, for me to visit. I drove up again in April, a month after the move; the city house had sold quickly. As soon as we were settled with a pot of hot tea, my mother blurted it out, her tone the auditory equivalent of her look of long-suffering.

"It seems I have a double."

A double! Immediately, my mind went into high gear. That mysterious other who is and is not you. Our mother, of all people, who wanted only to be ordinary and above all, unnoticed. This was the last thing I'd expected her to say.

"It's been going on since the first day I moved back here. I get it all the time: 'I thought I saw you on the street this morning, Irene. It wasn't 'til I was right up close, opening my mouth to say your name, that I realized it was Dorothy Goodman.'"

"Who is Dorothy Goodman?"

"I don't know. I don't know her."

"Have you asked around?"

"Of course not."

"Did you ask Vivy?"

"Vivian doesn't know her either. Let's talk about something else. How's David?"

"I do have a story for you." I took a sip of my tea, and settled into the easy chair with a view of the street and the narrow flower bed, where a row of evenly-spaced white narcissus with orange centers stood on guard. Our mother loved stories about David, who is the stereotypical absent-minded professor, and not a practical person.

I told her that David and I had bought a new bed and the delivery men had come while I was at work. Our bedroom is on the second floor of the house. The men got the bed halfway up the stairs and could get it no further due to the narrowness of the turn. When I arrived home from work at dinnertime, the bed was wedged on the landing. You couldn't get to the upstairs without clambering over it, no small feat.

I sprang out of the easy chair and mimed the action for my

mother. "Why didn't you have them take it away?" I said to David, clapping both hands to my head.

"They said maybe we could get somebody to bring it in the upstairs window."

"David, have you lost your mind? Look at the size of the thing. It would never go in a window. And, what would we do, advertise in the paper? Wanted: somebody to bring a bed in a second-storey window."

"Oh," my mother exclaimed. "Oh, oh, OH." She sounded as if she was in agony, but tears of mirth spurted onto her cheeks. She had a good sense of the ridiculous once you got her going. She jumped to her feet and hurried from the room.

"Where are you going, Mother? Don't you want to hear the story?"

"I have to shut the outside door. Mr. McTavish might hear me laughing."

"Mr. McTavish?"

"The superintendent of this building. I don't want him to hear me making noise. I don't want to be put out on the street."

It turned out she wouldn't watch TV in case Mr. McTavish heard the noise. She wouldn't let my brother bring her own grandchildren to visit. She wouldn't play her piano. She wouldn't let me look out the apartment window "in case the neighbours think you're gawking at them." She told me to keep my voice down at least half a dozen times during that visit.

This move was going to be more of an adjustment than we'd anticipated. I'd thought that moving back here to Rilling would be like returning home for her. Apparently not.

David and I had rented a cottage on Lake Huron for two weeks, not far from Rilling. On our way back to our city home, we stopped at my mother's apartment for a visit. I brought our wine bottles and cans to recycle in her bin.

She met us at the door, a look of alarm on her face. "Oh no, you can't do that."

"We can't?"

"Mr. McTavish might look in the bin and see the bottles."

"Mother, have you seen the beer belly on Mr. McTavish?"

"I never use the bin. I'm not having Mr. McTavish know all about me."

I set the cans and bottles by the door to take home with us, and asked how she was enjoying the town. She said that other than going to Vivian's, she just went back and forth to the nursing home to visit our father. Otherwise, she didn't go out much, only to church, and for groceries.

"How come? This is your home town."

"Up here, people stay on in their houses 'til they drop, you know. No matter what shape they're in. Literally drop in their tracks."

"Yes?"

"They look at me, and the first thing they say is, 'How's James?' I can see what they're thinking. They think I stuck him in the Home because I couldn't be bothered. I can hardly hold my head up when I go out."

"Mom, they're not thinking that; they're not judging you. Dad has advanced Parkinson's. You were getting up to him several times a night. Your health was giving out."

"Up here, women look after their husbands 'til they drop. They're judging me alright. I know them."

"Are people still mistaking you for your double?"

"Oh yes. It's got so I know the look. They come up to me, and I know what they're going to say." She pulled a tissue from the box on her end table and patted her temples. "Would you stop harping on this, Lexie? I don't want to talk about it."

"I'm not harping, Mom. I merely inquired. It's not everyone has a double."

"Get off it."

In October of that year, during one of our phone conversations, our mother surprised me. We'd talked for twenty minutes, and

I was saying goodbye, when she interrupted: "Well, I guess I'll be seeing Dorothy Goodman."

"Your double?"

"It's been getting worse. A couple of weeks ago, Edna Taylor spoke to me in the hardware store: 'Irene, I hear you was passing out pamphlets for the Conservatives on Friday. I thought you was a Liberal.'"

Our mother was a lifelong Liberal and she believed that a person's politics belonged in the private realm, along with their sex life and the contents of their garbage pails. She would no more have "displayed" herself by passing out pamphlets for a particular party than she would have walked naked to church.

"I don't think she believed me when I told her I hadn't passed out any pamphlets, then, or ever in my life. She gave me a queer look."

"Did you tell her it was probably Dorothy Goodman?"

"I did. That's when she gave me the look." There was a pause, then my mother said, "This has gone too far, Lexie. How can I hold my head up in town when a woman everybody thinks is me is parading around making a fool of herself?" She blew her nose. I realized she was near tears.

"Mom, she was only handing out pamphlets. You were going to tell me how and when you're going to meet Dorothy Goodman."

"I'm not meeting her, I'm going to set eyes on her. She's giving a talk on Africa, of all things, in the church basement. I've hardly slept all week, trying to decide whether to go."

"Maybe Vivy could go with you."

"Vivian has a hospital Board meeting. Don't keep on and on about this, Lexie. I'm getting off the phone now."

She went.

I can close my eyes now, and see our mother that fall evening, setting off alone under the streetlights of the town not far from where she'd been born, to encounter herself face to face. That's how I thought of it. I found out later that our mother had dressed in the navy suit and white blouse she wore to church. She'd worn her pearls. Maybe she stopped once or twice to allow the touch of burning in her throat, the slight tightening in her chest, to pass. We didn't know it, but she was having angina by then. She would have made herself as inconspicuous as possible, walking the eight blocks through the crumbling leaves that would still have smelled faintly of maple at that time of year, stepping carefully around the fallen crabapples and the acorns. I don't know where she found the courage to take that walk, when she'd avoided self knowledge her whole life. People can surprise you.

She told me the rest herself, the next evening, on the phone.

"I sat on a folding chair, in the back row, so I could get out of there in a hurry if the resemblance was too uncanny. Just before eight, two people came through a door at the front of the room. A pretty, slender woman with white hair, who sat down in the first row with her back to the audience. A stern-faced, dark-haired younger woman who went to the mike and performed the introduction; I could see her moustache from the back row."

"Wow."

"The pretty woman stepped to the podium and began to speak. This was Dorothy Goodman. I've never looked so hard at anyone in my life. She had white hair, yes. She's about my age and size. But I couldn't for the life of me see anything that would make all those people think she was me."

I knew already what it was, just from my mother's description. "How was her talk?"

"I don't remember anything about it. When she finished, they started putting out the date squares and the butter tarts and the tea. I didn't stay. I was buttoning my coat when Faye Steadman came sidling up. You know how she does. 'I seen you sitting there when I come in, Irene, and I thought you was Dorothy Goodman. You two are doubles.'"

"Oh my."

"I got out of there. I'd had enough. Faye Steadman doesn't have the brains she was born with."

Vivian and I talked about it on the phone. "I know why everybody mistakes Mom for Dorothy Goodman," I told my sister. "How many women of seventy-five do you know who have thick white hair, are slim and trim, and still pretty?"

Vivy agreed: "And the sad thing is that you'd never in a million years convince mom that she's pretty. In fact, she'd get mad if you tried to tell her that. She can't see herself."

"Well, she made a start, didn't she. I still can't believe she actually went, by herself, and faced her own double."

Eventually, our mother's angina progressed to the point where she realized that something was wrong and told us. Vivian was alarmed, and sent her to the family doctor, who made an appointment for her with a heart specialist in the city. I took time off work and came up to Rilling so that I could drive her to the appointment first thing the next morning. I stayed overnight at Vivy's and while there, dreamt about our mother. I decided to tell her the dream during our drive to see the specialist.

I picked her up at eight a.m. It was a beautiful morning and we had plenty of time, so we went the long way, by the lake. Stubble in the fields. The odd burning bush in the gardens. The occasional glimpse of Lake Huron, dark blue to the horizon. Heaps of leaves in the farmhouse yards, flashes of orange pumpkins on the front stoops. The world in its dying throes, sparking off colour. It was our mother's last fall, but we didn't know it then.

As we drove through this landscape, I told her the dream I'd had in the night.

"I was standing on a curb in Las Vegas, of all places. You and dad pulled up in a taxi. You were wearing that fitted, velvet suit of forest-green Vivy gave you for your birthday. A white limousine arrived. Dad faded into the dust. Fred Astaire and Ginger Rogers got out. Ginger faded into the dust.

"Fred Astaire opened his arms. You went right into them. He danced you under the Fremont East gateway. He twirled you past the Beauty Bar and Don't Tell Mama. All the way down and back. When you returned, you were lit up like the Vegas strip on New Year's Eve."

I told Vivian about it that night, back at her place.

"That's an amazing dream, Lexie. Our agoraphobic mother, who would barely leave the house her whole life for fear of making a fool of herself. What did she say?"

"She loved the dream. Her eyes got all green and shiny. She was lit up from inside. I got a flash of the beauty she once was."

"And never knew she was."

"She said the dream would last her the rest of her life. She was animated for the rest of the drive, talked about all sorts of things. She even mentioned her double."

"Really? Dorothy Goodman?"

"She says she's still getting it from people, but it doesn't bother her anymore. She says that after the night she went and saw the real Dorothy Goodman, the whole thing just seemed silly. 'The woman doesn't look like me at all. Some people don't have the brains they're born with.' That's what she said."

"What about the trip back?"

"Quiet. All that stuff the specialist said to us. A lot to think about. He's faxing the whole report to you, as well as to her family doctor."

The phone rang. It was the hospital about one of Vivy's patients. She went into the den to take the call.

I sat by the kitchen window. My mother and I had been quiet on the way home, but it was a good quiet. The countryside disappearing. As we drove, we could see the long shadows folding into night, and the small groups of cattle and sheep clustered around their feeding stations near the barns, barely visible against the last light. The mirage of mists and vapors rising from the lake, the lake evaporating into the sky. Eventually, the pricks of light that signified Rilling. Its reassuring, ordinary surface.

* * *

There's a postscript to this story. Years later, ten years or so after our mother's death, David and I were in Mexico with Vivian and her new husband Mike (Mike the Second). The four of us were sitting on the balcony in the warm darkness, escapees from the one of the coldest Ontario winters on record. You could hear the night chittering softly along the dark lagoon. A woman's voice crying an old song in the distance.

Our talk was desultory. Then Mike said that he had known someone, years ago, who was murdered in Mexico. The guy—he couldn't remember his name—and his girlfriend had been camping in the badlands. This was in the late sixties. Some bandits came along and raped the girlfriend. The guy tried to fight them off, and they killed him.

I asked Mike where and how he'd known the person who was murdered. "He was the son of my grade twelve English teacher. Dorothy Goodman was her name."

"Dorothy Goodman of Rilling?"

"Yes. My parents moved us from Fredericton back to Rilling the year I was in grade twelve."

"My God," Vivy and I said in unison. "Our mother's double."

Mike had never known our mother. We told him the story of the double, then I asked him something I'd always wanted to know. "What was Dorothy Goodman like, Mike? How did she seem to you? Our mother thought she was an outlandish person who passed out political pamphlets and gave talks on Africa."

"Made a spectacle of herself," added Vivian.

Mike's tanned face became animated and he spoke with

fervour. "Thick white hair. She was a beautiful woman, inside and out. A special person."

"When she taught you, that year, was the death of her son in her past or in her future?" I asked.

Mike thought for a moment. "It would have been in her future."

I flinched. "There she was, teaching you guys about Hamlet, no idea what was going to happen."

"It didn't defeat her. She lived her life."

We fell silent again.

After the others had gone to bed, I stayed on the balcony in the warm, dense darkness, and thought about the different Dorothy Goodmans, Mike's and our mother's. How we bring into being both our gods and our demotic others. That we do it with the artistry and the blindness and the skewed imagination of any creator.

Their lives, our lives, rippling down the years. On the lagoon's dark surface, a thin, glittery streak appeared. The gibbous moon. I sat on, watching its slow, hypnotic progression across the night sky.

XV.
Beneath the Mock Orange

WHEN I SET OFF THAT MORNING, I had no idea that this journey was my last chance. I didn't know what was at stake, didn't recognize the crucial moment, didn't even understand the territory.

The card I'd picked out for my mother's seventy-fifth birthday featured ruby geraniums against a background of indigo-blue delphiniums. With tax, the card cost $6.39.

"My God, I didn't check the price." This is what my mouth blurted, when I handed over a ten-dollar bill and saw it diminish to a handful of change. I caught on the cashier's face the look the young give you when you've revealed yourself to be an old fogey, got a flash of my young self, standing on one foot, then the other, as my mother expressed shock and disapproval at the price of something or other. The disgust I'd felt at those times was physical. Even today, I could taste it, could remember how my stomach had felt—shriveled on the inside. At least, today, I hadn't gone on to say, "When I was a girl, you could get a whole box of nice-looking cards for $1.00."

I jaywalked across the street and used the bank machine quickly and efficiently. (Watch me now, cashier.) Re-crossed the road to my yellow Pontiac sunbird, the August asphalt a blast of heat against my bare legs. Turned on the air, twisted my hair into a ponytail and applied the new sheer-cerise lipstick I'd bought on impulse after picking out the card.

It would be good to get out of the city, to drive north to the small town near the shores of Lake Huron where my mother lived now. Though I loved my mother and was close to her, she and I had clashed for as long as I could remember. She was an old woman now, though, and I was determined to get along with her. I'd taken two days of vacation to participate in her milestone birthday, and had promised myself not to react when she said, as she inevitably would, "Straighten up, Lexie. I don't know how you can breathe when you slouch like that," or "Keep your voice down, the neighbours will hear you." I'd promised myself to control the irritation I knew I'd feel the minute I walked in the door and smelled the Jergens lotion she used on her face. I'd given her my favourite French perfume one year for her birthday. She touched a drop to her wrist, sniffed, then shoved the pretty silver bottle across the table at me. "It's way too strong," she said. "I don't know how anyone could wear that. I'd have a sick headache in fifteen minutes." I was determined to be patient when I took her for a drive and she chose the same old route and told the same old stories.

My sister Vivian, who lives in the small town a few blocks from our mother, had the food for the birthday party catered and she brought a dozen purple helium balloons to decorate the common room of the nursing home where our father lives. We had decided to have the party there so our father could be present, though it wasn't clear that he'd know what was going on. The party was well attended and my mother seemed pleased.

The day after, Vivian went to work early, and mid-morning, I set out from her place, where I'd slept, to pick up my mother for the promised drive in the country. I saw her before she recognized the car, and for an instant she looked like a stranger. An elderly woman dressed up in a pale-blue skirt and pink blouse, thin hands holding her black purse so tightly that her knuckles were white. She looked lost, somehow, though she was standing in front of her own apartment. Then she saw me, and she was my mother again, purpose back in her face, frowning and smiling at the same time, smoothing her permed white hair, bending to open the passenger door and slide carefully inside. In less than five minutes we were on the highway and I felt my spirits rise—the new lipstick, the blue sky, a few white puffs of cloud here and there, the feeling of going somewhere.

"Wow, look at the fields, Mom. There's hardly any pasture left for the cattle."

"Oh, I think there's enough. Sit up, can't you? I don't know how you can breathe properly when you slouch like that."

I took a deep breath and sat up. "Such a drought. Look at that field."

"Keep your eyes on the road, please, Lexie."

I'd planned to drive her straight to the lake, but she insisted we go around by the farm, said she hadn't been out there since the summer before last.

I thought this a mistake. Now that my brother Graham was divorced and living there alone, the house was a wreck.

I quelled my irritation. Obviously, we were going to the farm. I knew that my mother probably understood on some level that going there was not a good idea, but that she was drawn by a force she didn't understand. I'd come to think of the farm as the other woman. It—she—destroyed both marriages. My parents had stayed together but their conflict over the farm ruined their relationship.

I turned off the highway, then, further along, onto the road that followed the course of the Maitland River. A little wind raised drifts of dust. The gravel road narrowed where high, old maples met overhead. Bushes had grown so close to the gravel that there was no longer a shoulder; the road had almost the feel of a tunnel. Once, our kin had lived every little way along here: small family farms that allowed them to survive. The houses and barns were deserted now, the countryside silent. Nature taking back her own.

"Stay back, can't you, so we're not eating his dust," my

mother said, pointing to a tractor pulling a farm instrument, far ahead.

"We're in a drought, Mom. That's why the dust is so bad. Even the established trees are drooping. Did you see the corn on the highway? Some of it has withered away. How much rain have you had up here anyway?"

"I have no idea."

This was our mother. She'd always tuned out when a factual detail was in the room. At the last intersection before we would reach the farm lane, I slowed the car and guided it across the stone bridge. The water had never been this low. I kept this thought to myself.

A rabbit skittered in front of our wheels; goldenrod and the white lace of wild carrot crowded the ditches. Halfway up the hill, I turned right into the long farm lane. Half-grown cedars lined it and grew into its space, their branches brushing, catching, scraping. As the Sunbird emerged, now, into the open, my mother and I gazed into the familiar valley on our right. Here and there, in its depths, you could see a glimmer of the creek. There was no sign of Graham.

We parked at the gate to the yard, and walked slowly up the slope to the back porch. In the kitchen, my mother picked up a glass jar from the counter and wordlessly held it out to me.

"What's that?" I said.

"The summer before last, when I was out here, the wallpaper was loose like that." She pointed up at the piece of mustard-coloured, flowered wallpaper that dangled over the stove. "I'm afraid of a fire. If he leaves a burner on, the wallpaper so close! So I made up a paste with cornstarch and water. Found a little brush. Begged him to bring it out here and step onto the stool and stick the paper back up."

She replaced the little jar on the counter. "This is it. Still sitting here. The paste turned to mold. He never used it."

"I can maybe do it, in a minute. First, I need to go up to the bathroom."

"You can't go up there right now, Lexie. There's a Mennonite on a ladder outside. Didn't you see him when we came in?"

"He's down now." I pointed out the back kitchen window. "He's over at the barn, standing in the doorway. Graham must be in there doing the chores."

From upstairs, I heard my mother trying to play the old organ. She could make any keyboard instrument sing, but the organ had been ruined by dust and mice, damp and cold; it wasn't possible even to tell what piece she was playing. When I descended the narrow back stairs and re-entered the kitchen, she was standing in the dining room doorway, surveying the mess of papers. She looked at me. "Do I dare brave the bathroom?"

"Yes, but look neither left nor right, and take a box of Kleenex with you."

Her semi-joking tone was a surprise. At one time, the state of this house would have sent her into outer space. Keeping up this huge decaying farmhouse and our small city home had been her life's work. But she didn't seem fundamentally upset. She was just dipping into it, playing with it, the way a child will toy with something that might be dangerous.

While she was upstairs, I checked the fridge. A loaf of doughy white bread. A bottle of Metamucil. A can of coke. Ugh. No wonder Graham was in such bad shape.

I heard my mother on the stairs, and went to meet her.

"I looked neither left nor right, but I couldn't help looking down. I've a good mind to get on my hands and knees and clean this place myself."

"Only to have it get dirty again. Come on. Let's go."

That evening, back home in the southern Ontario city where I live, I called Vivian, who asked how the drive went.

"It was uneventful. Not long after we sat down in the park, she was ready to head home. I think she just wanted to see that strip of blue from the top of the hill, and reassure herself that the place where she'd taken her kids and her mother for a happy picnic once every summer was still there."

"Yeah, probably."

"While we were in the park, an old guy told us there's been less than one tenth of an inch of rain in June and July, and none in August. It's been sunny all the time."

"True enough."

"You know what Mom said, Vivy, even after the guy told us that? 'I think it's like this every year. People forget from one summer to the next.'"

"That's typical of her, Lexie."

"You know, at one time, I'd have taken the Fact of one tenth of an inch and shaken it in her face. I didn't, though. I told myself I'd finally grown up. I didn't need to change her. But I reckoned without the coffee."

"What happened? She phoned me earlier tonight, said she thinks you're in poor health."

"Oh, great. Wow, Vivian, now that does make my gorge rise!"

"What happened?"

"What happened is—we get to her apartment and I make my own damn coffee, because hers is like dishwater. Which, I mean, probably insults her right there. She gives me a plastic cup and asks whether I wasn't going to make two cups. I'd told her earlier that there was nowhere to buy a decent cup of coffee on my two-hour drive home. I'd said I might make a second cup for the road, at her place.

"So anyway, I tell her, if I still want it when I'm ready to go, I'll make a second cup then. Right away, she says, 'That's ridiculous.' She spits this at me, Vivian. She really does spit, but I don't get mad, I monitor my tone, I suggest we go on her veranda, it's such a beautiful day."

"Yeah, okay. And?"

"Well, so then she asks if she can use my grounds to pour water through and make herself a coffee and I say of course, but it'll be pretty weak. So she comes out with her coffee and she's quiet and sips it and then she bursts out, spits out, in her same furious tone, 'This coffee is so strong I can't even drink it, and it's made from your grounds—the coffee you're drinking can't be good for you, Lexie, it's probably what's wrong with your health, how much coffee must you go through in a week, how can you afford that?'"

"I tell her not to be ridiculous, that there's nothing wrong with my health."

"'You always have something wrong,'" she says. "'You're sickly.'"

"I'm sickly? Mom, that's ridiculous. I just like my coffee stronger than you like your coffee."

"She got to you, Lexie."

"No, no, because I was aware, I knew...oh damn it, okay, yes she got to me. I mean, for Christ's sake, she likes weak coffee, I like strong, we're both okay. But no, she turns it into a personal accusation. And I'm a spendthrift, did you get that? And my health is poor. Whose health is poor, Vivy? Why does she always have to accuse me of what she is?"

"Oh Lexie."

"Well, it's true. So I decide to give her some of her own medicine. I tell her gourmet coffee is a big thing right now. I say most people, in the city, would consider her coffee weak and tasteless."

"That would cut her to the quick."

"Yes, I go to the bathroom and when I come out, she's sitting on the couch with her eyes closed and that long-suffering face on her. A strip of pink on her cheekbones. I ignore her and get ready to go. Then she says, in this little voice, that she wants to give me the money for my gas, for all the time I spent driving her around. Cause now we're enemies, see, and she doesn't want to be beholden to me."

"Remind me of this when she's dead, Lexie."

"What do you mean, Viv, 'when she's dead.' Do you know something I don't?"

"No, I mean that, one day, when she eventually dies, and

we're weeping at her grave, remind me how impossible she was, would you?"

"Ah, Vivy. I got along fine with her for two whole days. She seemed to enjoy it. I took her to the farm. We sat under the mock orange tree. We got along fine until the coffee."

Only months later would I put this day under the magnifying glass of my memory and examine every detail. Only when the day had been lifted out of the sleepwalk of the familiar did I do this, only when it had been transformed by its status as "the last time."

When my mother came downstairs from the bathroom, at the farm, we went out through the back porch. It smelled of wood and kerosene, as it always did. Outside, she stopped and looked up at the sparse branches of the mock orange. The leaves were drooping and browning in the hot sun. She sat down on the worn gray bench that's always been there. Looked up at me. "Do you remember the time I borrowed that relaxation tape of yours, Lexie? It was a silly thing, but I ended up listening to it quite a bit. You know how the tape asked the listener to imagine a special place, a place where you could relax and feel at peace, the place where you felt most like yourself?"

I looked down at her, wondering what was coming. My mother wasn't given to self-scrutiny. Her thoughts rarely left the daily world you could see and touch and hear—the meat thawing on the counter, the frying pan that needed cleaning. "That was the part I had trouble with," she continued. "Picturing my own special place. I got stuck there." She frowned and shifted over on the bench, patting the spot beside her.

I sat down. Both of us gazed up at the tattered mock orange; I could smell the fallen harvest apples in the west corner of the yard.

"I could never decide," she said. "I couldn't decide whether my special place was right here, under this tree, the way it is in June, with that little breeze blowing and those white fragrant blossoms opening wide, or whether it was in the city, in my own back yard." She brushed my knee with a thin, brown-splotched hand and sat up straighter. "And you know, I think that's been my trouble in life, too—I never had my own special place, never knew where I wanted to be, never found out where I belonged."

She paused. Maybe she even turned and looked at me right then. I was aware of her, and at the same time thinking about how the little girl I'd been had once sat in this very place, smarting from a scolding I never forgot.

"I never ... found out where I belonged." Her words chimed in my ears like the cicadas that chimed in the drought-stricken maples that surrounded the outer yard of the farmhouse. The pause between us stretched. I was aware, I have to have been aware, that she was waiting for some acknowledgement of what she'd just said—a few words, an arm around the shoulder, a touch on the hand. Yet I didn't move. I remained silent.

By the time I put this day under the magnifying glass, every mundane detail had become luminous with significance. Two weeks from our drive to the farm and lake, our mother was taken to the hospital with heart problems; three months later, she was dead.

That morning, she stood and brushed off her pale blue skirt. "Let's get a move on, Lexie. We'll never get to the lake if we hang around here. Graham must be busy in the barn with his visitor; I guess he figures he saw us yesterday at the birthday party and doesn't need to come out."

The two of us walked to the car. I backed it up, glancing at the barn door to see whether my brother would appear at the last minute. I saw only the swallows—their dips and dives through the air, and the gray cat on her back in the dust, lifting her head to take short, stabbing licks at her white bib. My mother and I drove slowly out the long lane as we'd done regularly for the past half century.

How unsuspecting I was. How ... timeless it all seemed. How

familiar the quality of the August light, the muted crunch of tires on gravel, the dust as it rose behind us in the rear view mirror, the goldenrod opening in the front field, the crying of the seagulls beyond the hill as they swooped and fell out of the late summer sky onto the ploughed fields below.

PART III

I've noticed the significant changes that sometimes occur in people's lives after the parents die. Palsied, humped, these elderly figures still hold surprising power over their middle-aged offspring.

—"Incestuous Ossuary"

xvi.
Incestuous Ossuary

VIVIAN'S THIRD HUSBAND, Mike, lasts fifteen years, long enough for us to know him, to take him for granted, to be mighty startled when suddenly, shortly after our parents' death, he abruptly disappears.

I've noticed the significant changes that sometimes occur in people's lives after the parents die. Palsied, humped, these elderly figures still hold surprising power over their middle-aged offspring. After our parents' death, not only do my sister and Mike break up, Pascale sues my brother for divorce. I'm the only one of the three of us to stay married.

It takes some time for me to realize we'll never see Mike again. "Wow," I venture, during a telephone conversation with Vivian. "Imagine how...surprised Mom would have been at this, uh ... development. She was so fond of Mike."

"Oh, I never would have split up with him as long as our parents were alive," says Vivian quickly.

"But ... what happened, Vivian? I can hardly believe this. A month ago, we're all there around your table, eating that marvelous Mexican dinner Mike prepared. Then, last week, Katie announces she's moving to the prairies with her boyfriend. Yesterday, Julie phones to tell me she's quit her job in Toronto and she's moving to the south of France, for how long she doesn't know. Pascale is gone; our five nieces and nephews are gone. Now you're saying Mike is history. I feel as if my world is falling apart, to tell you the truth."

"Lexie, it's a lot of change. I know that. But surely you understand that Mike and I have been unhappy for a long time."

"Well, I do and I don't Viv. I didn't understand it was that serious. Do you think this might be just a temporary separation? People often get back together."

"No, I don't. He's moving his stuff out this weekend. I'll call you Sunday night, okay? We have a bowel resection at seven tomorrow morning. I have to get to bed."

It's not until two more weeks have passed that I find out what's happening. On the Saturday morning, I leave Vivian a distressed message. My phone finally rings around nine, Sunday evening.

"Lexie, I'm in my bathtub. I just got home now. I listened to your two messages and picked the phone right up. I'm really sorry."

"I'm not sure I can take this. Another loss."

"It's unbelievable, I know."

"Is this what it is to be middle aged? First Mom and Dad die, six weeks apart. They could probably get in the Guinness Book of Records for that one—Parents Dying Closest Together."

"Yeah, about the only way they were ever close."

"They were close. They were completely involved with one another. But in a relationship of struggle and misery."

"True."

"Then Pascale and the five kids. I miss them, Vivy. Really miss them. Then you and Mike. You know how I feel about that—I never even got to say goodbye to him. Then Julie and Katie, both moving away. Now I find out my job will be gone for sure by the end of next year. My life is evaporating around me."

"I know, Lexie, it's incredible. Please don't cry."

"And you're still burning the candle at both ends. I'm so afraid you won't last. I'm telling you, if you don't, I'm going to throw myself into the coffin with you."

"Good. I'll be glad of the company."

"Graham feels the same way about you, you know. He told me last week that life wouldn't be worth living without you.

He was serious. Things are even worse for him of course."

"Good Lord—sister and brother! What a responsibility the two of you are."

"David's away again."

"He is?"

"Yup. California this time."

"How long will he be gone?"

"You know what, Vivy? I don't even know. Either he won't say or he doesn't have a clue."

"Lexie, I think men do this when they're newly retired. Feel their oats, get out and see the world. I'm sure he'll settle down."

"On another topic, Vivian, our brother sent me a one-sentence email this morning: Ask your younger sister what she did Wednesday night in Ephram's bed."

"Our dear brother's been telling tales."

"That's all he said. Come on, you've told him, you can tell me."

"Graham knows because I had to phone him at his office in Toronto to ask him where the key was hidden."

"The key?"

"To the farm. Graham keeps the farmhouse locked since he got the contract in Toronto, you know. There's nobody there during the week."

"Okay. What's going on?"

"I had a clandestine assignation, that's all. In the dead of night. At the farm. In Ephram's bed."

"My Gawd, you don't let grass grow under your feet. Who with?"

"Believe it or not, he too is named Mike."

"Where did you find him so fast?"

"I've known him to say 'hi' to for years. So there I was, crawling around the stable on Wednesday night in my best seduction outfit, looking for the key to the house, then rutting in Ephram's bed with the portraits of our ancestors looking down on us. They didn't look too happy. Mind you, they never did."

"Who is he?"

"I've known him socially for quite a while. When Mike and I split up, a third party told me that this new Mike had had his eye on me for a long time. This is very much on the QT, Lexie. There'd be hell to pay if anyone found out at this point."

"My God, Vivian. Here you are, sober physician by day, and drunken wild woman by night. You're playing with fire."

"Funny you should say that, Lexie. I went out to the farm before Mike came. The house was cold. Really cold. I built a fire. It turned into a conflagration. I had to open all the windows and doors. Mike arrived soon after. 'Well, now you know one thing about me,' I said. 'I can build a damn good, rip-roaring fire!'"

"That's all he knows about you, Vivian?"

"That's right. We don't really know one another at all."

"Sounds like you're fast getting acquainted."

"I have to tell you the part about your journal, Lex."

"What about it?"

"Your March journal came in the mail Wednesday morning. I knew I'd be beside myself, waiting out there at the farm, because there was some question as to whether Mike would be able to make it. He'd been up all night the night before, traveling, and he had to go to Belgium the next day. You know how I haven't been able to concentrate lately, can't read? So I thought—what can I take that'll distract me while I'm waiting. I picked up the mail and there was your monthly journal. Just the ticket. I built the fire and opened all the windows and doors. Then I sat down by the little table where Mom used to roll out the dough for her cinnamon buns. You know why she chose to work there? You can see all the way down the lane to the road.

"I start reading. I get so engrossed that I don't even see the lights coming in the lane, don't see the lights till they come in the washroom window, at the west side of the house. Such is the power of your words. I'm so glad you've been sending me this stuff—I feel closer to you than I have in years."

"Uh huh."

"So afterwards, Mike and I are sitting side by side on Ephram's bed, getting dressed. I always wear these black socks, like a man's, under my trousers. Mike puts on his socks and says they don't feel right."

"I wish you wouldn't call him Mike."

"It's his name, Alexia."

"It seems indecent, somehow. I keep thinking you're talking about Mike. Mike the First. I suppose the socks were yours and only went on over his big toe."

"They were mine, but they fit him. He's the same size I am. He's a small man, like dad was."

"Does he have a small willy?"

"No, his willy is of normal size."

"You would know."

"Yes, I see them every day at the office. Did I ever tell you that when I was sixteen I gave Billie Mayhurst a blow job in Ephram's bed?"

"Really? When I was sixteen I was still galloping down the lane on a stick, day-dreaming about a teacher who was twenty-five years older than I was. Ephram's bed? Where was Ephram?"

"He would've been ninety-six or seven by then. He was in the nursing home."

"Where was mom?"

"She wasn't there, obviously!"

"But she was always there. She had nothing to do but hang around and live through us."

"It was winter. The water was turned off in the winter and nobody went there. Don't you remember?"

"Yeah. I'm just being silly."

"You know how my hair was really long then - to my waist? I got semen in my hair. And there was no water."

"What did you do?"

"I forget. Melted snow on the wood stove, probably. Do you know they give courses in Toronto on how to give blow jobs?

One of my friends told me that and the next weekend I read it in the *Globe and Mail*."

"It doesn't sound as if you need a course. Oh, Vivian, be careful. You're playing Prometheus, you're stealing fire from the gods."

"I seem to remember there was a rather ghastly price to pay for that. I've got an overworked liver as it is."

"So tell me the whole thing. What did you do when Mike Number Two's lights came through the washroom window?"

"Don't call him that. You make him sound like a bowel movement. I met him at the door, so he'd know he had the right farm. Gave him a beer. Put him in Ephram's rocking chair and got on his lap. As I said, I had my best seduction outfit on. I'd drunk half a bottle of champagne. Usually I drink a whole bottle."

"Why did you drink only half a bottle?"

"I had to drive back to town. And I'm trying to reform."

"Why didn't you give him champagne?"

"Because men his age can't get it up when they've been drinking."

"What age is he?"

"Fifty-two."

"I hate old men who can't get it up."

"Old men? He's younger than you are."

"Yeah, but I'm eternally twenty-seven."

"Luckily, we have Viagra now. I have a stack of Viagra on my desk at work. I'm stockpiling it. Two drug salesmen came by this afternoon and I invited them to sit down in my office. One of them was kind of cute. He said, I see you're planning quite a weekend. Yes, I said, what can you two boys come up with that tops that?"

"Did Mike the Second get it up once you got him into Grandpa's bed?"

"Oh, yes. He got his blood pressure pills changed, just so he could. He went to Dr. Hayhurst last Monday morning, after our first time, and he said, 'Listen, you've got to change my blood pressure pills so I can fuck Dr. Kerr.'"

"He didn't say that to James Hayhurst. Did he?"

"Of course not. He told me he did, though, for a joke."

"Ephram's bed has been getting quite a work-out since Pascale and the children left. That's what Graham said this morning in his email. He's taking the woman he met through the *Globe and Mail* to the farm again this weekend. She's bringing her dog this time. Did you know she's a writer? A playwright. She's won writing awards. Real ones."

"Maybe she'll write the family up in a play."

"What if mom is in heaven watching you screw Mike in Ephram's bed on week nights, and Graham screw a woman with dreadnaughts in Ephram's bed on weekends!"

"She'll get quite an eyeful."

"She'll feel her life was a failure. That she raised us wrong. She really liked Mike, you know."

"Oh, I could never have broken up with Mike as long as mom was alive."

"Yes, you told me. I guess this is why mom donated her eyes to science. So she couldn't look down from heaven and see us after she died."

"You're right, Lexie."

"You know how she was - pure Irish intuition. She knew she'd managed to hold dad down all her life, and that she'd mostly held us down too—well, not you and Graham so much, but me, that's for sure. She knew we'd break loose after she died. She didn't want to see it."

"It's to be hoped she doesn't still have the frontal lobe damage she got after her heart operation. Up there in heaven, know what I mean? If she does, she'll be doing what I'm doing, here on earth. Remember how she hiked her skirt to her waist to show the minister her scar when he asked about her swollen leg?"

"She'll be doing her best to give God a hard-on."

"She might do better with Jesus. He's younger."

"Yeah, Vivian, she could give him a blow job, and maybe get semen in that long hair of his!"

"Nah, she has a bad neck, she couldn't."

"Are we drunk?"

"No, we're wide open because we've had multiple losses."

"It's called middle age."

"Lexie, I have to go to bed. I'm so tired I could die."

"I really do feel that way about you, you know, Vivy."

"What?"

"I love you more than anyone in the whole world. If you go before me, I'll throw myself on your pyre. I feel, in some ways, as if you're all I have."

"For Christ's sake, Lexie."

"I mean it. Graham feels the same. It's been that way since you were a little kid. I want my bones beside yours for eternity. Graham does too. We've discussed it."

"Please stop, Lexie. You're making me cry."

"They can put the three of us in one coffin. An incestuous ossuary, that's what we'll be. Death has taken our parents, the world has taken our children, our spouses are defecting at the rate of one a year, soon it'll be only the three of us left."

"No kidding."

"I've never even gone back to look at mom and dad's grave, you know."

"I planted daffodils on it. They're in bloom right now. Listen, I know you're alone there and feeling badly, but I have to go to bed. I'm on call for twenty-four hours starting tomorrow morning. I didn't get any sleep Wednesday night, you know why. I didn't get much sleep Thursday night because a woman delivered at two in the morning. I have to get to bed."

"Goodnight, sweet prince."

"Goodnight."

xvii.
Pilgrimage

Our real journey in life is interior
—Thomas Merton

WHEN I AWAKEN IN THE NIGHT to hear the noise at my shutters, my first thought is that the Only Begotten has come to make love to me in the French way. I raise myself onto my left elbow. The closed shutters render the room utterly dark. Someone is rattling the heavy, wooden boards, pushing and working at them in a persistent way.

The town is Prades, in the south of France. I've travelled here from Canada to join a study group of strangers. Spain thrums behind lavender mountains to the west, and orange poppies shout from the ditches. In the bakery window, an orange cat curls around sun-warmed loaves of bread.

I've come here for two reasons, one in the open, one known only to me. Prades is the birthplace of Thomas Merton, a man who lived as a Trappist monk, and became one of the most significant writers on spiritual themes of the twentieth century. Merton is the subject of the study group. My hidden reason is to strengthen myself by travelling alone in another country. Companionless, surrounded by the unfamiliar, can I continue to exist or will I dissolve like a pill in a glass of water? One of my first memories is of my mother, who was almost agoraphobic, panicked by a knock at the door, ordering me to crouch with her behind the sofa. All my life, I've carried a fear of the stranger.

Although my room is on the second floor of this one-star hotel, my window, at the back, opens onto a flat roof. It would be easy enough for anyone to hoist himself up. Whoever is trying to get in is as awkward at opening the shutters as I was at closing them. This fits with my mental profile of the Only Begotten—a dreamy, intuitive type who, like me, has trouble with the mechanical workings of the physical world.

The reason the Only Begotten jumps into my mind is a conversation I had with my brother before I left Canada. My brother was not able to understand my reason for going alone to France. He has been spared my agoraphobic tendencies. Put another way, he doesn't need the grounding properties of the familiar. My brother believed that I was going to France to find a lover, this being his reason for travelling as frequently as possible to his favourite country on earth.

"You haven't lived until you've had a French lover," he said. "In the south of France, you're sure to find one."

"Even the hot-blooded men of the Midi won't be interested in a woman of fifty-four," I told him. Besides, what about your brother-in-law? Have you forgotten that, unlike you, I still have a spouse?"

This was unkind, but my brother was as persistent as a horse-fly.

"He won't know what you do across the ocean in a foreign country."

"I'll know what I do."

"The French appreciate older women."

I lost patience and flared, "God Himself couldn't find me a lover, unless, of course, He sacrificed his Only Begotten Son for the cause."

My brother giggled. Dimples appeared in the top of his cheeks, and a becoming shade of peony-pink overwhelmed his tan. The pink drained away and he expressed shock at my blasphemy. I heard no more from him on the subject of lovers.

The determined rattling and scrabbling at the shutters is

escalating. I'm out of bed now, feeling my way to the door that opens into the corridor. If the intruder is not the Only Begotten, or someone equally harmless, my plan is to open the door and scream, "*Au secours!*" I know that this is what you do when in trouble in France, having read Ludwig Bemelman's *Madeleine* books to my children.

Two days ago, I saw a sculpture of the Only Begotten in a Catholic church. The marble Christ lay upon a bier, a white linen cloth edged in a stepping-stone pattern beneath his body, a brown-striped towel sculpted around his private parts. His torso, legs and arms were muscled and gleaming, smooth and copper-brown. It was the body of a man in the prime of life.

I stand at the door now, ready to flee, my hand upon the knob. The most remarkable aspect of the body of this Christ was the blood. Copious and tomato-red, lurid to my Protestant eyes. The result of Mary's union with God had been Christ. What sort of entity would I conceive if I were entered by divinity? I turn the knob of the bedroom door, open it a little, and tense my muscles for a sprint. The racket is at its height, the curtains shaking from top to bottom. I switch on the light.

A huge black cat jumps onto the floor. His gleaming fur is the colour of the night sky. A pair of yellow eyes looks up at me. The two of us stare at one another. If this is Christ, He has once again arrived in a form that's unexpected and difficult to recognize.

I gently close the door and move towards the cat. He springs upon the bed, crossing my path. One of the most widespread superstitions in the world is that a black cat crossing your path is bad luck. I prefer to think that divinity has entered my bedroom. France is full of black Madonnas. They are about strength. Darkness and its possession of us seems to be an essential part of the spiritual route.

I switch off the light, open the curtains and leave one shutter ajar, so that my visitor may leave easily if he wishes, then lie down on the bed beside him and marvel at the human mind. How, set off by a silly conversation with a sibling, it can busily concoct a fantasy about the Son of God that is ridiculous enough to be a dream, while the body rushes adrenaline to the limbs and moves towards the exit.

When I awaken the next morning, my visitor is gone. I think about my wine-enhanced fantasy and admit to myself for the first time that I have a growing interest in matters spiritual, brought on, perhaps by the recent death of my parents. This may have been just as important in bringing me here as the second goal of testing myself to see whether I have vanquished agoraphobia.

"A pilgrimage is a journey to a sacred place in the expectation of transformation." It's the voice of our leader, Professor of Religious Studies David Steadman, from Louisville, Kentucky. We're in class, here in Prades, and he's beginning his lecture.

This is the sort of sentence that is life blood to me, though I have not entered a church to worship in thirty-five years. As a young woman in my first year of university, I took a course in Religious Studies. My paper was *The Fall of Man*. The Professor called me in. He was a short, heavy man with football shoulders, bloodshot eyes, sagging bulldog cheeks, and the full lips of a Gina Lollobrigida. In class, I had spent more time marveling at those lips, on that face, than in listening to his words; I expected to be chastised.

He handed me my paper and told me soberly that it was better than anything he'd received from his students at Columbia. He leaned forward. His sad, gray-blue eyes looked into mine. "This is your field," he said.

I didn't understand the significance of this. I had led a limited existence in rural Ontario, and did not know what Columbia was. I did know what a field was: a fenced, grassy expanse in which reddish-brown creatures in various stages of rumination and regurgitation stood around or clambered unsteadily upon one another's rumps. As for my field of study being God, I had rejected Him at age thirteen.

The memory is vivid. I am sitting beside my parents in the little country church we attended, a scent of new mown hay coming in the window, cicadas whining in the old maples outside, the wooden pew hard at my back, all my being focused on the new hat I'm wearing—white, wide-brimmed, tiny daisies in the ribbon that circles the crown—and the looks I'm attracting from a boy in the choir. The minister begins to speak. His words register with a clarity that burns through my haze. "No man can serve two masters: for either he will hate the one and love the other; or else he will hold to the one, and despise the other. Ye cannot serve God and Mammon."

I look around at the perspiring congregation. No one else seems to have heard this. My face burns with the force of it, the shocking thundering simplicity of it. There are two paths. A person can choose only one. Fine, then, I will serve Mammon. I have only to look at my parents to see where serving God gets you.

The light from the tall windows that give on Prade's main square shows up the gray in David Steadman's dark, tightly-curled hair. "No one," he is saying, "no one undertakes a pilgrimage who does not have an inborn yearning for an encounter with the divine." I shift on my hard wooden chair, thinking again of the intruder at my shutters and how my first thought had been of the Only Begotten.

Not until my late forties did I begin to discover that the water of life lay for me in the realm of image and mythology, in that liminal place where the world known to the senses intersects with the world beyond the visible. A friend lent me books on Thomas Merton. I read the autobiographical writings, and the biographies, but still did not understand. This fun-loving, talented and intelligent man voluntarily removed himself from life. He went to prison—what I thought of as prison—shut himself away in a monastery, a young man of twenty-six. There he endured plain food, scorching heat in summer, brutal cold in winter, an arising time of 2.15 a.m., severe restrictions on travel, and limited access to a phone. All because of God.

"Thomas Merton was a man who refused to live a collective life, but rather built for himself, consciously and often painfully, a life that expressed his unique soul," says Dr. Steadman. "To do so, he found it necessary to give up much that his individual self enjoyed."

Again, I feel the *frisson*, as when I saw the ad for this trip in the *Globe and Mail*. It summoned me with the authority of fate. I was afraid to go alone, but knew that I had to; fear had already cut me off from too much of life. When I set down the phone after booking the trip, my entire body broke out in red, raised hives.

Back up three days, pre-Prades. I'm sitting in a sidewalk café—a hiatus in the old city of Toulouse, on the way to Prades—engaged with the secret purpose of the journey. It's my first day alone in this country. The waiter brings me *limonade* and soundlessly I throw down my challenge to France. Surround me with the unfamiliar. Encircle me with strangers. Engulf me in the sounds, smells, textures, expressions, language of a world that is foreign to me. I once read about a woman who was reduced to gibberish when confronted by the chaos of India. This isn't India, but it's not Canada, either.

At the top of a postcard to my sister, (this being Before Email), I write the words "God's Mistake." She has recently split up with her man, and will be visiting Paris in May. She plans to wear a black, see-through jumpsuit on the plane. "You never know who I might meet," she tells me, running her hands over her breasts and her newly svelte hips.

"But I thought you were going to Paris to meet your new lover, Vivy. I thought that was the whole idea."

"Yes, yes." My sister waved her slim fingers dismissively.

"But I don't know how long he'll last. I'm forty-eight, you know. This is my last kick at the can." She laughed aloud. "I can't let any potential lovers get away."

It was only a few days later that my brother advised me to find a lover in the south of France. What siblings! Practiced in the art of "taking" a lover, as if lovers were delicacies on a plate passed at a cocktail party. Whereas my out-of-bounds, amorous encounters consisted of surreal fantasies conducted in my own bed.

I begin to fill the postcard with small print.

"My seat-mate on the way over was a physician, in the same specialty as you. Between takeoff and "bedtime," he managed to extract from the Air France crew three *demi-bouteilles* of champagne, one *demi-bouteille* of red wine, and a cognac. He found the courage to speak to me only after thus fortifying himself. He described the frustrations of his job, said he wanted to pack it in. When I told him I was travelling alone to meet a group of strangers, he said, "That takes guts." I kept looking at the guy's face. There was something familiar. Finally, I got it. He had the same full lips as the long ago professor of religion I've told you about. How strange that Dr. Brown's lips would come along now, thirty-five years later, just when I'm on my way to the field he identified as mine.

"It should have been you, Vivy, in your see-through jumpsuit. This guy was wasted on me (as well as wasted!). Instead of initiating amorous activity, I wrapped myself in the red Air France blanket and read the letters of William Carlos Williams and Denise Levertov.

"God got mixed up, *ma soeur*. He sent me on your trip. It's understandable. One can't expect God to be on top of every fine distinction in His creation. You're going to Paris in June, I'm going to Prades in May. You can't expect God to read to the end of every single word. He may even be dyslexic."

By now, I've had to buy a second postcard and label it "Continued." On both, having filled every blank space with small script, I sign my name and look up. The street stretches away, lined on both sides with plane trees, each equidistant from the next. Their variegated bark has the gunmetal sheen of a greyhound. None of my loved ones knows where I am at this moment. The trees repeat themselves as far as the eye can see. At home, surrounded by the familiar, with meals to prepare, errands to run, a husband reading the newspaper in the next room, it's easy to feel that I know who I am, easy to imagine that my individual life has purpose.

Here, not one person within a radius of thousands of miles knows who I am or cares whether I live or die. In the face of such monumental indifference, can I maintain a belief in my own meaning?

One morning, Dr. Steadman tells us about Mechtild of Magdeburg, who lived in the thirteenth century. She considered God her bridegroom, loved him with her body and her senses, as well as her heart. The professor goes on to give us other examples of religious figures who loved God in this way. He finishes: "In some people's eyes, sleeping with a human lover is the earthly version of union with the divine."

From the first day, I wonder about my fellow travelers—their motivation for coming to Prades. Like me, many have a covert reason. A surprising number have the same preoccupation as my brother and sister.

"You will have guessed that I sleep alone," says Dorothy, a faded blond woman from Vancouver. In the depth of her amber eyes burns something that will never forgive, never forget.

"They are answering your needs?" Rosa asks me, on returning from the Prades hairdresser. She fluffs the coiffure that shows off her Latin cheekbones. "You are finding what you came for?"

"How do you mean?"

She leans closer and drops her voice. "What you think of the men in this group?"

I shrug. Rosa's perfume is cloying, pervasive. She moves closer; her arm and hip graze mine. "How old you think I am?" She arches a carefully plucked brow.

"Fifty-four."

"Sixty-eight," snaps Rosa. She nods her head and gives me a tragic look. "I am sixty-eight." A cunning expression inhabits her dark eyes momentarily. "Fifty-four was one of my best times."

"A man?"

"Of course." She looks me over. "How old you are, anyway?"

"Fifty-four."

"Ah, you are so lucky. What I will give to be that age again." And she sashays off.

At dinner, Caroline, from New Hampshire, sits beside me. "I've carried a package of condoms in my suitcase on more trips than I can count and I can tell you right now that I'll be carrying them home unused yet again."

"How do you know?"

She waves her arm to encompass the three tables. "Take a look around you."

But that's only surface, I'm thinking. How many times have I made the mistake of judging on appearance, then discovering, once I got to know the person, how wrong I was.

Anne is a tall woman in her early forties with a rippling mass of curly, strawberry-blond hair. I learn Anne's story by overhearing a snippet of conversation between her and Dorothy. Dorothy has just asked her what had brought her to Vancouver the year before.

"My husband was having a bone marrow transplant."

"Oh. How's he doing now?" said Dorothy.

"He's dead," said Anne.

Anne sits beside our leader at every meal. Her husband was

only forty-one when he died six months ago, leaving her on an isolated farm in the Yukon. She rests her arm along the back of David's chair, twisting strands of her shining hair around two fingers.

"What are your criteria for a new lover?" she asks, on a Sunday morning at breakfast. "What's your bottom line?"

David shrugs and purses his lips. "That she be operationally finished with her stuff."

"I guess that lets me out." Anne flips her hair over her shoulder. "Just listen to me."

Anne's an extravert. It's all out there, on the table, at every meal.

I have the impression that none of my companions sees their search for a human lover as a search for God.

Thomas Merton's journal reveals that at the age of fifty-three, he fell passionately in love with a twenty-two-year-old nurse who looked after him when he left the monastery, temporarily, to have a back operation. He refers to the nurse as 'M' in his journal. The pair met secretly in the woods and in town. Merton describes their encounters, and his anguish at breaking his monastic vows for his love of a woman. On and off, he can convince himself that being with an earthly lover is the temporal version of union with the divine. After five months in which he is torn, and seesaws back and forth, Merton decides that for him, the two are mutually exclusive. He chooses God. His connection to God, his work for God, evidently gives his life a larger purpose, and this feeling of having found meaning wins out over personal intimacy, personal pleasure.

There's another common reason for this pilgrimage, I discover. Teresa's husband died two and a half years ago. They had only eight years together, having met in mid-life. Lee's husband died recently, in his early seventies, which, she says, "probably seems to most people like a normal life span, but doesn't feel that way to me."

Michael lives in Windsor. Tall, balding, a trace of a German accent. Two of his three adult daughters have come close to death: one through a car accident, one through anorexia. The first will never leave her wheelchair.

Ginny is a pale middle-aged woman who wears rimless glasses and fastens her straight brown hair into one long braid. A malignant melanoma was removed from her leg a year ago. She bends over, pulls up her jeans and rolls down her sock. There is a hole the size of a golf ball in the back of her leg. Ken was told seven years ago that he had only three years to live.

Again I consider that the recent loss of both parents may be one of the reasons I'm here.

Death. The ultimate loss, threatened or a recent fact. Pilgrimage as a search for meaning in the face of the end of our physical life, or that of a loved one's.

I find no one with my other reason for coming here. David Steadman is curious. A couple of times, he's probed for details and I've put him off with a joke. To tell about my fears embarrasses me.

"Smile," a friend advised me, before I left for Prades. "People often mistake shyness for unfriendliness. Smile, even if you don't feel like it. And force yourself to speak up in class. If you do, people will talk to you afterwards."

On a Sunday morning, I walk to the town square. Church bells are ringing. Unlike the regular, modest *Angélus* that chimes hourly, the sound this morning is peremptory. Insistent and incessant, it drowns out human conversation. Almost a temper tantrum of the bells: come worship or else.

I take a seat at the outdoor café, order a *café au lait,* and think about the ubiquity of both the human dread of death and the human search for a lover.

Around me, people from this village sip their drinks and talk.

The smoke from their cigarettes drifts effortlessly beyond their fingers and into invisibility. Only a few elderly women make their way across the square and into the church.

I have relaxed, I realize, as I sip my *café*. The strangers of this group have turned into friends. Though they believe in God and I doubt His existence, I feel comfortable, interested, not especially an outsider. My notebook has become the companion to whom I tell my intimate thoughts. There is no danger of my dissolving. I am more substantial than I thought.

Two days remain. Anne and Rosa and I sit on a stone bench outside the front door of the hotel, waiting for the call to dinner. A man is standing in front of us, crying. It's Jim, a middle aged collector of Merton arcana. He's telling us how, for five years, he's been cancer free, then a routine test revealed that the cancer was back. He repeats for us the conversation with his oncologist, sobbing now as he did then.

Rosa stands up and offers him a tissue. She pats his arm. "It's God's will," she says.

"Oh, I know, I know," says Jim. "It's God's will." He blows his nose and tells us he's going to Lourdes after Prades.

Anne stands up too. "Is there any way we can help right now?" she says.

Jim brightens. "Actually, there is. I'm looking for a fourth person to go up the mountain with us tomorrow morning. We'll be missing class. With four, we're eligible to hire the driver with the special permit to take us up."

He's talking about *Le Canigou*, the sacred mountain of the Catalans. Anne explains that she and Rosa were part of a walking party that made the ascent several days ago. All three of them look down at me.

This is how I come to be sitting in the back seat of a jeep driven by a stranger. The road up the mountain is superlatively steep. Every turn is a hair pin. A jeep cannot make a turn in one try. In order to complete the turn, the specially-licensed driver must go partway around the curve, then back the vehicle right to the edge of the drop. He must do this for every turn. I did not know this when I got into the jeep. There are no guardrails; this is France.

I'm in the back seat of the jeep. I make the mistake of turning my head and looking out the window behind me, the first time we back up to the edge. The lip of the drop is invisible because our back tires are right on it. I'm looking straight down into the void. A moment of exquisite terror. The only other time in my life that I've been this afraid is back home, when I booked this trip.

I must have made a universally-intelligible sound, for the driver says, in French: "All the world has fear on the way up, Madame. The way down is not so shivering."

I face forward, close my eyes, and say the prayer I was taught in childhood. "Thy will be done." On the skin of my entire body is a sheen of cold sweat. My knees are literally knocking on each other.

Thy will be done.
Thy will be done.
Thy will be done.
(But surely Thy will is not to wipe me out.)

We reach the mountain top at last. On jelly legs, I climb down from the jeep. The driver takes my arm and walks me towards the monastery of *Saint-Martin-Du-Canigou*. "Vous allez bien maintenant, Madame."

I free myself from his grasp and indicate a wooden bench. "I'll just sit here for a moment." I gesture at the door so he'll leave me.

When the others have disappeared inside, I walk quickly away. The tour of the Abbey will take an hour and a half. Everyone has told me it's a special place, that I'll sense the presence of God as soon as I step through the door. But having so recently experienced the centimeter between life and death,

I don't want to go inside and be part of a group experience. I need to be alone.

I take a path that leads uphill, away from the monastery, and find myself in a little woods. It's silent, but for the occasional chirp of a bird. The air swirls with streams and eddies—sweet lift of pine scent, fragrance of dew-touched wildflowers. The clouds are ghosts slipping between hemlock trunks. The path ahead climbs into denser clouds. It's easy to pretend I'm approaching the gates of heaven.

Another ten minutes of walking, and I come out of the woods at the highest point of *Le Canigou*. There's a sort of lookout—a small stone wall and stone bench. I sit down and the clouds lift. The vista is incomparable. I can see all the way to Spain.

Here is where something should happen, I muse. On the top of this sacred mountain, far from home. Spared the void, brought here safely by a stranger. Here is where I should have a life-changing experience. God could come down those few steps from heaven and assure me that He exists, that the fullness of time is here, now, that all will be revealed.

I wait, but nothing happens, nothing visible at least. What I do not realize, sitting on the top of *Le Canigou,* is that it will take months before the amazing effects of facing down a major fear become obvious to me.

I take out my notebook, read the most recent entry and begin to write. Two or three pages later, I'm enveloped by a womb of cloud. I feel secure in my invisibility. Strangely at home.

xviii.
Puke Birds

It's pretty confusing there for a while.
"Have you heard from Mike at all?" I say to Vivian, over the phone.
"Heard from him? I'm sitting on his lap."
"You're back together?"
"Lexie." Her voice is dry ice. She thinks I'm doing it on purpose. She thinks her new Mike is as constantly on our minds as he is on hers. But when things started to fall apart with Mike the First, Vivian declared that she'd never marry again, never even live with anyone again.

Graham and I were glad.

The truth is, both of us want our sister for ourselves. We grumble to each other that if Vivian had to take up with another man so quickly, she could at least have picked someone with a different first name. When we refer to them as Mike the First and Mike the Second, Vivian says we make it sound as if she's ruling a petty dukedom. Her new man is Mike, period, she insists. If ever we find it necessary to refer to her previous relationship, we're to use his last name.

You can tell she means it and I decide to make more of an effort. Graham persists in calling them the First and the Second.

Mike the Second, from now on Mike, is a true blond, like our father. He has our father's blue eyes, their exact shade of chicory blue, their exact shape. He's slight, with our father's fine bones. Strong and wiry. A hard worker, just like our dad. A family man, a self-made man who started at the bottom and ended at the top. It's as if our father has served his time in limbo and been reborn.

He and Vivian are demonstrative in public. They French-kiss during cooking, during dinner, during conversation, at red lights, and in the dentist's waiting room. It's enough to make you gag, if you've been married for as long as I have. Even if you aren't married at all.

One day—the 24th of May weekend, to be exact—between the entrée and the dessert, Vivian purses her lips and looks tonguingly at Mike. My older daughter, Julie, with us for the weekend, grabs her flute and plays an arresting, tingling riff.

"What's that?" says Vivian.

"It's the call of the puke-bird," says Julie.

Vivian shrieks and jumps to her feet; she's high all the time, since meeting Mike. "Perfect." she says. "Perfect! You've put the picture of the puke-bird into my head, Julie."

"Love-birds—a close-sitting pair with crazed, spiked-out feathers in not so subtle colours—devouring one another with undistracted looks and smooches," I add.

Vivian runs around the table and hugs her niece. "Julie, you're brilliant!"

It catches on. Vivian tells the story around Rilling, and she and Mike become puke-birds to friends and family alike. Whenever they start their sloppy tonguing and drooling, one or another of us will attempt, with our vocal cords, a flute-like trill that comes out, usually, sounding like a piccolo screech.

As the puke-birds become increasingly amorous, I begin to wonder whether Vivian's declaration that she's finished with marriage and co-habitation is to be trusted.

Mike's job is temporarily in Budapest. He's starting a branch plant of the company he works for, head office in Rilling, Ontario. After New Year's Day, he returns to Hungary.

One January evening, Vivian and I happen to be on line at the same time. Most evenings, I don't have access to my sister. She's almost always working Emerg or at a Board meeting, or trying to recruit physicians for Rilling, or attending a social event, or....

This time, we're both doing chores around the house. Exchanging short emails, leaving the computer long enough to put in a load of laundry, or clean up the kitchen, returning to read the reply and respond, leaving to do another chore, coming back. It's a conversation.

Vivian is sounding frail, wistful: "I'm so glad I have a sister and a brother, a big sister and a big brother. Sometimes I feel like a little child. I want to climb into my mommy's arms."

"Well, remember, I'm your mother as well as your big sister. And you're my mother as well as my baby sister. I think that when all else has fallen away, this is what will remain. It's very strong, when you have it, the love of your kin. The bonds go back so far—right to the beginning. There's something almost ... what's the word ... atavistic about my love for you. When mom first brought you home, you cried a lot. Every time you cried, I'd beg her to let me feed you, and she'd let me give you a bottle of lukewarm water. Every morning, I'd wake up and remember that there was a new baby in the house and I could actually feel the happiness in my body. The same thing happened, by the way, after I had Julie and Katie. In some ways, it's like you're my own kid."

"Yes, I do understand how that could be. Just to change the subject for a moment, I saved two lives this week, Lexie. One was an older, heavy smoker with pneumonia. The other was a microcephalic, vegetative child with pneumonia. Both had to be intubated and ventilated and they're both home now and doing the same as ever. For some reason, there was little pleasure in either ... I think it's being tired and burnt out and frustrated."

"Are you missing Mike, now that he's back in Budapest, or is that whole thing cooling off, now that he's gone?"

"It's Mike being away that's the problem, Lexie. I don't feel like this when he's here."

"But Vivian, you need to find your centre in yourself, not in someone else, don't you think?"

"I don't know. All I know is he's gone and life seems a slog. I'm just, you know, putting one foot in front of the other."

"Not to sound as if I'm lecturing, Vivian, but I don't think happiness lies in another person. All of us need to try to find the sweet among the bitter in our everyday lives. This is our life, right now - this trip back to the drycleaner's because they made a mistake, this repetitive conversation with the same patient, this chat you have in the supermarket with an acquaintance. It's not somewhere in the future, it's not in Budapest, it's right here, right now."

"I was happy when Mike was here, Lexie. I truly was."

"What I think about happiness, Vivy—not to go on too long about this—but to me happiness doesn't reside in having another. No one ever lived 'happily ever after.' Happiness comes in how you give meaning and awareness to the individual bits and pieces of your daily life. Am I sounding like a preacher?"

"I think I've fallen in love with Mike, if you want to know."

"What? Wow, that's a bombshell. Really?"

"Really."

"I'm phoning you."

"No, Lexie, wait…"

I'm already dailing her number. She picks it up right away. "Lexie, I'm too tired to get into this on the phone tonight."

"Vivian, listen. Being newly in love isn't happiness, it's… euphoria. And the nature of euphoria is that it doesn't last. That kind of love—the 'falling in love' kind of love—it doesn't last very long."

"I know all that but it breaks my heart. It tortures me because I don't want to make a mistake. I know it needs time. But time runs out."

"You don't want to make a mistake? What are we talking about here?"

"Okay, I wasn't going to tell you this yet. Mike has asked me to marry him."

"You've got to be kidding."

"Far from it. And, okay, I'm thinking about it. Whew. I'm glad that's out. I tried to tell you on the phone the other day, but I couldn't."

"Actual marriage? Are you serious? You said you'd never even live with anyone again, let alone marry someone. Vivian, you've only been going with Mike for ten months."

"Like I said, I'm only considering it. But it's torturing me, Lexie. What if it's a mistake?"

"You haven't known him nearly long enough to make a decision like that. You can't really know a person for at least three years. And you did say you'd never marry again."

"I know what I said."

"Time doesn't run out, Vivian. There's all the time in the world to make a decision like that. It doesn't need to torture you, because there's no deadline on this. I mean, has he given you an ultimatum, or something?"

"Of course not. I won't jump in, but I have to follow it. All my being is reaching for him. I know that what you're saying is right, but isn't it okay to wallow a little in the joy of the present?"

"Of course. The present is all that exists. But you're not asking me about wallowing in the present, you're talking about 'til death do us part.'"

"Well, one thing I am going to do is go to Budapest for four to five weeks in September. Live with him there. See how it goes. Is that okay?"

"Yes. I guess so. That's okay."

"Is everything okay as long as I don't commit to tying the knot?"

"Yes. For God's sake don't even come close to that without asking me, Vivian."

"I find life so hard at present."

"Why? You're in love. You're separated, but soon you'll be with him again. Enjoy that, anticipate it. Don't imagine there's something better than what you have right now. Don't spoil it by defining the situation in such a way that you have to torture yourself."

"I'm going to bed now, Lexie. Night night."

It's ten o'clock when we hang up. I open the kitchen closet and lift out the warmest coat I own. Pull on my lined, calf-high boots, a hat that covers my ears, sheepskin mitts. The snow squeaks beneath my feet as I walk. My forehead aches from the cold. I wrap the long wool scarf around my head so that only my eyes are uncovered. Walk and walk and walk, until my toes are numb and I can no longer feel my nose. The handwriting is so clearly on the wall. I am going to lose my sister again.

xvix.
The Dinner Party

EVEN NOW, I CAN'T DESCRIBE the farm objectively. It's been a powerful force in our family, so much so that I might say we never owned the farm, it owned us. It held us in thrall. We lived elsewhere, yet my father and my brother Graham served it every spare minute of their lives. The women of the family felt the effects of this. The farm destroyed both marriages. My parents', my brother's.

Today, the hilly countryside is green and lush; it's been a rainy spring. About an hour after leaving home, I get into real country. The farmhouses are freshly painted and prosperous looking. Cattle, sheep, and horses graze the fields, the gardens are vivid with tulips, daffodils, narcissi, muscari. I turn off the radio and roll my window halfway down to let the country smells blow into the car—grass, wildflowers, manure.

As I travel further northwest, the roads gradually become narrower, and the farms take on a rundown look. The countryside here has a deserted air, many of the farms no longer inhabited. Two hours of driving, and my car crosses the small stone bridge and starts up the steep gravel hill. When I was a child, you could see half of Huron County from the top of this hill; my father would put the Austin in creeper gear to climb it. The County has reduced the hill's size since then; I think there's change enough in this world without altering the grandeur of hills.

As I drive in the long lane, the cedars that line the narrow track reach for my car, their branches brushing, catching, scraping. Grass trails its long fingers along the undercarriage—a hollow sound. My brother, my sister and I—all three of us, in our childhood, absorbed our father's feelings for the farm. Its creek runs in our blood, its forests are part of our inner world. As children, we lay on the beds of dark decomposing leaves formed by the roots of the old maples in the bush. We lay on the sun-warmed stones along the creek, smelling silt, willow, and summer water. The farm made us outsiders on the city street we called home.

Today, I park in the outer yard and walk up the slope to the farmhouse. My brother Graham lives alone here now. His wife, Pascale, divorced him and during the mid-nineties, he was "downsized" from his job at one of Canada's big banks. She and the five children live three hours distant, in the city. The mock orange that used to transform the farmhouse yard at this time of year, with its fragrant white blossoms, seems to be dying, despite the rainy spring. The pines that line the path to the outhouse look brittle and stressed. The outhouse itself is about to collapse into a pile of weathered boards. A jagged torso of exposed heartwood is all that remains of the big maple that used to be at the foot of the hill that rises behind the house. I walk across the creeping Charlie feeling as if I've entered some strange afterlife. Yet when I open the back door and smell straw, rubber boots, manure, old wood, ashes and the hard-packed earth of the cellar floors, it's the smell of home.

The kitchen table is dirty, the floor strewn with bits of straw and dead flies. Eva is at the small counter area, labouring to turn out a multi-course dinner. Eva is only ten months old as a girlfriend, new enough to think she has to impress Graham's sisters. My brother is still in the besotted stage, fetching and carrying for her. The dinner was my idea. I thought it might be the saving of us. A first step, anyway. I see at a glance that dinner's nowhere near ready.

One of these things is not like the others, and that's our sister Vivian. Wearing a tiny black pantsuit, her platinum hair shaped into a sophisticated cut, she looks as if she belongs on a fashion runway. "Lexie!" she exclaims, jumping up and hugging me hard. "You look fantastic in that jade green. And I love your hair—it's beautiful."

I hug her back. My feeling that I'm in a strange dream evaporates; I'm myself again.

"Can we help?" says Vivian, directing her words to Eva.

Eva shakes her head. Her face is flushed. Two strands of dark hair hang in her eyes. Sweat slowly traces a track on her temples. She looks at Graham. Her sultry black eyes say—get them out of here so I can concentrate.

Always a quick study, Vivian stands and takes the hand of her new man, Mike. (Mike the Second!): "How about some wine, Graham? We can sit outside at the front until you're ready, okay? I've been in an air-conditioned office all day."

Graham has spruced up since Eva became part of his life. His white hair is cut short; he's freshly shaven, wearing a pair of clean jeans and a white T shirt. He pours glasses of Beaujolais, and asks Mike to take a quick look at his computer. Vivian follows the two of them into what used to be the dining room. It's storage space for our mother's furniture now, the computer crowded into a dark corner.

Vivian warned our brother right at the start not to get in too deep with Eva. She knew Eva's background from a friend. Eva is thirty-five to Graham's fifty-five and beautiful in an unkempt, smoldering sort of way. Her dark hair contains streaks of natural red, her cheekbones are high, her eyes black, her derrière so shapely that everyone remarks on it. Eva has had no relationship that lasted longer than a year, Vivian told Graham. One of her two marriages was to a Transylvanian, who beat her up.

Both Graham and Eva have a passion for horses. This is

what brought them together; Eva started out as Graham's vet and ended up his girlfriend.

I climb the narrow back stairs to the bathroom and wash my hands with soap that looks dirtier than anything it could be asked to clean, then walk along the upstairs hall. Stacks of books and papers cover every bed. What is all this paperwork? The bloodlines of Graham's horses?

The floor of every room is littered with hundreds of tiny bodies. Too big for house flies. I kneel to look. Lady bugs. The new, yellowish kind with mutant tails. They were a plague on all our houses last fall, like the locusts of old.

I descend the back stairs and go outside. Walk around to the front of the house. The front steps are rotting. I climb onto the broken-down porch and sit in the one rickety lawn chair, beating time with my feet to the old nursery rhyme that's begun running through my head. Lady bird, lady bird, fly away home. Your house is on fire, and your children—they are gone.

Vivian and Mike come in sight, carrying two lawn chairs. Before me lies the deep green valley of the front field, the creek barely visible for the lush vegetation that grows on its banks. A goldfinch-yellow swath of buttercups sways in the field, right up to the emerald edge of the forest. I know this landscape as I know my own body. Every hillock and stone holds memory and meaning. The farm's disintegration feels to me like the long, continuous rending of a vital organ. It seems a visible image of the riving of our family—our parents dead, Pascale and the children gone from our lives, my children grown up and living far away. And now, trouble between my sister and brother.

Vivian and Mike pick their cautious way up the broken steps. Besides the chairs, they're carrying a bottle of wine, and glasses.

"What kept you two? Did you take the computer apart and rebuild it byte by byte?"

"It wasn't just one quick thing," says Mike.

Vivian unfolds her chair and sighs loudly.

"What's the matter?"

"Oh, you know." She waves her arm in the direction of the farmhouse. "Mike and I just heard the latest." She accepts a glass of wine and pulls a melancholy face: "My water pump broke on Monday. It cost me two hundred and fifty dollars to have it fixed. The new scythe blade broke on Tuesday. I'd only had it a week. That cost me fifty dollars. The storm we had on Thursday knocked out my computer and my phone. It ruined my modem. Last month, I had to buy $640.00 inserts for my shoes because my hip and my knee hurt so much, but the inserts make the shoes rub against my skin and give me blisters. I had visitors coming from France, so I hired two Amish girls to clean the house. I haven't been able find the inserts since."

Vivian has our brother's tone and his gestures to the very life. Mike laughs, his face flushed, his chicory-blue eyes clear.

"The mare that just foaled has an abscess in a tooth," Vivian continues, her face as long as a Sunday afternoon. "Jake's gone to live near Wawa for six months. Now I have nobody to fix stuff when it breaks. Guy needs almost three thousand dollars for his fall tuition. He never phones me except when he needs money. The house is overrun by mice and crickets."

I slump in the broken chair: "I know, I know. He's driving everyone away with his obsessive litanies of despair. But his troubles are real. His health is terrible, for one thing." I stop myself abruptly. Who do I think I am to be lecturing Vivian? She's the one who has been an ever-present support to Graham her whole life.

My sister raises her glass. "God, what a lovely evening. This view. Everything's so green. Like Eden, or something. It almost hurts to look at it." She looks over at me. "Do you realize that this is the first time Graham has ever invited us to dinner?"

"I think he's starting to come out of his depression about the divorce and the loss of mom and dad, and his job. Since he met Eva."

She nods. "It's still beautiful here, isn't it, in a gone-to-rack-and-ruin way."

"With an emphasis on the rack and ruin," says Mike. He reaches out and touches Vivian's cheek with a cherishing finger. A robin races across the neglected grass. Two kildeer and a bobolink perform on a high wire. From one of the lilac bushes, a wren sings its distinctive song.

Vivian takes another sip of wine and sighs again: "Everything seems fine so far with Graham and Eva, anyhow."

"How long do you give them?"

Vivian tips her glass and swallows a third of the wine it contains. "Another few months, maybe. Then there'll be hell to pay, because this time, she's not only his lover, she's his friend. This one's not a virtual relationship, it's real. She's his vet, for God's sake. This'll be the worst loss yet."

Vivian and Graham were close, from childhood on. Between them was a life I knew little about. Adventures in Europe. Trips to horse races. Vivian dating her older brother's friends. Graham was an adventurer. He travelled widely and had long passages of Shakespeare and other English poetry off by heart. He could recite French poetry on demand. Women were charmed.

Since the second Mike's arrival on the scene and Graham's increasing bitterness and degenerating health, my sister and brother have grown apart. Graham hasn't accepted Mike. He's jealous of him and resentful of Mike's big family, who now take up much of Vivian's time. Over the winter, he turned to me, phoning me, complaining that he rarely saw our sister, that he didn't even feel free to drop in on her anymore.

I passed on some of this to Vivian, toning the bitterness down. "Why doesn't he invite me to dinner for a change?" Vivian muttered. I was surprised at her response, then shocked at my own blindness. Vivian's legendary generosity has flowed down the years like a Niagara. Why wouldn't she want Graham to return her hospitality for once? The next time Graham phoned, I suggested that he host Vivian and Mike, told him cheese on toast would be okay, it was the thought that counted. Told him it couldn't always go one way, from Vivian to him.

"Graham is his own worst enemy," says Vivian.

"I know, I know. But ... he's lost everything. How would any of us be?"

"Di-nnerrrr." It's Graham, calling us in.

We trek around the house and enter by the back door. The smell of cooked food rises to meet us.

"Sit down," says Eva. "Anywhere." The beautiful face is red, beaded with sweat. She looks knackered. A lock of black hair hangs over one eye.

Eva has scrubbed the table and the floor. We take our places, the three of us automatically sitting where we sat as children. I glance upwards. The light bowl contains dozens of dead flies. Live flies buzz against the kitchen window panes. The kitchen floor linoleum, butter-yellow in our mother's time, has faded to mustard-beige.

Before each of us, Eva sets a bowl of Hungarian goulash. Large chunks of fatty beef float in the brown liquid. I sip the broth from my spoon and leave the beef in the bowl. I'd told Graham that the only meat I ate was chicken, hoping he'd pass that bit of information on. The last thing I wanted to do was insult Eva. Graham looks happier than he has in years and Eva has obviously put major effort into this meal. She announces that she's purchased trout from a commercial fish pond in the area. She wrapped them in newspaper and baked them in the oven.

"I didn't know you could put newspaper in an oven."

"You cannot," says Vivian, sitting up straight. "Some people can, but you, Lexie, cannot. And don't let me catch you trying." Her blue eyes pierce me for an instant. "Remember that your children have predicted you'll die by fire."

"Pshaw! My kids exaggerate."

Eva brings the trout to the table. She unwraps the fish. The skin comes off with the newspaper and the grin comes off my face. Eva slides one of the trout onto my plate. The fish is pallid, white, rubbery. Worse, it still has its head. I regard the eye. That flat, unseeing look of the dead. I'm ambivalent about fish at the best of times. My stomach lurches. I cannot eat this flaccid thing with a head and no skin and a staring glass button of an eye.

I look at Vivian, who carefully avoids my gaze.

I cut the fish into chunks, and one by one, as we eat, and when Eva is looking elsewhere, slip the pieces from my fork into the serviette on my lap. When Eva goes to the sink, I bend down, wad the whole into my purse, and close the zipper.

I cannot bear the thought of the head in my purse and Eva surely would not expect me to eat that anyway. I bury it beneath the salad greens, then eat the risotto. As I chew the thick gummy rice, I pick up the nude backbone of the fish. It doesn't feel bony, as I expected, it feels delicate, like a spider's web, but it too gives me the willies and I drop it onto my plate.

It's hot in the kitchen. There's a hole the size of a dog's head in the screen door, which means that the glass door has to be kept closed so the winged creatures of the night won't come in. Mosquitoes. Bats.

Eva serves asparagus on its own. "Forty percent of human beings produce urine with a strong asparagus smell when they pee after eating asparagus," she says, as she sets down the bowl. She's relaxing with us, the effect of the wine no doubt.

I lean forward. "Oh really? I know I do. I'd assumed everyone did. Do you mean that we who pee asparagus pee are in a minority? Who at this table does?"

Mike, Vivian and Eva raise their hands. Graham says that he does not.

Forty percent is probably wrong, I think. Graham wouldn't notice such a thing.

"I suspect that everyone produces the smell," says Vivian. "You probably just can't smell it, Graham."

"It's due to a compound called methanethiol," says Eva.

"Methanethiol contains mostly sulphur, with a bit of hydrogen and carbon thrown in."

I remember that Eva's a veterinarian, versed in things medical.

"Oh, I nearly forgot!" says Vivian. She leaps to her feet and runs out the back door.

"Where's she going?" Eva and I say this in unison, looking at Mike, who shakes his head and shrugs.

A car door slams, then Vivian is back. She hands a large poster to Eva. The photo is of a skinned, partly-dissected horse. "Your birthday present," she announces. "I bought it in England. It's from an art show I saw this spring in London when I was over for a medical conference. Humans were skinned and dissected and on show. There's one horse in the exhibit. That's it for mammals, other than human."

Eva holds the dreadful image of the mutilated creature under the fly-trap light fixtures. "Oh, I just love this," she exclaims.

"I do too," says Vivian.

"That was an art show?" says Mike, staring at the poster.

"This is amazing," says Eva.

"Oh yes, Mike," yells Vivian. "It was ART." We're all half-drunk now.

Underneath this dinner, I can feel all the other meals I've eaten beneath these lights. Millers and moths cluster on the outside of the south window, as they've always done at this time of year. The old wood stove is a presence in the shadows. The dark opening to Ephram's bedroom. We still call it Ephram's bedroom, though our elderly cousin, who was like a grandfather to us, has been dead twenty years, having lived to be one hundred years old. I've sat here to eat countless meals prepared by our mother and consumed in the company of kin. Everything scrubbed "within an inch of its life," one of our mother's expressions. The layers of dinners contribute to the unreal caste of the evening.

Eva has propped the laminated poster on the unused wood stove, where the large, ghoulish image of the horse without its skin presides over the dinner. Quite appropriate.

Every time Eva sits down, Graham's hands are on her. She doesn't seem to mind that he smells of the barn. Maybe she can't smell him; after all she is a country vet.

Eva brings on the crème brulée. She's made it in special cups that, upended, allow the custard to keep its shape. Garnished it with wild strawberries. She says that she and Graham crawled all over the farm to find them. "Well, actually, we were looking for morels," she says, with a darkly electric look at her lover, "but we found these."

I try one of the tiny carmine-red berries, green leaves, stems, and all. Finally, something I can enjoy. "You'll never find morals, crawling the farm," I say to Eva. "Either your parents inculcate them or not."

"Very funny," says Eva. Yes, she's relaxed with us now. Vivian and Graham are engaged in drunken repartee. Things are going well. Again I glance up at the hundreds of dead cluster flies. In our mother's day, even one fly up there was too many.

"Change is the only constant in human life," I muse aloud, for by now there isn't an original thought in my head.

Graham lifts his glass to the level of his glowing cheeks. "To The Dinner!" he proclaims. "It was Lexie's idea to have it and Eva's idea to cook it."

My throat burns. I have to bite my tongue to keep from calling Graham an idiot. I'd wanted Vivian to think the dinner was his idea; that had been the whole point. My worst fear is that the three of us—the kernel of our family that remains—will break apart, each of us falling away into separate lives. No matter how Graham has behaved, he's our brother.

"This is cleaned up?" I interrupt Graham to distract Vivian from his disclosure. "What are those things all over the bedroom floors? Why are the beds thigh-deep in books and papers?"

For answer, Graham mashes his face against Eva's neck and snuffles like a pig.

Vivian gets unsteadily to her feet. "Thank you so much, Eva.

I don't know when I've had such a good dinner."

I stand as well: "Yes, the fish was amazing. So fresh and flavourful."

Eva smiles and nods, "It was swimming in a pond this afternoon."

"There you go. So tender. And the risotto. I haven't had such wonderful risotto in years."

"My Eva, my beauty," slobbers Graham from his chair, his left hand making its way up Eva's leg, his right pawing her famous derrière. "Come to me, my beauty."

We coast out the lane. Mike presses the button that rolls the windows down. An ode to joy by the frogs in the swamp almost drowns out the crunch of our tires on gravel and the occasional ping of a stone against metal. Dark shadows, the black sky, a moon one night away from full. Smell of the creek.

"I put the fish in my purse." I say this as Mike makes the turn from the lane onto the concession line.

The car gives a small lurch. "In your purse?" say Mike and Vivian in unison.

"I couldn't eat it."

"I forced it down," says Vivian. "And the risotto was glue. She didn't stir it long enough. You didn't really like it, did you, Lexie?"

"Of course not. And I almost gagged at the mere sight of the goulash. Those huge chunks of fatty beef."

"I can't believe you two," says Mike.

"Why?" Vivy and I chorus the word. "Did you like it?"

"No, it was an awful dinner. But the way you two went on, I thought you loved it."

"Well, of course we went on, Mike. Look at all the trouble she went to," says Vivian.

"Exactly," I say. "We don't want her to think we didn't appreciate her work. Besides, who could turn out food worth eating in that kitchen!"

Mike laughs. "What pieces of work the two of you are," He shakes his head. "You were so convincing. I'd have sworn you thought it was gourmet fare."

"The evening was a success," I say.

"Yes indeed," says Vivian. "Eva was pleased and proud. We bonded." She flings her arms high. "We bonded over the skinned horse and the asparagus pee."

"And that's good for Graham," I finish my sister's sentence. "Eva will feel more at home in the family now."

Mike shakes his head as if to clear it of a fog. "Where millions wouldn't. I think maybe Eva is the right one for Graham after all."

"Graham's fallen hard for her, that's obvious," I say. "But what's going to happen six months or a year from now, when Eva moves on?"

"Maybe she won't move on," says Mike, the optimist. "Maybe she'll settle in at the farm with Graham. I'm going to take the back road home."

Vivian hasn't said a word about me engineering the dinner. Maybe she didn't hear Graham's comment. I ask her to pass me the glove compartment flashlight, then open my purse. The strip of serviette has come apart. The handbag stinks intensely of fish. I stretch my arm forward, hold out the purse, order Vivian to take a whiff.

My sister snorts. "Get that away from me, Alexia. You'll have to throw it out."

"But it's my favourite purse. It's leather."

"You'll never get the smell out."

As so often, Vivian is right. The purse will end up a casualty of the evening.

Mike leaves the windows open and drives slowly on the gravel road. There are no other cars. We fall silent, listening to the spring night, feeling its young, hopeful breath upon our faces.

XX.
This Is History

An hour to go and one last party. More flowers and a framed portrait of them as a group. Cake around the workroom table. At a minute to one, they form a circle around me and chant the seconds to zero. Clapping, cheers and shouts. I kick off my shoes. One of them hits the ceiling, lands on a desk and knocks papers flying. I strip off my stockings, say I'll leave the building "footloose and fancy free."

Jean's laughter turns suddenly to tears. She grabs me. "Oh no, this is it, this is really the end!" Jean has for years been one of the sharpest thorns in my side.

"Are you crazy?" says Gillian, pulling her off me.

Though I have been taking things home all week, I have five full shopping bags, three bouquets, a purse and an umbrella. The staff help me to load the elevator. Can they come with me to my car, help me to carry all this? I smile at them—Nope.

I want to bear these last fardels alone.

Outside the building, people stare at my bare feet, the almost un-carry-able bag lady paraphernalia, the flowers sticking every which way. I'm the fool in a play of my own making. My working life of thirty-one years is over.

Somehow, I make it to the car, dump my unbearable load in the trunk, get behind the wheel, switch on full blast Mick Jagger's "Turn the Girl Loose," and rock up the long boulevard to the highway.

Can it really be? The mortal coil of myself can barely contain this tornado of euphoria: "Thank God Almighty," I shout above the music. "Free at last!"

Ten days later, the Budapest airport. A woman with platinum hair and stylish black leather pants rushes towards me. Her arms are full of red and pink and yellow and white. My sister. Scent of Shalimar and leather. Spicy tickle of carnations on my cheeks. She takes me to the curb, where her new partner, Mike, holds open the door of a black company car. Mike the Second is how I think of him, privately, though I no longer say it aloud, because it irks Vivian. He has the same first name as his recent predecessor, my sister's former partner.

We speed through the narrow streets of Budapest. Nose among the flowers, I turn my head this way and that, trying to see everything. Just before I left, a colleague reminded me of one bit of history and it runs through my mind now. On June 28, 1914, a militant Serbian nationalist assassinated the heir to the Austro-Hungarian throne. The chain reaction led to the First World War.

Mike drops Vivian and me at his flat in the hills of the Buda section of the city and returns to work. I lie down for a nap and have a vivid dream.

> I am in a large, bright flea market in Budapest. A stall owner says she has something new, shows me a group of dolls. I am shocked to see they are the childhood dolls my grown daughters in Canada have just thrown away.

I retired at the end of August, summer school over. My daughters were home together that week for a vacation. I asked them to clean out the attic, to get rid of childhood toys, to pack what they wanted to keep for storage in the basement.

To my surprise, they were ruthless. I watched them stuff into Amity boxes dolls and toys I thought they'd never part with. I rescued three of my old favourites. They laughed and took a picture of me pretending to nurse the baby doll. Now the dolls have turned up in Budapest, in my dream. So what's that supposed to mean? That you can't throw anything out? That it returns in another form?

On my first full morning in Budapest, Vivian and I wait for the bus on a hilly street near the flat. A light rain pitters on our umbrellas. My sister is annoyed. Last September, when she came here to visit Mike, who is working temporarily in Hungary, it was sunny and warm for the whole month. I assure her that for all I care, it can rain toads. When I fly, I turn into stone-age woman, astonished that I can walk into a heavy piece of machinery that rises into the sky and in one night can take me from Toronto to Budapest. This is Hungarian rain, I tell her; every drop is of interest to me.

Settled into our seats, we jolt over rough pavement, smell the damp cloth of people's coats as they get on and walk past us down the aisle. Sway around a queasy corner. Vigilant as always, my sister checks the map, determined to get us off at the right place, to look after me.

Months later I will re-read the email I wrote when we got back to the flat that afternoon. I will note that I chose to send it to my husband, two children and brother. My nearest and dearest, chosen automatically as recipients. I will note the small inaccuracy and the strange mélange of inconsequential and significant, how I spoke of the weather and my night's sleep along with what we had seen when Vivian switched on the television for a weather report.

Tue, 11 Sep 2001 11:37:47 -0400

Dear David and all,
 Here in Budapest we have just got the terrible news of the attacks—4 hijacked planes crashing into the

World Trade Center and Pentagon.
Also that all American and Canadian airports are closed. I hope we are not going to have a World War.
It is late afternoon here, and raining. Usually in Sept. it's warm and sunny.
Vivian has visions of us trying to survive in Hungary with no money and no medications. She doesn't think I'll be able to get home as planned but I'm SURE Canadian airports will be open by the time my week here has passed.
Try and write to me soon. I slept 12 hours last night, am already on Buda time, feel fine.
love,
Lexie

My husband David reads this and thinks that I've smoked dope or downed a bottle of Slivovitz. He's been painting our basement. My brother reads it and thinks that I've flipped out at last. He's been cleaning out the stables. Both of them reluctantly log on to internet news, to check anyway.
"The horror, the horror," reads David's reply.

Every day, Vivian switches on CNN as soon as we come back to the flat. Budapest is being coupled irrevocably for me with images of the planes, the burning towers, the collapse, people running for their lives. Vivian feels that the end is nigh, the towers of Mammon sliding into a heap of stinking burning rubble, all of us soon to follow. An event that feels as if it will change the course of the twenty-first century, just as the shot fired in 1914 changed the course of the twentieth.

The Budapest market. The minute we enter, I recognize it and turn to my sister excitedly. This is the market of the dream of my arrival day. Large and bright, a stunning multi-coloured display of fruits, vegetables, meat and crafts. Ostensibly, we're looking for a glass rooster. But I can't stop myself from looking for the dolls of my daughters' childhoods. I take my sister to the place where the dream stall was located. It's piled high with crocheted, white, lace tablecloths.

There is every kind of glass bird in the market of Pest but a rooster.

We sit for coffee beside a stall hung with thousands of red peppers. So what's this rooster thing, Vivian wants to know.

"You know how the rooster appears on the border between worlds?"

My sister's blue eyes look into mine as she raises her coffee, holding the warm mug with both hands. "Between worlds?"

"Between darkness and light. Dawn. An in-between space, a liminal space." I lean towards my sister. "A space with the potential for something to happen."

Vivian looks thoughtful. "Your old life is over, your new life just beginning—is that the idea?"

"That's it."

Back at the flat, I go into Mike's study, to his laptop. It's morning at home in Canada; there are messages for me.

> A friend: Things in NY are in a state of war—fires burning out of control and untold people dead. Heads of state gone to secure locations, air and navy forces protecting NY. Bob called us from Dubai, said the Arabs are cheering in the streets.

> My younger daughter: Hi Mom, can you believe it?????? Bush said "make no mistake we will hunt them down and punish 'them' so maybe we Will be in a war. You may indeed have trouble getting home.

> David: Today's papers: 40% of Americans are born-again Christians; U.S. *got what it deserves*; Falwell: *this*

is God's retribution for sinful behavior by abortionists, gays, lesbians & feminists; Bush calls himself a born-again who found Jesus in '80s; U.S. had it coming for a long time (Canadian newspaper); *We have to thoroughly demoralize the enemies of God* (Arab media).

The next morning, Vivian goes to the store. I'm still in my nightgown, writing emails. She sets the security system when she leaves. Mike's flat was broken into in the summer, his computer taken, though there is a locked fence around the apartment building. Some are doing well in Hungary's new economy, others are desperately poor.

When I go to the kitchen to make tea, the security system (I'm later told) thinks I'm a burglar. Screaming high-pitched noises in the flat. What sounds like sirens outside. A neighbour at the window of his apartment, looking over. I don't know how to turn the system off. No sense standing here. I return to writing to friends and family and am soon oblivious to the racket. Just as I finish, an email arrives, a nighthawk friend quoting John Ibbotson of the *Globe and Mail*:

By this time next year the world as we know it may be unrecognizable.

I want to wash my hair, but the alarms are still shrieking. A thief would long since have made off with her loot. I decide not to go in the shower. What if Security arrives!

As soon as I'm bent over the kitchen sink, hair wet and soapy, I hear people in the flat. Two men appear at the kitchen door and begin to question me. I can't understand a word and reply with a Trudeau shrug. My nightgown and sudsy face seem to exonerate me. They appear intensely amused, turn off the alarms and leave. The trap designed to catch the outsider catches only me—the sister, the insider.

I am not here primarily to see the castles and cafés, the wide flowing river, its Parisian bridges; I'm here to spend time with my sister. In real life (these days do not feel like real life) she's a doctor, her days jammed with appointments, nights broken by emergencies and deliveries. We haven't spent so much time together since the autumn of our mother's last illness. We take the bus downtown to Pest, walk along the base of a cliff for half a mile and arrive at the Gellert baths, part of the grand old hotel on the Danube.

I have forgotten my bathing suit, so rent one for eighteen dollars Canadian. It's one-size-fits-all. The big hole in the side seam is what makes it fit all, I say to Vivian. We change in a slimy-footed cubicle and are issued a sort of shower cap. As we climb the steep stairs, I take Vivian's arm, and mock-stagger onto the next step. "I am one bath away from death, my sister." I clutch my chest. "Pray that 'taking the waters' will cure me."

Vivian puts her arm around me. "Are you listening, God?" she shouts.

As we reach the top step, we emerge, miraculously, under a blue sky with fluffy clouds. It will be the only hour we see the sun during my eight day visit. More stone steps to a pool. The water receives us with warm, buoyant arms. Our bath-mates are speaking German, Czech, French, and languages I don't recognize. Vivian in her cap looks like our mother. Later, she will tell me she was thinking the same of me. We drift, we rock gently. I look at my sister and experience an inundation of happiness so intense that it's a material presence. The only way to tempt happiness into your mind is to take it into the body first, says the poet Mary Oliver. I believe it.

When we leave the bath, there's a lightness to my being that feels as if it will endure. *Wash me,* I say to Vivian, *and I shall be whiter than snow.*

Later Vivian treats me to a cappuccino and poppy seed roll in the tearoom of the Gellert hotel. Through the arch to the grand lobby, we watch a film crew shoot a movie called *I Spy.* My napkin flutters to the floor. Vivian bends to pick it up and her face floods with red. She crunches the napkin in her hand. "You look a fright," she says. "Poppy seeds stuck between your teeth and shower cap hair."

"Oh well, who cares. Vivian, what's the matter?" My sister has tears in her blue eyes.

"Lexie," she says. "Tell me the truth. Am I a complete idiot to attempt this for a fourth time? It's Mike's fourth too; did you know that?" Wet eyes and red blotches on her cheeks. "What if we fail?" Her voice catches. "What if we fail yet again?"

I hand her my untouched glass of water and she slurps a mouthful.

"Vivian, don't say 'fail.' You haven't failed."

Her red-rimmed eyes look into mine.

I touch her hand. Vivian's hand is little and slender and soft. My hands are soft too. Vivian says it's because neither of us has ever done a day's work in our lives. Vivian, who routinely works fourteen hour days. She means what our mother would have called work. Scrubbing floors. Stripping wallpaper. Milking the cows.

"You're on your fourth relationship because you've grown. You're no longer the girl who married your cousin. You've changed—inside—so much that you wouldn't recognize the girl who got married in front of the outhouse if you met her on the street." My index finger traces the skin at the base of Vivy's fourth and fifth finger. "You've delivered babies, sat with people as they died, crouched over the critically injured in the back of an ambulance, sick to your stomach, keeping them alive 'til you got to the big city hospital. You've sat across from a mother with five kids and told her that she has three months left to live. You've dragged yourself out of bed in the middle of the night to go to a sick person more times than anyone knows. You've deepened as you coped with all this. You've grown, you've changed."

Vivian picks up the water with her free hand, takes another sip: "Do you have a tissue?"

"No. People stay in dead marriages for the children's sake, or because they're too insecure to move on, or because they're afraid of being alone or of being poor." I pick up her hand again. "You haven't failed. You've been courageous. You've gone through the deaths of three intimate relationships. And each time, new life has come in. Someone who's right for you at that stage."

"Do you think Mike and I will make it, Lexie? Do you believe we will?"

"Make it where, Vivy? I don't think of life that way. It's not a race. It's not somewhere you end up. Life is right now. It doesn't matter whether you or any other married couple crosses the finish line together. No one's going to be there to give a medal. What matters is each day—how we are with one another. If it goes bad and stays bad, you will stay, or you will move on. No one knows what will happen in this world."

"But you've been married forty years, Lexie."

I laugh and let go of her hand, half-stand and beckon the waitress for a tissue. "That doesn't mean I'm a role model. I've lived one way. There are others. Besides, have you forgotten Zack? The divorce?" I look down at her white hair. She had it dyed platinum after our mother died, but to me it looks white. It looks like our mother's hair.

I sit back down. "And yes, I do think Mike is the right person. He's a kind, intelligent man, and he adores you. He's good to his mother and father, good to his children."

Vivian sits up straight. "Are you still jealous of him, Vivian?"

"What makes you think..." I'm stopped by the look on her face. "Oh, okay. Yes. I'm jealous of how much of your time he takes, he and his big family. I'm resentful of how you seem part of a 'we' now, no longer just you. You and I aren't as close as we were." Vivian is trying to say something, but I shush her. "But at one and the same time, Vivian I'm happy for you. Happy that you're happy."

When I say the last "happy," it comes out like the cracked groan of the cello Katie used to saw on when she was little. Vivian and I look at one another and start to laugh. We laugh until our eyes stream and our noses run and our ears block up. I call the waitress and ask for more tissues. Vivian was right. I look such a fright that on the way back to the flat a Hungarian youth jumps up and gives me his seat on the bus, stands for the duration of the long ride back to Buda. Later I will learn that as usual I've constructed a fellow journeyer's life in a way that reflects myself only. In Budapest, the young routinely give up their seats to their elders. It is, after all, the old world.

Back at the flat, it's a jump cut to the new world.

> A friend: What a strange time to be in Europe. Here, there is a general mood of heartsickness that transcends borders & politics. I tear up at the most unexpected moments—standing with a co-worker in the hospital lobby, watching the TV, phoning to set up an appt. to donate blood, looking at the photo of people falling in midair from unimaginably high up. Tomorrow night I am going to a church prayer vigil. I keep seeing in my mind's eye the Tarot card "The Tower"—struck by lightning, breaking off at just the same point, people falling ... a card that signifies humbling of human hubris & pride in our intellectual and technical mastery. There is a sudden, painful illumination, delivered with all the force of nature—an opportunity to explode out of small mind into a greater understanding.

From the embassy last night, we went directly to a concert in an ornate castle. Liszt then Dvorak cascading over and through us. I looked away for a moment, heard the audience catch its collective breath, and looked back. A princess from a dream, the coloratura soprano in a magnificent white dress with three black dots on the hem, a crown that sparkled. When she sang full out, her voice carried over the entire orchestra: the human voice the mightiest instrument of all.

In the washroom, I asked Vivian if, like me, she looked around at those our age and thought that they were a generation older than we are. She nodded, and we giggled at our foolish images in the mirror.

I fall asleep with four lines from the poet Tony Hoagland's "America" drifting through my mind:

> *When each day you watch rivers of bright merchandise run past you*
> *And you are floating in your pleasure boat upon this river*
>
> *Even while others are drowning underneath you*
> *And you see their faces twisting in the surfaces of the waters*

Dear David,

I write to you in a state of frunkeness. Tonight, Mike took us to Artichoke for dinner. Artichoke has melon walls and palm trees. At each place, an apple cut in the shape of a rooster. Vivian and I complain that the white wine isn't giving us a buzz; there's something wrong with it. He orders more. I take out my notebook and copy words from the menu: naked chicken; fress greens; vegetable pudding; thorn for dessert. My pen falls to the floor.

Vivian crawls under the table to fetch it. She's wearing a blood-red blouse that clashes with the melon walls. Shiny, black, vinyl pants. "I see the wine was okay after all," says Mike.

The waiter comes and looks at his patron crawling

under the table. I've never really seen eyes bug out before, David. I swear, the waiter's eyes are maybe two centimeters in front of his face. He leaves the table to find his buddy. He shows his buddy Vivian crawling under the table. They laugh and laugh. They sag against the bar, they fall against one another. They're as red as Vivian's blood blouse.

She finds the pen, finally, and comes up. She goes to the washroom. When she comes back, Mike tells her that we told the waiter 'Lewinsky' because, really, what else could she be doing down there? Vivian believes us. She laughs so hard that she matches her blouse. Every time the waiter looks in our direction a smile comes spreading on his face.

I am still stiff in my stomach from laughing. One day here is as long as one week at home. Time is stretchy—it includes whatever you want to do. I am expanding too. I keep running into my stomach where it didn't used to be.

Even in my frunkeness, David, I do realize that we are fiddling while Rome burns.

love,
Lexie

I awaken the next morning with pounding heart. Another vivid dream.

I have signed up for a course in art history. The teacher is "new age," and has us lie on the floor and do nonsensical, time-wasting exercises. She goes to the back of the class, gets her baby, starts to nurse it in a gross, gobble-gobble manner. I am disgusted by this class, and ask for my money back.

"What's all this about dolls and babies?" I say to my sister at breakfast. "The Jungians think that when a baby recurs in your dreams, a new part of you is coming to life."

"Yeah, and the new part is one half of a pair of drunken-sot sisters," she says, shaking the bottle of Tylenol. "You might, like me, need two of these with your coffee."

After breakfast, she switches on CNN and I go to Mike's laptop.

> A friend: "They" keep saying that everything has changed. Yet for us, here, in our daily lives, everything is exactly the same. The same round of getting up with the alarm, fighting rush hour traffic, work, evening classes, grocery shopping, meal preparation, bed, alarm, start over.

I reply with a quote from Slavenka Drakulic, a Yugoslavian journalist I'm reading who is writing about the war in the Balkans:

> *I'm afraid that we will have to live with this war for years. But you too will have to live with it, and it will change you—not immediately but over time... We all thought that the war would not come to us, that it was impossible.*

Keeping the apartment in basic supplies is a task. The hills are steep and groceries heavy, we learn, when they have to be schlepped home on foot. It's still the old European way here—daily shopping for vegetables, fruit, bread.

Before he left for work, Mike said there was a piece of turkey in the freezer. Vivian says she'll stuff it and make mashed potatoes—a comfort meal. She gets her dictionary; the meat doesn't look like turkey to her. Sure enough, the label doesn't correspond to the word for turkey. Nor does it correspond to chicken, beef, pork, or lamb. She has a mystery meat.

Though it's pouring, she ventures out. The butcher is closed, she tells me later. She goes down the hill. There, the butcher is open but no fresh meat. She turns to leave and notices whole roasted chickens in the window. She pays her five dollars and returns. She decides to make a risotto to serve with the already cooked chicken.

As my sister shops and cooks, I lie on the burgundy couch, feet up on the polished wooden sill. Still reading Drakulic. The heavy rain beats hard against the window. I'm aware of the sounds and smells of domesticity, of the familiar guilt I felt as my mother worked and I read. Like my mother, my sister has said she doesn't need help.

As she stirs the risotto, I go to stand near her, admire the loaves of fragrant, fresh bread she's brought home. The bread reminds me of a passage in Drakulic. I sit on the kitchen stool and read to her as she stirs.

This little flat in Buda is redolent of the sounds and smells of home. My sister has made it so. I break off a piece of bread and watch her stir, thinking that I have my mother back again. We have become one another's mother. But we are still the little kids we used to be, as well as the middle-aged women we'll never believe we are. I get off my stool, put my arms around her, tell her how much she means to me. She nuzzles me back. I return to my reading, she returns to her stirring, the rain continues.

By the time Mike arrives, dinner is ready. We eat by candle-light, lulled and comforted by the steady rain, the wind from which we, in our circle of family, are sheltered. As I taste the fragrant risotto, I realize that Mike the Second has become Mike. The other one is history.

More wine, thoughts beginning to swim. The other one is history. But history repeats itself. The shot heard round the world becomes the airplanes felling the towers. The ancient image on a Tarot card becomes the falling towers. The dolls of my children's childhood become the dolls of my inner world in Budapest. Mike One becomes Mike Two, Mike Two becomes Mike. What are we really saying when we say someone or something is history? The opposite of what we think? That it is bound to return?

David: Dominos fall, and nations. Reprisal begets reprisal. Unimaginable horrors slouch toward us as, helpless, we wait to cross the next threshold.

I reply: The cure for the panic of the moment is historical perspective.

My last day. In a shop window, Vivian and Mike see a glass rooster. The shopkeeper speaks only Hungarian. Vivian crows and flaps her wings. The woman fetches the rooster, presents it to my sister. Vivian jumps up and down and the old woman catches her joy.
There they were, Mike tells me—two jumping jacks.
The miniature glass rooster has a red comb, an orange tail, yellow feet. Magnificent. Early every morning, I've heard roosters in the hills of this old world city on the Danube. Their call—that miraculous cracking open and letting go that's both joy and submission—to your fate, to whatever history has in store for you.

At the Budapest airport, Vivian and Mike hug me goodbye. In the boarding line, we passengers round a bend in the corridor. A wide table. Behind it, three tall, bulky Hungarian men, uniformed, guns visible at their belts. They search everything to be carried on the plane. Women set their purses on the table without complaint, but our bodies reveal reluctance, embarrassment. What is in our purses is our most personal, our most private.
As I stand in the lineup, I think of the Jews, the lines they waited in and marched in, the stripping away of possessions, clothes, family, identity, life. The Jews and all the others, the endless lines of human history.

The woman beside me is pregnant. White face, huge dark eyes. She trembles as her carry bag goes on the table. The guard opens it. Looking up at us is a crouched black and white cat. The guard's big rough hand with its scraped knuckles moves forward. I stop breathing.
    He pets the cat gently, zips up the bag, hands it back into the woman's keeping.
    As we leave the table, her dark eyes meet mine. We exchange a smile.

The flight home is long. I'm surrounded by old women, crones with markedly individual faces, written on by their lives. All the way across the Atlantic, the gabble of aunts and grandmothers warms and lulls me. It will go on no matter what happens. I'm glad for this time alone, this space between the old world and the new.

David has forgotten where he parked the car in the multi-level airport garage. For twenty minutes, we wander the concrete landscape, dragging my suitcase. It becomes heavier and heavier, a return of the quotidian fardels I bore and bear, that all humans have borne and do bear in one form or another. "There's the car," says David at last, bringing my fantasy to an abrupt end.

The house seems huge, my computer screen gigantic after Mike's laptop. There on the bed are the three rescued dolls of my Budadream.
    The September night is hot and humid. In such weather, our cat usually sleeps at my feet. But tonight she sleeps beside my face, the tip of her whisker just touching my cheek.

xxi.
The Love Bites of Twenty-Three Rogue Monkeys

MY FIRST DAUGHTER HAS SETTLED in Montreal, my second daughter in Winnipeg. Both of them were raised in southern Ontario, where some winters you can almost get by without boots. Montreal has the largest annual snowfall of any major city in the world. Winnipeg has fifty-eight days a year of minus-twenty degrees centigrade. Both first daughter and second daughter hate cold weather. Go figure.

I call them first daughter and second daughter only to myself. I called them this in fun when they were children, but when first daughter became a teenager, she stopped laughing and said that the practice was dehumanizing and demoralizing.

First daughter, Julie, travelled in her twenties, moving from job to job, country to country. At one point, she spent fifteen months in northern Japan.

On this winter morning, fifteen years after Julie's sojourn in Japan, I phoned my daughter in Montreal to tell her that I had read in the paper that a rogue monkey looking for a partner had bitten twenty-three women in rural northern Japan as they went to work or took out the garbage. I expected that first daughter would laugh. I thought both of us would laugh, then have a warm, chatty, mother-daughter conversation. It was a Sunday, before noon, and my husband was away for the weekend.

Julie said that fifteen years before, when she lived in northern Japan, I had sent her an article on rogue monkeys who bit women in rural northern Japan and that not one of the

Japanese women she'd talked to had heard of such a thing and that she had told me this at the time and why was I contacting her to tell her yet another rogue-monkey-in-Japan story? Julie was cross and brushing her teeth as she spoke. She said she was on her way out, and she ended the conversation.

I had no memory of having sent Julie a previous rogue monkey story. I went to the stove and put on the kettle. I filled the coffee grinder and pressed the button. Along with the racket came that wonderful aroma of splintering coffee beans releasing their essence. When I poured the boiling water, the aroma deepened, as expected, and I inhaled it deeply, hoping that this pleasure would replace the pleasure of a warm, chatty conversation with first daughter.

It did not, of course. The pleasures of the senses are intense and undeniable. But they don't go as deep as the pleasures of meaningful communion with one's own flesh and blood.

I carried the white china mug to the kitchen table, sat down, cupped my hands around it, and looked through the window at the snow, which was falling in a lazy yet steady way straight down from the sky onto the garden. I tried to think why I would have sent Julie the same rogue monkey story twice. I was not in the habit of phoning Julie spontaneously with stories of any kind.

And I tried to think why Julie had not laughed.

Perhaps it had something to do with Japan. I remembered how, after fifteen months in Japan, Julie had been frightened on the expressway home from the airport—so many cars, going so fast. How Julie had said the dinner plates seemed monstrous, the portions huge. How she'd eaten only one bite of her welcome home cake, then explained that she'd lost her taste for sweets. I had looked at Julie, experiencing the miracle of her return but something else as well. My daughter was at one and the same time deeply familiar, and a stranger. Best friend said it out loud.

"You've changed, Julie. You've lost weight and put on

muscle, that's part of it. Your forearms look strong. Capable of anything."

"That's probably from the swimming," Julie said. "And from practicing my flute. My room had no bathtub or shower. So every day I cycled across town to the gym. I swam lengths and showered. And most days I practiced my flute for hours. Eleven hours every day, over the New Year's holiday. There was nothing else to do. That was their family time."

I came to with a start, and uncurled my fingers from the cold cup. The snow was still falling, transforming the garden into something soft and white, mounded and mysterious. Yes, I decided, first daughter's reaction had to do with Japan. She had undergone both solitude and loneliness. She'd been hungry. She could see her breath in the air, mornings, in her unheated room in that small town in the mountains. Most likely, she viewed her time in Japan as a hard-earned achievement, something she was proud of. She probably thought that I was belittling it, sending those monkey clippings. This was the answer.

There was nothing funny about the rogue monkey story, I decided, and I was an insensitive loser to have told it to first daughter not once, but twice. I stood up and went to the window. I would call Winnipeg. I would ask second daughter's opinion, and that would result in the warm, chatty, mother-daughter conversation I still craved.

I called Katie. "Good morning, Mother," she said. "What's on your mind?"

I told Katie that I had phoned Montreal to tell her sister that a rogue monkey looking for a partner had bitten twenty-three women in rural northern Japan as they went to work or took out the garbage. That her sister had been cross and brushing her teeth and etcetera. I said that I had forgotten that I had done a similar thing fifteen years ago, and, like Julie, wondered why I had done this once, let alone twice, what did Katie think, after all she was in Psychology.

Katie laughed and laughed and laughed. She laughed so hard that I caught her laughter, uncertainly at first, but giving in to it. We laughed ourselves weak. Of course the story was funny; how could I have persuaded myself otherwise! When the two of us had straightened up, I told Katie that I had spent the last half hour sitting quietly at the kitchen table, trying to think why I would have sent Julie a rogue monkey story twice, and had decided it was because I was an insensitive loser. This set Katie off again.

Once we'd blown our noses and composed ourselves, I asked Katie why her sister had not laughed. Katie said all she could think of was that Julie must have thought that I was being over-protective.

"Over-protective?" This was an angle that had not occurred to me.

"I can only think that she thought you sent the story to warn her to watch out for rogue monkeys."

"I could see that if she still lived in northern Japan," I said, "but in downtown Montreal there are no rogue monkeys looking for partners. Besides, would she think that I would think that a rogue monkey would think that it could be a desirable partner for your sister, who is very beautiful?"

Katie laughed loudly. This was turning into the kind of conversation I had been longing for.

I asked Katie if she knew what a rogue monkey was. Katie said it must be a breed of monkey. I asked her if she knew what rogue meant. Katie said "Mother I'm in fourth year, it means scoundrel or tricky person."

I said that a rogue monkey was a monkey who went his own way and behaved unpredictably like, for instance, a rogue wave. Katie had never heard of a rogue wave—this was before the tsunami—and said she didn't believe in such a thing.

I said, "A rogue wave is not like God—something one believes in or disbelieves—its existence is a scientific fact." Over Katie's protest, I said that yes, yes, a little family could be picnicking in Prince Edward Island and a rogue wave could crash onto the beach and pull them into the ocean and drown them all.

"Mother," said Katie. "You have always been a catastrophizer. In fact, on second thought, I understand why Julie didn't laugh. Whether you know it or not, your subconscious has made rogue monkeys into metaphors for danger." Second daughter's minor was in English literature. She continued. "You are using metaphor to insinuate to Julie that rogue monkeys are dangers that erupt without warning from the trees or from the oceans or from the bucolic sweep of McGill's green sward."

Katie actually said that—"bucolic sweep" and "green sward." Perhaps I should have steered her away from literature. She said that moreover, my sending of articles on rogue monkeys to Julie was the same as my posting a description of the of-course-never-needed Heimlich maneuver on the back of the kitchen door for all those years of their childhood and by the way was it still there?

I swallowed this meekly, not wanting second daughter to clean her teeth and leave for a pressing engagement. When we had finished our conversation and hung up, I took down the stained, yellowing poster of the Heimlich maneuver. It was true that it had never been needed. I opened a bottle of red wine to use in the beef stroganoff I planned to make, as my husband would be home by dinner time. And why not have a few swigs of the wine as I cooked! Receiving the ire of both first and second daughter in one day had felt to me like the love bites of twenty-three rogue monkeys. As I cooked and sipped, I decided that both my repeating of the story and first daughter's response would and should remain mysteries of the human psyche, its reach being even more vast than that of the heaven and earth of which Horatio did not dream.

That evening, a rogue mushroom I had failed to cut in half while making the beef stroganoff and drinking wine lodged itself in the entrance to latest husband's windpipe and he began to turn blue. New status hovered in the hall like a ghost. Late husband.

I stood behind my husband, encircled his slight girth with my arms, placed my two fists beneath his diaphragm and shoved in and up with sudden force; in short, I performed a perfect Heimlich maneuver. The mushroom popped from his throat and shot across the kitchen. The pink of life returned to his skin. New status evaporated.

I broadcast that shot around my world, especially to Winnipeg and Montreal, where the long, shining icicles snapped and sang with it for the rest of the winter and the two mighty rivers could not help but giggle beneath their smooth, unreadable faces.

xxii.
The Play of the Gods

NOT WANTING TO BE MARRIED in the heat of summer, Vivian has chosen September for her wedding day, thinking September as in blue skies and dry air you can breathe. Cicadas by day, crickets by night. Harvest apples, peaches and corn. The stasis of summer giving way to mutability. The season of getting on with things.

I speak with Vivian by phone on Wednesday of the wedding week. "Three days to go," she says. "I just got back from the site. The big tent is up and the grounds look spectacular. Half of Rilling seems to be employed out there this afternoon—deadheading flowers, scrubbing bricks, weeding, sweeping. What a whirlwind."

Vivian's wedding is being held outside, on the grounds of her longtime friends Nancy and Ted. "That's a big property, Vivy. Did you check the entire area?"

"I walked all around it, yes. There was a row of sunflowers at the back that had grown to a ludicrous height. They looked like giraffes. Off with their heads, I said to one of the gardeners. Nancy had given me free rein, so I was Queen for a day."

"Is Graham ready to give you away?" Graham is our brother. "I assume he made good on his threat not to buy new clothes?"

"Thank God Graham has a girlfriend. I've put Eva in charge of his appearance. I reinforced with her that there was not to be a hint of horse dander about his person. We don't want the flautist slumping to the concrete in a wheeze, mid-tune."

The flautist is my daughter Julie. "I don't think Julie is all that allergic to horses anymore."

"Best to be sure. I'm off to the board meeting tonight. I'd much rather sip a glass of champagne on my back deck, but there you go. By the way, you and David and the girls are the only people allowed to stay with us at the house the night before the wedding and the night of. Everybody else has to find a motel!"

"It's nice to feel we're special."

"Just wanted you to know that, Lexie."

Gloucester's words stick in my mind: *As flies to wanton boys are we to th' gods/ They kill us for their sport.* Certainly the gods have a weird sense of humour. They like to play with us. Vivian has worked so intensively on this wedding, she's gone to such lengths to ensure that it be perfect, that I expect trouble. She has flow charts, a wedding planner, and numerous helpers. There's a little industry going on. I'm expecting the gods to step in. One of their favourite games is to take an extreme of anything and tip it over into its opposite. Especially, it seems, an extreme of perfection.

When Saturday arrives, the hand of the gods is immediately evident. We're more than two months beyond the summer solstice, but you'd never know it. Huron County is at a rolling boil beneath a fiery sun. There are desert mirages on the highways. The sky is a super-saturated blue, the earth parched, the ground cracking.

The ceremony isn't 'til four, but David and I arrive early for the last of the picture-taking. It's only a fifteen-minute walk from Vivian's, but it's far too hot to walk. As we drive in the long, curving lane in our air-conditioned car, I notice the contrast between the lush, well-watered lawns of the estate of Vivian's friends and the parched fields that creep to the fences around the grounds. Thin drooping corn. Stunted grain. The crops lean against the rails, looking as if they're comparing their dull vegetal lives to ours of ceremony and intermingling flesh.

There are already a fair number of people here. Women coiffed and gussied up to each's ideal of fashion, men stuffed into tuxedos and suits on what has to be the hottest September day in my memory. I move into the shade immediately and fan myself with the paper that holds my readings. Even the flowers that border the lawns are dressed in their best; they've been cajoled and cosseted into a third blooming, and the curving beds seethe with colour.

Is it too much to say that a wedding is all about the clothes? For the female of the species, that is. The bride's dress is the centerpiece of course, but the clothes of the matrons and maids of honour, the guests themselves—how many hours, how much agonizing, how many tears, how much euphoria goes into costuming oneself for this ritual where two people are joined into one unit until death or divorce do them part?

Vivian conceived her dress in January, nine months before the wedding. She set off for the city an hour away with her best friend Maeve. They had an appointment with the designer who would create Vivian's outfit. That morning, Lake Huron was lashing the shore, sending squalls of fury inland. There was snow under their tires and inundations of white coming off the fields in such quantity that visibility was periodically nil. By the time they arrived, Vivian told me, her hands were stiff white claws that had trouble letting go of the wheel.

"Did you consider postponing your meeting?" I asked.

"Lexie," she said. "This is my wedding dress we're talking."

"Of course. One's life is nothing by comparison."

"I'll ignore that. Anyhow, I'm excited. The designer is making me an ivory skirt of *peau de soie* that's dead straight, with a slit up the right side. The blouse is ivory crêpe. A wrap-around with a big portrait collar. It ties at the side with a sash that hangs to the floor. She measured me today and it'll be ready to try on in July so I hope to hell I still like it then!"

I'm going to be wearing a dress I still can't believe I bought. A dull navy-blue job, long tight sleeves, lacy bodice, full-length skirt. It's a dowdy, invisible, older-woman dress. I bought it when I was tipsy in the local Ladies' Wear shop. Overpriced, tasteful clothes sagged from the hangers. I should have run from the store.

Our younger daughter, Katie, came home for a week in early July, and we met her at the Toronto airport. She swung through the door and strode swiftly toward us—tall, blond and composed, child of my heart and flesh. I knew better than to say this aloud; her independence was new and strongly guarded. She was wearing the piercing she'd acquired the last time she was home, a fearsome set of silver claws that jutted from her lip. Was the claw meant as a warning? A kind of "keep off the grass" sign? I kept my thoughts to myself.

On her second day at home, I took Katie shopping for a dress for the wedding. I'd finally learned to set aside my own shopping style—strike, pluck, try on, buy, depart—and allow my daughter her pace. Katie is a slow, dreamy shopper, vegetal almost, her pulse seemingly harmonized to the leisurely tempo of plant life. I took her to a discount mall where graduation dresses were marked down to twenty-five bucks. There was a long line up to get into the few, tiny, mirrorless change rooms.

Katie tried on fourteen dresses.

Halfway through the process, I began to wonder if I still possessed the stamina to be a mother. After each change, her tall, majestic form flung open the door of the room and stepped forth, clad in combat boots and the dress of the moment. In the exposed white space between hem and boot, a tattoo. Fourteen times, she stood and regarded herself in the floor-length mirror, asking my opinion. She turned this way and that, light glinting from her silver claw. This she did as if there were not a lineup of people staring at her.

Every time Katie disappeared to try on yet another dress, the lineup buzzed and seethed—"Do you *believe* it? How many is that? When did she go in there?" On display in the small area outside her change room door, I looked at the floor and tried to be deaf and invisible.

It came down, finally, to an agonized choice between a red strapless dress and a short-sleeved mauve. The mauve was dull, but the red showed several inches of cleavage; the space between Katie's neck and the top of the red dress seemed an endless white steppe. I finally suggested we get an tailor to add black straps. An asphalt highway across the steppe. That did it. Katie chose the red, releasing me from the potential lynch mob of waiting women.

Katie took over the matter of her father's clothing. David had not worn a suit jacket or dress pants since he retired. He declared that his outdated clothes were still good. Katie informed him that new clothes would not be wasted—he would need them for funerals. She had her father drive her downtown, shoved him over the threshold of the stores and supervised the purchases. She accomplished the whole business in two hours. David would never have taken it from me.

I haven't seen the set up for the ceremony until now. The guests will be on rented, folding chairs on one side of the large, oval swimming pool. The bride and groom will stand on the far "shore," in the dappled shade of a linden tree. I choose a chair, lay my superfluous shawl on it, and look across the blue water to the spot where my sister will soon stand to enter the portal of a new life. White, angel-perfect cabbage butterflies flutter above the gardens. A honeyed buzz seems to infuse the hot, heavy air. I'm conscious of a moil of emotions. Happiness for Vivian one minute, sadness for the closeness Vivian and I have lost the next. Admiration of Mike and liking for him one minute, wishing he'd never appeared the next. Guilt for feeling the way I feel. Silently I scold myself: *"Let us not to the marriage of true minds admit impediments."*

David and I move into the area where the photos are being taken. It's then that I see a second manifestation of the hands of the trickster gods, in the form of the photographer's assistant, Janet.

Janet is middle-aged. She's wearing a fitted, black, sleeveless sweater. Tailored black pants, black sandals with heels. Her streaked blond hair is done up in an artful chignon. Her copious jewellery is gold-plated, her long fingernails a polished, manicured copper. She's beautifully turned out. Except for one thing.

Her breasts are unconfined by a bra, and they are by no means small or perky or nondescript. Their large, pendulous forms hang from Janet's chest. The nipples flop around the area of her navel. They poke and prod from within at the thin fabric of the fitted black sweater, as their owner, seemingly unselfconscious, moves around the photo subjects. The breasts sulk and brood from behind the fabric when she stands still. My eyes return repeatedly to these free-flapping objects with their pointed ends. If Janet were an old slattern with whiskers and broad buttocks and lank gray hair or a hippy type with a loose flower-power shirt, her breasts would be unremarkable. It's the oddity of her having used artifice to make the rest of herself conform to an expected image, yet having allowed these cow udders to remain in their natural state and on plain view.

Not only this. Clad completely in black, Janet is a dark shadow of the bride in her full-length white. The gods have arranged to have a bride and an anti-bride at this wedding. On which will the guests' eyes be focused?

I knew we should have built in a trickster element. Otherwise, the gods arrange one themselves.

As four o'clock approaches, David and I take our places. The chairs are in full sun. Seated, we face its undiminished force. White napkins, tissues, even handkerchiefs appear in sweaty hands. Men mop their sweltering temples and foreheads, women pat their noses and chins. Silently I curse the long, dark sleeves of my dress, so fitted that I can't roll them past my wrists. I long to rise in place and belly flop into the pool. I'd like to watch and listen to the ceremony while treading cool, blue water, an added benefit being destruction of the hated dress.

The harpist and the flautist are in place, across the pool, also in full sun, playing a series of short classical pieces as we wait for the bride. I imagine Julie riffing into the Call of the Puke Bird when her aunt appears. The harpist seems to be in a terrible mood. The furrow that gores her forehead appears to be permanent, though I know she's only in her twenties. She holds her black eyebrows tense, as her fingers pluck the strings and elicit a haunting, ethereal music that's at odds with her cross appearance.

Half an hour ago, Vivian went into the house to have a bath and recover from the rigors of the picture taking. Then she planned to get back into her clothes and have Maeve re-do her makeup. Still, knowing my sister, I expect her to appear sharp at four o'clock.

It was when I went to see the movie *Monsoon Wedding* that I realized I'd bought the wrong dress. The intense, primary colours of that movie—orange, saffron, red, gold—the rich fabrics, the huge fragrant tropical flowers, the thousands of marigolds, the dancing, the singing, the chanting, the incense, the chaos, the life force. I emerged onto the winter street feeling as if I'd missed out on my life in this cold, northern, broomstick-up-the-arse country. Went home and played "Sympathy for the Devil" full blast. Katie's red dress was hanging in the kitchen; I'd just picked it up from the tailor. I threw off my clothes and tried it on. It fit me perfectly! Maybe I would fight her for it. Katie wasn't missing out on her life; that was obvious.

Vivian enters at exactly four o'clock, from our left.

She stops and kisses our uncle, who is sitting in his wheelchair. Our mother's brother, the last surviving family member of his generation. Vivian has had him driven here in a white limo from his nursing home thirty miles distant. Our brother has Vivian by her left arm. He looks serious, as if he's concentrating on keeping his feelings locked up. Originally, Graham and I were both to give Vivian away, but I've been demoted to wedding guest without portfolio. It might have been something as simple as Vivian fearing that I would fall into the pool on our way around it.

Vivian and Graham follow the white curve of the pool's concrete edge without mishap. Floating on the blue water are dozens and dozens of flowers—red, pink, orange, purple. Mike waits on the other side. If I were to half-close my eyes, I could believe Mike to be our father, small-boned, slender and blond. Eyes blue as the summer sky. I think of Vivian's first marriage—the outhouse, the plopping cow rain, our father holding Vivian's left arm, the breasts popping from fuchsia gowns. What a journey my sister has been on. What a trip.

The minister squints, or maybe smiles, at Vivian and Mike and adjusts her glasses: "Dearly beloved, we are gathered together in the sight of God and in the face of this congregation..."

Beautiful words, but no longer true for us. God is gone from our sky. We have only the freakish, unpredictable gods. Dearly beloved, we are gathered together in the sight of the gods, who play with us according to their whims. The ceremony progresses smoothly. As in a dream, I rise and read *Let us not to the marriage of true minds*, and later, *Though I speak with the tongue of men and of angels*.

My sister stands, slim and lovely in her pale ivory skirt and blouse, speaks her words at the appointed time. As the ceremony draws to a close, I wonder what the gods will do to this free spirit once she's been transformed from bewitching lover to familiar helpmeet. The lover is exciting and exotic. The wife is of the daily world. Up to her elbows in duty and role.

After the ceremony, champagne and hors d'oeuvres are served by white-shirted, dark-vested waiters circulating among the guests. The band arrives.

Dinner is in the garden under a large canopy. I am by now locked into such a mood that I don't approach anyone, even those I haven't seen in years. If they come up to me, I answer them and grind out of myself a modicum of polite conversation, feeling as if my face will crack, as the earth cracked when Persephone was stolen from her mother by a man. Does every mother feel this, in some hidden part of herself, as her daughter pledges allegiance to a stranger? Never mind that Vivian isn't my daughter; it feels as if she is. And never mind that Mike isn't a stranger. Tonight, anyone who isn't my own flesh and blood is a stranger.

Dinner is beef. As we don't eat red meat, David and I have asked ahead of time for the option of the vegetarian meal. A small bright salad is set before us, red and yellow peppers arranged to form a teepee that nestles in soft green lettuce. Saffron rice. That's it. Vegetarian seems to mean that you're served the vegetable portion of the meal and nothing else. I can smell the steak on the other guests' plates. My mouth waters. My stomach wants it. My head or maybe my pride forces me to make do with the vegetables and rice. At dinner, an eighty-five year old cousin says that my navy blue dress is quite the nicest at the wedding. I rest my case.

The bar has been stocked with twice the normal amount for one hundred and fifty guests. Vivian had a brief tiff with her wedding planner over that, who said that the regular amount would be enough. Vivian knew the drinking habits of her friends and relatives. She was vindicated when the caterers narrowly avoided running out of liquor.

Our brother Graham's youngest child, Annelise, is fourteen. She drinks a glass of champagne, then a glass of wine, on an empty stomach, and quickly becomes drunk, swooning and running off at the mouth. Just as I exit from the downstairs bathroom of the house (which is decorated by a floor to ceiling poster of a cow) Graham's new girlfriend, Eva, appears. She is helping Annelise down the stairs to the bathroom. Graham's ex, Pascale, follows close behind.

Eva is a vet. She has developed a fondness for Annelise, and Annelise, who loves animals, has accompanied Eva on her calls over the summer. When Eva hears that Annelise is in a state, she hurries to the scene and shepherds her young admirer to the bathroom, apparently giving no thought to the fact that Annelise already has a mother. Dwarfed by the staring life-sized cow, my brother's estranged wife and his new lover swab and succour Annelise as she lolls and slobbers and sobs that she "loves them both the same."

Pascale has an indestructible sense of humour. On the phone to me the next day, she says that she had to make four stops on her three hour drive home to the city, after the wedding, so that Graham's assorted progeny and their dates could variously "puke, pee and gag in the ditches." She finds nothing funny in Graham having a smoldering, Hungarian beauty twenty years his junior on his arm. Eva may be a vet; she is also a knockout who exudes sexuality. Can there be anything more gall-inducing for a woman than to see the man you have discarded end up with someone younger and more beautiful than yourself, especially if you are at the same event without a date.

I have a story to trade with Pascale about her oldest child, who happens to be my favourite nephew. Yves is at the wedding with his shy girlfriend, Lin, from whom none of us has ever heard an improper word. At some time after midnight, Yves and Lin sit down across the table from me and several other guests. Lin says that Yves has a fat ego. "It's become so fat that he has trouble breathing," she says, sliding Yves a sidelong glance from behind her curtain of straight, black hair. Yves, fortunately, is so wasted that he doesn't take this in. "In fact," says Lin, to howls of laughter from her listeners, "Yves has ego-induced asthma." She puts her little hand over her mouth, then: "Oh, I must apologize. I am a little tipsy." She sways in her chair: "Yves' ego is so swollen that he says he is very nice and very sexy." Lin puts her hand over her mouth again, and says, "Yes, he is very nice, but I don't know about sexy." Her drunken audience wipes away laughter-tears. I ask if anyone has noticed the breasts of the photographer's assistant. This elicits an immediate chorus of yays and a series of raunchy comments. No one, it seems could take his or her eyes off the breasts. I have not been alone in my staring and my unseemly curiosity. Hazily, I discard my theory of sulking, brooding nipples and decide instead that the breasts were hidden pistols ready to fire from the waist—a mammary blast against the institution of marriage, a turning upside down of the established order. An instrument of the gods in their favourite pastime.

Dinner has long since been cleared away, the band is on its third set of the night, couples are on the dance floor under the open tent. Vivian has fastened up her skirt and she's in the midst of the revelers, dancing with abandon with her husband of three hours, whom she referred to in her short after-dinner speech as the love of her life. *We're gonna rock, rock, rock, 'till broad daylight, We're gonna rock around the clock tonight.* The sax is going crazy. Vivian's arms pump, her legs are move in time to the music, she's whooping out the chorus. From the shadows, I watch her, feel what it's like to be her. The ground shifts.

It's me. Me I'm mad at, forever on the sidelines, the observer, whereas Vivian flings herself into life and lives it. I take a deep breath and flop onto my arse, my back against a tree. This will take some thought.

If you can't find a partner, use a wooden chair ... let's rock, everybody, let's rock. Everybody in the whole cell block. The stars have a gleam in their eyes. Every last one of them.

Crash. The daughter of the matron of honour jumps into the swimming pool in her good black dress. It's 1:15 in the morning. Her mother follows, wearing the gold outfit in which she stood up with Vivian. She does remove her shoes first.

Her friend jumps in, wearing her pale-blue suit. One after the other they go.

Not wanting to be thrown in, Vivian and Mike decide it's time to leave. Julie too—she's wearing her best friend's borrowed dress. I'm torn between going with them and drowning my navy-blue. "Come on," says David. "You can sell your damn dress to Second Time Around."

The bedroom David and I occupy for the night is right below the newly-wedded couple, but we hear nothing. It isn't until the next morning that we learn of the wedding's conclusion.

"Bring your coffee in here," Vivian calls from the living-dining room, when she smells bread toasting in the kitchen, a sure sign that David and I are up.

My sister is sitting at her long dining room table opening presents. A rectangle of sun lights up her platinum hair and the collar of her pink sleeveless blouse. She has stacked her thank you notes, written beforehand, in a neat pile on the table. As she opens each gift, her small, efficient fingers retrieve the note from an alphabetized file and lay it for customizing on top of the present. Mike is sitting at the table drinking his morning coffee and looking on, Julie is blowing her nose and wiping tears from her cheeks. "Sit down," she says. "Oh my God, you have to hear this. I've been laughing so hard I'll be sore tomorrow."

I look from Julie to Vivian. "What's going on?"

Vivian smirks. "Mike, you tell the story this time." She looks over her glasses with mock severity at David and me. "The story that was not, let me tell you, funny at the time!"

Mike clasps his hands behind his head. I note that the blue of his shirt matches exactly the blue of his eyes. This will be Vivian's doing. She has always dressed her men. "Oh," he says, "it's just that I spent my wedding night trying to get the bride's skirt off her body."

"What?"

"That's right. It was harder than removing a chastity belt."

"What happened?"

Vivian raises her eyebrows. "The invisible zipper in my skirt broke when I tried to take it off. Remember how the skirt was narrow all the way to the bottom?"

"Yes. Dead straight is how you described it to me."

"Straitjacket would have been more accurate," says Mike. "I worked and worked and worked at the damn thing as my bride became more hysterical by the minute."

"I'd woken yesterday morning with a sore throat," says Vivian. "By bedtime, it felt like a raw flame. I wanted to wear the skirt on our honeymoon to the Big Apple, so I didn't want Mike to wreck it."

"I have to get my toolbox, finally," says Mike. "I take my pliers and work away at the zipper. Vivian keeps croaking at me not to damage the material."

"He brought the full force of his considerable ingenuity to bear on the problem," says Julie, with a giggle.

"As my bride rails at me and writhes on the bed," says Mike.

"Finally he goes and gets a scalpel that I happen to have home," says Vivian.

"I did," says Mike. "I'd had enough. I fetched that scalpel and I took my puke-bird tongue in my teeth, and over the hoarse protests of my brand new wife, I ruthlessly slit the skirt from top to bottom."

"I might just as well have jumped into the pool with the others," says Vivian, "for all that's left of my wedding outfit."

I place my hand on my heart and lean towards my sister, "Never did you imagine that your beloved would end up slicing it off you with the very instrument you use every day to better the lives of others! See what I mean about the hand of the gods?"

"Yes, but think what could have happened," says Vivian. She removes a gold bow from a long, flat gift wrapped in silver paper and looks at her audience of Mike, David, Julie and me. "Remember how I had a bath to cool off between the picture-taking and the ceremony? Then dressed again in my outfit? What if the zipper had broken then, when I tried to put the skirt back on? What would I have done?"

"You would have had no alternative," says Mike, "but to be married in your ivory crepe blouse, your exquisite white shoes from Italy, and your panties."

"Nothing of the struggle to remove the bride's clothing filtered down to me, and it's just as well," I tell Mike. "If I had heard the clank of the toolbox lid, the whine of the electric drill, the scritch of pliers, the muffled hysterics of your bride," I nod at Vivian with mock solemnity, "and finally, the fierce rip of scalpel along white silk, what would I have thought?"

Mike laughs and looks at his new wife. "Perhaps that your sister and I had moved on from puke-bird hijinks to darker erotic activities..."

"Exactly. So, my darlings, I was wrong with my dire predictions. Wrong. In the end, the gods let you off easy."

We left for home at noon. That evening, David and I drove Julie and Katie to the airport in Toronto's west end. They caught their respective Air Canada flights, one east, one west. Behind my sunglasses, I shed a few tears. Another family milestone over, all of us back to our separate lives.

There has been endless speculation about the anti-bride's breasts. A cousin who lives in Rilling made discreet inquiries, and could discover hearsay evidence of no other occasion on which the photographer's assistant had appeared without that crucial item of underwear. The whole incident was strange enough to confirm my belief that she was but an instrument for those invisible forces that insist on being a part of our human lives.

The gods choose the strangest things to spangle in mystery.

xxiii.
The Mothers, the Daughters, the Sisters, the Brother

IN APRIL OF THAT YEAR, a foal was born on my sister's birthday. A chesnut stud colt with a large white blaze and four white socks out of Graham's mare, Little Gently. As the birthday was my sister's fiftieth, my brother Graham named the foal "Cinquante." He dropped off a birthday card and a bottle of champagne at Vivian's place in Rilling, along with a note about the birth of the foal.

At first, the foal did well. Graham's girlfriend of two years, Eva, gave him a tetanus shot. The next day, she castrated the two yearling stud colts, Maestro and Arpad. She gave booster shots for West Nile to all of Graham's horses. Eva was Graham's vet as well as his girlfriend.

This was Little Gently's first experience of being a mother. When her foal was five days old, she kicked him in the head. Little Gently seemed to be irritated by the foal's constant presence at her side, and his repeated nosing at her nipples.

I was shocked. I'd never heard of a mare behaving in this way, but Graham told me that it does happen. He was troubled and began keeping an even closer eye on the pair. When nothing more happened, he let them briefly into the front pasture that slopes towards the creek. Little Gently seemed to be learning how to be more motherly, and no mishaps took place. The foal was getting stronger.

A few days later, Little Gently stepped on her foal's right hind leg, injuring it enough that Cinquante had trouble getting up in the stable. The next day Little Gently stepped on Cinquante's left front leg. Trying repeatedly to get up, Cinquante broke open the scab on his umbilical cord, and it began to leak urine. He developed navel ill and joint ill despite the fact that Eva had put iodine on his navel cord at birth. He became virtually unable to get up on his own, even outside, in the fenced area between house and barn.

Graham agonized and spent two nights in the stable. Cinquante was only sixteen days old when Graham and Eva decided that the foal would have to be put down. Eva looked after this, and she helped Graham dig a grave at the farm our father called the Other Place. They buried Cinquante beside the frog pond. I could picture the spot. One spring I had seen the area teeming with new life.

Graham said that not only did Eva provide kind and professional care to the horses, but that she helped him physically by digging the grave, and supported him in his decision and in his sorrow. He said that he didn't know how he had ever got along without her.

Five months later, in September, Eva broke up with Graham, giving as her reason the twenty year difference in their ages. When my sister and I received the heartbroken phone call from our brother, each of us sat down and wrote one another identical emails that crossed in cyberspace: "Eva has a new man." We hadn't expected Graham and Eva to last, but we were disturbed. Our brother had lost his job, his wife, his five children, his home, half his money, and his parents—all in the same year—and he had been deeply depressed until he met Eva.

Eva's mother was scheduled to arrive in Rilling for a long-planned October visit. Vivian had been going to have Graham, Eva and her mother over for cocktails. Graham begged Vivian to stick to the plan; he still believed that he could convince Eva to come back.

Vivian was intrigued by what she'd heard about Eva's mother and, as always, she was hoping to give everyone a good time.

If Graham thought that he could yet salvage the relationship, she was willing to do what she could—she'd always entertained our brother's girlfriends and whoever they brought along.

Eva had by now bought a little house in Rilling and she'd taken in a boarder—a twenty-eight-year-old Hungarian who had known Eva's mother back in Budapest: "Zsa Zsa is pretty good for a sixty-eight year old," the boarder had said to Graham. "She has a gay husband in the front room and a lover in the back room."

Eva herself had said, of her mother: "My dad was Zsa Zsa's third husband. He was a doctor. He died penniless. Zsa Zsa took all his money." Eva had looked at me then. "My mother's fashionable, very well-preserved. You'd like her." I'd smiled and silently filed away this view of me.

Zsa Zsa wasn't Eva's mother's real name, just the name everyone called her behind her back. She was reputed to drink only champagne.

On the day in question, I almost fell down Vivian's stairs in my haste to descend and set eyes on the guest. I rounded the bar at a trot. So often, the creatures of my imagination are more compelling than their flesh and blood incarnations.

This time, my imagination had not outrun reality.

Who would believe that this woman was two years from turning seventy! Not a line on the beautiful Slavic face that looked intensely into mine. A dark flame flickered in the black eyes. Her full lips were painted a glossy dark red. Wavy, jaw-length chestnut hair framed an oval face. The dark eyes glittered as they ripped me up and down. Immediately, I felt like an ungainly, new-world hick.

Zsa Zsa stepped forward and aligned her cheek briefly with mine. An exotic scent. I watched her out of the corner of my eye as Vivian's new husband, Mike, poured me a glass of champagne. It was hard to imagine this woman at either Graham's farm or at the house her daughter had purchased here in town. Ropes of pearls decorated her neck, she wore a glittering diamond on her pinky, a huge sapphire on her fourth, gold rings on the other hand. Her nails were manicured to a polished carmine sheen. She wore a beautifully-cut suit of fine black wool.

Vivian had described Eva's house in Rilling in an email after her one visit: "An absolute pig stye. Much worse than the farm, if you can conceive of that. A bungalow with the original carpet from thirty years ago. She has two dogs and at least three cats in residence. It stinks of urine, and I mean the entire house. Amazing. Her mother will faint dead away when she arrives, I am quite sure."

This, I had seen the minute I entered the room, was not a woman to faint dead away. Her presence was regal. I welcomed her to Canada and asked what she thought of Rilling, population three thousand. Zsa Zsa adjusted her black and white lace cuffs. She raised her eyebrows and looked over at her daughter, who was slouched at the end of the bar in beaten up blue jeans. Eva's hair was askew and her fingernails were dirty. She looked as if she'd come straight from delivering a foal.

"I am enchanted to see my darling Eva," said Zsa Zsa. She smiled, her teeth a sheen of identical pearls in the pink pod of her mouth. "I cannot stay long. I must attend a ball in Vienna. My companion, Dirk, will be honoured."

"Lovely. And what is Dirk being honoured for?"

"He is walking from Budapest to Northern Europe."

Again Zsa Zsa looked at Eva, who returned her look briefly, and said, "has walked." Then Eva turned her head away and pointedly asked my brother, on the other side of the bar, to refill her beer glass.

"My goodness, that's quite a walk," I said, hurriedly. "Why did he do that?"

Zsa Zsa set down her glass and stepped back from the bar. I became aware of her unforgiving backbone. "I am on the board of the Red Nose society of Europe. We raise millions for hospitals. Dirk is raising thousands of dollars in his walk. I am extremely proud of him." Her dark eyes willed her daughter to turn and respond. Eva continued to show her mother her profile.

Vivian came down the stairs with plates of appetizers in both hands.

Zsa Zsa raised her chin. "My daughter the surgeon cannot live in a house like *that*," she said. Her nostrils flared. "Eva will come to Budapest at Christmas and I will come back in June and I will furnish and re-carpet her house and by then she will have removed the old carpet and painted all the walls." She looked at her daughter. "Right, darling."

Eva returned her mother's gaze, but still didn't speak.

"Oh, are you going to Budapest at Christmas?" I stuttered, in Eva's direction. The tension was as thick as overcooked gravy.

"Apparently," Eva replied. She swigged her beer and flashed her mother another black look.

Mothers and daughters. In these two, the familial resemblance was clear. Yet the mother was artifice-enhanced, a fastidious woman of the world, an artist of makeup and fashion and seduction, living in the sophisticated heart of the old Magyar empire. The daughter cared not a fig for any of this. Cared for its opposite—for animals. Her home reeking of the creatures, her person hinting of them. She chose to live in a backwater of the new world where the favourite pastimes are getting drunk and killing one another off on the roads. I wondered whether this was the real Eva, or whether she was reacting to her mother, behaving in a way that would be most irritating to her.

Zsa Zsa and Eva ate pieces of smoked salmon on flatbread, and sipped their champagne and their beer. Zsa Zsa talked to Mike, Eva talked to Vivian and Graham. I mused that while it was entertaining for us to meet Zsa Zsa, what could it have been like to be raised by this woman? What scars did Eva carry, scars that would affect her intimate relationships in the way that all of our scars do? Add those scars to Graham's and it wasn't surprising that the liaison had crashed and burned.

Vivian and Graham and I sat on at the bar after the guests left. Graham told us that Eva had dumped him in France. Graham went there every fall to help his friends put on a horse event. This year, he had paid for tickets for Eva to accompany him. She was to join him two weeks after he arrived.

She did join him, but only to say, on her first day there, that she was breaking up with him. Graham was devastated. He told her how much and in how many ways he loved her. He would quote Elizabeth Barrett Browning's poem in its entirety, I knew that, would say the words as if they'd been composed by his own heart: *How do I love thee, let me count the ways...* Not only was Graham losing Eva, he felt shamed in front of his friends. He had told them all about her, had described her wild Slavic beauty, her brilliance, her knowledge of horses, her ass. After his tears, and the poem, they danced all night and lasted another week.

Mike and my husband David were watching sports on the upstairs television. Vivian and I, at the bar with Graham, would normally have been properly sympathetic. He was open and bereft. Eva had always phoned him several times a day, telling him what farm call she was on, getting his advice about the sick horses. He had opened doors for her, had helped her to establish her business in the area. He was so lonely now he could hardly bear it.

Vivian and I had had too much champagne. When Graham got to the place in his narrative where he told us about the dancing, we began to sing in a goofy way. *I could have danced all night, I could have danced all night, and still have begged for morrrrrrrre.* I started the singing and Vivian joined in.

Too late, I saw Graham's hurt expression. He turned and threw the contents of his glass of red wine in my face. It went down my front, over my sweater and skirt, and onto Vivian's carpet.

Vivian was livid. Furious at Graham and distressed about my clothes and the carpet. I followed her to the laundry room and tried to tell her that I wasn't upset over my clothes, that I'd deserved it—what are clothes, they can always be washed. Our singing of the song had come across as mockery when Graham had just told us how lonely he was.

Vivian said that in all his drunken obnoxious behavior, our brother had never thrown anything. She said that she would have slugged him. I said that I probably would have too, if I had been the kind of support to Graham that she had. But I hadn't been much of a support at all. Vivian picked up the phone and called her best friend, who knew exactly how to get the stains out. Vivian washed the clothes, went to no end of trouble to restore them to their former state. She dressed me in a tan skirt and a purple sweater that were too tight on me.

We got through it. Graham apologized and we returned to the bar. Vivian popped the cork from yet another bottle.

"You're going to have to learn to assess a woman with your hard-nosed banker's brain," I said to Graham.

"Vivian did tell me that Eva had had a colourful past."

"The word was checkered," said Vivian.

"I know it's not easy to be hard-nosed when you've been shot with Cupid's arrow, *mon frère*. But you'd save yourself a lot of suffering if you did." I said this even though I knew in my drunken swimming state that that's not how it works. "When you were with the bank, would you have given a farmer a loan if he had gone bankrupt twice and failed with eight farms?"

"It wasn't eight men she'd had, it was fourteen," said Graham. "Just to set the record straight."

We went to the dinner table. Mike and David joined us. We had wine and got drunker. As we ate our dinner and told stories, we laughed, at nothing and everything.

Eventually the talk wound back to Eva. "She has the most

shapely ass and the smallest waist I have ever seen on one body," I said. "Has everyone noticed her ass, or is it just me?"

"Of course. We've all noticed it," said Mike.

Vivian raised her eyebrows.

"My roommates used to tease me," I went on. "They said that my ass had been shot off in the war. I've envied Eva's ass since the day I was introduced to her."

"You and Vivian and mom all have the same problem," said Graham. "You go straight down at the back. You have no ass."

"'Had,' in the case of our mother," I said.

"Excuse me," said Vivian. "I have an ass."

"No, you don't," Graham and I said, as one.

Vivian looked at Mike and stuck out her lower lip. Mike said that of course she had a lovely ass. I said that Mike's life wouldn't be worth a pinch of coon shit if he didn't say that. That there were things in the Sears catalogue that you could wear to give yourself an ass—underwear with padding. Vivian said that you could get those anywhere.

"And I'll tell you something I'll bet you didn't know," she said. "Mom was interested in those things!"

"She was? Our mother was interested in padding her ass? Gawd, you never really know a person."

Graham said that Eva liked to make love with a light on. All his other women had made love in the dark.

"Even that floozie from Ferny?" I said.

"The first time Eva kissed me, she stuck her tongue down my throat as far as it would go."

"Jesus, Graham," I said. "You should've known enough to back off right there. Didn't you feel as if a viper was after you. Didn't you feel as if you might gag?"

"No," said Graham, "it was heaven." His head dropped to the table and he began to weep.

I told David I was going to put my tongue down his throat as far as I could. He said no, and sprang to his feet. I chased him around Vivian and Mike's dining room.

Vivian tried to put her tongue down Mike's throat. He didn't want it either and joined David on the run. I felt myself sway, and collapsed on the couch. Passed out, missing the end of the evening.

At breakfast the next morning, Vivian told me that Graham had drunk a bottle of wine as well as the champagne. He had passed out on the other couch and left for the farm in the wee hours. I hadn't heard a thing.

Vivian said she greatly feared the winter. Graham at the freezing-cold, dark, dreary farm, no human beings around for days. The place uninsulated and rundown. Him subsisting on doughy white bread and peanut butter: "Even last night, between all the laughing, he'd say every little while that he wanted to go back to the farm and die."

"You forget about his specialty," I said. "Rat compote with a base of strong pee. That'll keep him going."

Vivian put her head down on the breakfast table and wept. When I tried to touch her arm, she shook me off, then jumped to her feet and hurried from the room.

I had said a dumb thing. Vivian worked sixty hours a week, she was exhausted, she was hung over, the farm was only twelve miles away from her, whereas it was a two hour drive from me. She had most of the worry about Graham on her shoulders. My remark had thrown the whole mess back in her face, the way our mother had thrown the contents of the chamber pots over the fence, in the days before we had running water at the farm.

I sighed and began to clear the table. Mothers! I thought of Little Gently, Zsa Zsa, my own mother, myself as mother. That whole business of being charged with nurturing, yet separating from, what is flesh of our flesh. It was a task like unto the impossible tasks of the old fairytales.

Like the image of a finished print emerging from the darkroom, it was beginning to come clear to me that I was a lot more like all mothers than I liked to think. Imperfect. Making the kinds of mistakes that have always been made down the great chain of the generations.

I held the dishcloth under the hot water tap and wrung it out. Began wiping Vivian's counters and kitchen table clean. As I wiped, I resolved that next spring I would visit the frog pond on the Other Place where Cinquante had been buried at the end of his sixteen day life. One year, I'd been there at the right time to see the borders of the pond inhabited by hundreds and hundreds of tiny golden frogs. They were leaping in the mud, tumbling over one another, seemingly playing. Maybe I'd be that lucky again.

xxiv.
The Festival We Call Christmas

As we drive down the main street of Rilling on December twenty-fourth, I am reminded that here in Huron County the festival we call Christmas still exists. Sparkling red and green angels fly from the lamp posts. A large crèche squats unashamedly on the front lawn of the United Church. Infant Jesus lies on his back, halo larger than Himself. Three wise men lift their chins as they continuously bear their gifts from the east. Mary and Joseph hover close to the nest of straw by the stable, like any pair of mammals with newborn young. The word Christmas is emblazoned here and there.

In the city, where we live, the word Christmas has become politically incorrect. *Happy Holidays,* everyone says. I've been surprised at the speed with which city people have discarded *Merry Christmas.*

Vivian is waiting for us when we enter her house through the garage and step into the mudroom. "Merry Christmas," she says. "Now let go of your suitcases, hang up your coats, and roll up your sleeves." The four of us obey without protest. She stabs each of us in the fleshy part of our upper arm, and announces that we are now protected from influenza A. Vivian's authority in the family is so pervasive that even our grown daughters Julie and Katie submit without a word of protest. The four of us joke about this unique beginning to the festivities.

Katie happens to be looking at me when I laugh. "You've got a seed stuck between your front teeth, Mom," she says.

"You need to floss them."

I stand on tiptoe and bare my teeth at my five-foot-ten daughter: "Is there a seed?"

"Oh. I see, it's a space," says Katie. You need to get that bonded."

My sister's fourth husband picks up my suitcase and purse. "May I carry these downstairs for you, Lexie, or will you be running straight out to the dentist?"

"Ha ha ha. Yes, Mike, You can be our bellboy anytime."

Mike shoulders my luggage and heads downstairs. Vivian disappears into the kitchen. We remove our boots and carry the rest of our suitcases and the shopping bags of presents into the living room, where Vivian has strung Christmas cards several layers deep. Her main floor Christmas tree is a real evergreen. You can still smell the forest on its branches.

"We're in the middle of doing the vegetables for tomorrow," says Vivian, once I've unpacked and David has disappeared downstairs with our daughters. "Could you sweep up for us?"

"Of course."

Now that we've lost our mother to death, and our sister-in-law to divorce, I've resolved to help my sister in the kitchen instead of lolling in the most comfortable chair talking to the men. Vivian knows that I don't have the skill even to be a sous chef, so she assigns me scullery maid duties such as washing the pots and pans that are too sticky for the dishwasher, clearing the table, stirring the risotto, breaking hunks of stale bread into tiny pieces for the dressing, sweeping the floor.

I pick up the broom. "When's Graham coming?"

A shadow passes over Vivian's face at the mention of our brother. "He should be here now."

"How is he?"

"Not good."

"Sorry to interrupt," says Mike, "but what would you like done with this turnip?" Mike has become a skilled sous chef to his wife. He even knows how to manage and defuse

Vivian's occasional tendency to short temper in the kitchen. From beneath their feet, I sweep the by-products of their creations. Even vegetables produce waste when dressed up to look their best by humans. Their peels and scabs and wilted fronds and wayward juices fall to the floor, and I feel happy in a village-halfwit sort of way as I sweep and scrub and sweat.

Minestrone soup simmers on the back burner, two loaves of olive bread and a tray of stuffed peppers sit on a rack atop the stove. Leaves of dark-green spinach and Boston lettuce show above the top of the red salad bowl. The chores are done, dinner is ready, but still Graham hasn't arrived.

Julie pokes her head into the kitchen, long dark hair shining, brown eyes alight. "Not to be rude, but are we eating anytime soon? If not, could I have a crust of bread?"

"We're waiting for Graham," says Vivian, the sadness back on her face. She looks at her watch. He should have been here an hour ago.

Katie follows her sister into the kitchen. She's a vegetarian who does not eat even dressing because it has "touched the inside of a dead animal." Vivian has remembered this and has made a small amount of dressing and with it stuffed a medley of yellow, green, orange and red peppers to go with the soup. They were beauty itself before they went into the oven, the colours, the cut-out lids, but when they emerged, they were dull and semi-flaccid, collapsing in upon themselves like a penis that has done its work. Katie touches one of them with a fastidious doubting finger, on her face the expression of the disillusioned aficionada.

"Vivian made those peppers especially for you," I hiss into her ear once we're in the dining room.

"I'm going to call the farm," Vivian says, from the kitchen.

It's Graham's answering machine that picks up. We give up waiting and sit down to Christmas Eve dinner. Only when we're blowing on our first spoonful of soup does our brother arrive.

He enters the dining room, his face long as a winter shadow. His white hair sticks out over his ears and his shirt collar. He sits down in the empty chair beside me, redolent of profound melancholy. His hazel eyes are dull, the whites shot with blood.

A fog closes in on the table. Vivian, Mike and I row vigorously, attempting to keep us moving. David, Julie and Katie hunch in the stern, glum in the face of the inevitable. The occasion teeters, founders, and sinks.

"Glug," I murmur to Vivian in the kitchen, as we scrape plates in the silent hiatus between the main course and the mincemeat tarts. "Glug, glug, glug."

"I know," she whispers, through her teeth, dropping a handful of cutlery into the dishwasher. "Damn him. I mean, it's Christmas Eve."

As we eat the tarts and sip coffee, Julie and Katie get into a discussion of whether Handel's Messiah or Christmas music from around the world should be played while we open the presents. "Hey," says Mike, as the discussion shows signs of becoming heated. "Why is this either/or? How about both/and?"

The girls stop abruptly and stare at him. "Well!" says Julie. "You're more than just a pretty face, aren't you!"

To be fair, it isn't just Graham who's responsible for tonight's melancholy mood. Two years ago, our numbers around the Christmas table were reduced from fifteen to six. From one Christmas to the next, we lost our parents to death, Pascale and the five children to divorce, and Vivian's "Mike the first"—to divorce as well. The modern, rational part of us carries on with the Christmas rituals. It feasts and plays cards. It knows that the absent nine will not return. Another part of us waits for our family members as we always did, sitting up alertly each time there's a knock at the door, each time the phone rings, straining our ears for a car to pull up outside, wondering again and again why it's so quiet downstairs.

After dinner and a subdued present opening, Graham returns to the farm. The rest of us turn in early. Christmas Day is quiet, with Vivian being on call, and all of us go to bed by ten. In bed, I tell David that the arrival, on Boxing day, of our first cousins and their spouses will be sure to remove the Kerr gloom, just as the sun dissipates the foul mist of the fens (or so a certain type of British novel implies).

David rolls his eyes at my simile and says that maybe Vivian's stabbing of us as we came in the door on Christmas Eve was symbolic.

"What do you mean?"

"My husband props his head on his arm. I can see only his outline. "Maybe it's an indication of how she feels about us moving in for three days."

"Oh, come on. Don't be silly. She was inoculating us against sickness and death. Protecting us from harm. It was a gesture of love."

"I don't know, Lexie. Don't forget, she's got a big, new family of her own now."

Several minutes later, David is asleep, snoring lightly. I lie awake, thinking about how much this family gathering means to me, whether it's happy or sad, lively or quiet, and how empty this time of year would feel without it. What would I do, what would any of us do, without Vivian?

After coffee the next morning, I sing along with *And the Glory of the Lord,* and slap together the layers for the two grand pans of lasagna for which the peppers alone cost a small fortune. Vivian has made me responsible for the main course on Boxing Day. She knows that I'm competent to make only one dish, so she assigns to me the vegetarian lasagna for which Elyse Baker gave me the recipe all those years ago when we worked "together." Elyse of the darting vacant bird-brain eye. She did not have the concentration of a louse. Her recipe calls for "wheat germs."

Vivian escapes the chaos by going to the hospital to make rounds. The water roils to the rhythms of "Walk the Line,"

Mike having substituted Johnny Cash for Handel. He and David sit at the kitchen table over a second coffee discussing the state of the world.

Without warning, the noodles are *al dente*. I shriek for Mike and bless his springy heart he is immediately at my side, shouting the location of the colander and carting the hot pot of bothered water to the sink. As the kitchen heats up, I step onto the front stoop to cool off and to sing out *Merry Christmas* to the naked trees.

The kitchen mess is no longer merely unholy; it is profane in its desecration of the orderly sanctuary that is my sister's kitchen at other times. Mike helps me to clean it up, then we sit down to hear our cousin Charlotte's stories of the recent past. Our cousin Georgia arrives. Georgia is a lanky, no-nonsense woman with a tall neck that commands as much attention as her face. In her rich, authoritative voice, she tells us about Christmas Eve service in the village church a few miles down the highway. A child made a baby Jesus from dough and put it the toaster oven and it burned and Jesus was black. The children of the congregation sat still for only five minutes, spent the rest of the service running around the perimeter of the sanctuary making a ruckus.

"Hearing that makes me wish that Jiminy Slaughter would rise from his grave and give them all a good clout," says Vivian, back from the hospital.

"Who was Jiminy Slaughter?" says Julie. "Was that his real name?"

"Yes," says Georgia. "He sat in the back pew at church, with his five children in a row to his right."

"He had a preternaturally long arm," I tell Julie. "When one of the children acted up, he would look to see which one it was, counting, and if—say—it was the fourth, his arm would extend like a crane and give the kid a hard whack on the back of its head."

Julie winces and for an instant, I see Jiminy Slaughter's cruel face and sloped posture as if it were yesterday, the few strings of greasy hair that stretched across his skull like starved worms.

"You'd think there could be a happy medium between that and the kids running wild in church," says Georgia. "Honestly, our entire world is like the last days of Rome, and there doesn't seem to be a damn thing any of us can do about it."

Around noon, I stand up. The second wave of Boxing Day guests will soon arrive. My armamentarium of cosmetics is laid out on the bed off the family room. I tell Charlotte that I'm going downstairs to shore up the shell. She looks blank, and I quote Alice Munro: *She broke open the shell of her increasingly expensive and doubtful prettiness; she got out.* Charlotte understands instantly, as all women our age do, even those who have never constructed a shell in the first place. She says that certainly I may be excused for this worthy purpose. Vivian, home from the hospital, says that the same task awaits her. Charlotte says she put her shell on first thing this morning, but she'll go and polish it up. We agree that not one of us is ready to break it open.

The bedroom where David and I sleep opens off the family room, and Julie and I can hear Vivian using the phone at the bar. She finishes her conversation and comes to the door of the bedroom. "That was Graham."

"How is he?"

Vivian drops onto the bed. "He just talked on the phone to his five kids. They answered him in monosyllables. All except Yves have refused the invitation to come up today."

"Oh dear. How depressing."

"He told me he's the failure of the family, Lexie. Says he wants to 'lie down and die.'"

Julie is sitting on the bed beside Vivian, taking this in. She makes a sudden movement. "Graham needs to grow up and take responsibility for his life."

Vivian nods, touching Julie's hand. "I know. You're right,

honey. But he's so alone. He's lost everything—his parents, his family, his job, his lover. And his health is going." Her lip trembles. "He's my big brother, Julie. We used to be close. I rode his horses, went out with his friends. We went to France together, several times. We go back a long way." Streaks of mascara run down her cheeks.

"Whereas I was mean to him when we were children," I tell my daughter. "He was three years younger than I was. I put him down at every chance."

Julie looks from her aunt to me and back to her aunt.

"I'm so afraid we'll find him hanging in the barn," whispers Vivian, the tears starting again.

Julie moves closer to her aunt, and hugs her.

"Oh my," I say. "This is messy, for sure. But it's life. And this is Boxing day. I do not believe that Graham will hang himself in the barn. For one thing, he wouldn't be competent to do so. He wouldn't know which knot to use, he wouldn't have the manual dexterity to tie it if he did."

Vivian laughs. She blows her nose and wipes her cheeks.

Julie pats her aunt again and leaves the room, my "humour" as always too black for her.

Graham is our brother, our only brother. We remember him when he was high on life. We'd be devastated if he died. But sometimes there's nothing to be done but laugh.

The Boxing Day snow begins mid-morning. By noon, it's falling so heavily that if we were to lie down on our backs in the yard, every trace of us would be obliterated in half an hour. It is not true that Eskimo has more words for snow than English, just as it is not true that swimming after eating is dangerous or that getting chilled causes the common cold. On this day alone, we will speak the words blizzard, ice pellets, powder, flakes, drifts, squalls, and banks.

Vivian is pacing from window to window. I know she's not worried that the guests won't arrive. In this part of the world, no one stays home because of a blizzard. But two weeks ago, Graham begged her to let him invite Eva for Boxing Day. Though Eva broke off the relationship in September, he still wants to be friends. Life is meaningless without her, he says. Some part of her is better than none at all.

Vivian said okay, with the stern proviso that Graham not get drunk. She knew that inviting Eva wasn't a good idea, but didn't have the heart to turn her brother down.

At noon, Vivian gets another call from Graham, who tells her that this morning he called Eva repeatedly. He was unable to reach anything but her answering machine. Therefore, he went to her house in Rilling and knocked on the front door.

Eva's sister, Ione, opened the door, newly arrived from Washington D.C. "Hi," she said. "Are you a friend of Eva's?"

Graham nodded. "Come on in," said Ione. "Eva's out for a couple of hours with her new flame."

Only a week before, Graham had taken Eva her Christmas present. He'd broken down and begged her to return, had asked her repeatedly if there was someone else. She had sworn there was not.

Graham told Vivian that when Ione said those words, he wanted to flee and never return. But Ione had drawn him in the door and had begun talking in such an interesting way about her aspirations to be a science broker in Washington that he had stayed. When Eva returned to the house, Graham said nothing. "I bit my tongue not to lash out at her deception and dishonesty," he told Vivian. "I took the high road."

"Let's hope he stays on the high road for the rest of the day," I said, when Vivian had finished filling me in. "I see now why you're pacing the floor. The low road won't be a pretty sight."

The back door of Vivian and Mike's house opens and shuts, opens and shuts. Gusts of cold air whistle down the hall and bite our ankles. There is a grand stamping of feet. Each set of new arrivals appears in the hall, adjacent to the living room.

People blow their noses, adjust their hair in the mirror, look for a place to leave their purses and gloves. Various and assorted cousins and their spouses.

Drinks and appetizers. The room hums and buzzes. After a time, and with a little persuasion from Vivian, Julie picks up her flute, and her friend Louise, one of the Boxing Day arrivals, sits down at the grand piano. In our mother's day, we all gathered around the piano and sang while our mother played our requests by ear. Hymns, Christmas carols, popular songs of the forties. Nadine and Julie are playing Mozart, Bach, Scarlatti. Vivian clears the coffee table of empty mugs and glasses, loads the dishwasher, descends the stairs with an armful of dirty tea towels. When she returns, she leans over me from behind the couch. Quietly, she points out Graham and Yves in conversation around the kitchen table, the card players by the window, Julie and Louise now ad-libbing on their instruments. The medley of conversations, regular shouts of laughter from the card players, the music stopping and starting, aroma of lasagna baking in the oven. Many of us will not see one another again until next December. The voice of the flute is resonant, the piano pitters lightly in the background. The waning December sun slants through the big window and across the girls' heads, highlighting their hair with gold.

"This is what I aim for every year," Vivian murmurs into my ear, "but usually it doesn't come together quite this well."

I muse that the beautiful, dark-haired flautist is my replacement on this planet, that the music will go on without me one of these days. Live all you can, said Henry James. It's a mistake not to. Silently I second that thought.

Somehow I miss the late afternoon entrance of Eva and her sister. I say "entrance" because these three days of Christmas at Vivian's are a play; they always have been. Today, the bit parts are having their hour. One of the things Vivian and I sorely miss now that we, unbelievably enough, have become the oldest generation, is our audience. Our parents, our aunts, our uncles—the generation before us. They observed, commented, howled with laughter, fondly advised and sometimes preached moral outrage. They were easy to get a rise out of. And they loved us more than anyone ever will again.

At dinner, I find myself sitting across from Eva and sister Ione. Having met "Zsa Zsa," the mother, it's interesting to see the second daughter. Like Eva, Ione has not even begun constructing a shell, and probably never will. Her look is sporty, plain. Unpolished, squarely cut nails. Where Eva's black eyes are spaced far apart, like her mother's, giving her an exotic appearance, Ione's lively chestnut eyes are spaced a little too close together for beauty. Her nose, shaped like her sister's but twice the size, dominates her face. Her chestnut hair is dyed straw-blond and she hasn't bothered to touch up her roots for the Christmas season.

Ione is indeed an interesting woman with a vast knowledge of science and a creative way of thinking. However, she puts off the others at table immediately. She plunges into talk of her post-doctorate, her fellowships, her large salary, the husband who left her because she was always the one to get the better job and the better grant. This produces in me not dislike but something akin to sympathy. Someone who doesn't know enough not to say these things immediately upon sitting down at a dinner table of strangers in rural Ontario is probably a person without many friends.

Graham is drinking. He simultaneously puts the make on Ione and involves Eva in an intense conversation intended to draw her back into his life. Lori by the imported German Hanoverian Lorbas is due to foal to Mancel in the spring, he tells Eva. Lucy, by the Hanoverian Leperello and a granddaughter of Delight on the bottom side is due early to mid June. Flo and Gently by the thoroughbred Romulus Star, who was by Greek Jab, who sired "Sloopy," who was on the U.S. equestrian team in 1976, have spent three weeks with Mancel, the grandson of Northern Dancer, and hopefully these two half sisters, three years old, out of the full sisters Party Dancer and Freitag, will produce another good family line.

Graham increases his tempo. Flo, he says, his eyes now on Ione's, even as his hand wanders the table in search of Eva's, is a beautiful dapple gray. You'll have to come to the farm tomorrow and see my horses, he says. Gently is a gorgeous chestnut. Her coat is the exact colour of your eyes. Mancel is a dark bay with the head of an angel, the neck of a swan and the ass of an Irish cleaning lady. Graham's left hand finds Eva's as she reaches for her wine glass. "I'll always love you," he interrupts his horse narrative. Tears swarm his eyes.

Vivian's eyes release an arrow that lands on Graham's Adam's apple. Her eyes attempt to remind her brother that Eva was welcome under one condition: that he not get drunk.

Graham is oblivious. "I'll leave you a horse in my will," he drools, in the general direction of Eva. "Oh my beauty." His eyes squirt a fresh spate of tears. His nose begins to run.

Vivian gives Mike a look that means—get Graham downstairs, away from the Boxing Day table. Always a quick study, Mike jumps up and hands Graham a tissue, then guides his brother-in-law down the stairs. David follows, then Eva and Ione.

After coffee, our cousins, spouses, and friends crowd down the back hall. There are hugs all around. The whole posse disappears into the snow. Vivian and I begin clearing the table. Vivian mutters about our brother's drunkenness as we walk back and forth to the kitchen.

Downstairs at the bar, Graham gets into the whiskey. When they come back up, he's staggering. His left arm is around Ione and his right hand massages her stomach, even as he continues to importune Eva. Ione says that she wants to go home. Vivian helps the two women detach themselves from our brother, and sees them to the door.

Graham lurches to the kitchen table and puts his head down on his arms. I start in on the pots and pans. My brother and I are alone in the kitchen. I'm thinking about our mother's deathbed request of Vivian and me: that we look after our brother. That we turn the other cheek. Vivian has carried far more than her share of this.

"I didn't answer your emails all fall because I was too depressed," Graham says. "And I was offended by your vulgar tone. Our father would not have liked it."

My brother's tone is severe. He speaks as if repeating a lesson learned by rote. Graham is turning into our father, the negative side of our father, yet he never got along with him. Maybe that's what happens if we don't make peace with a parent. The very characteristics that we could never accept rise to the surface of our own personalities. Our father's rigidity, his inability to let go of the rules his mother taught him in another century, his dislike of spending a dime, his habit of working long hours with poor equipment at impossible jobs in punishing weather—these are taking Graham over before our very eyes.

My brother raises reddened, work-roughened hands to his face and rubs his eyes. "Eva came out to the farm two weeks ago. Her moustache was gone. I knew right then she had another man. I should have listened to myself."

"Did she get rid of her moustache when she first knew you?"

Graham begins to sob. I wring out the dishcloth.

"My very last conversation with Mom was about forgiveness," he says, through his tears. "That I should forgive Pascale for the divorce. But I've never been able to forgive Pascale." His voice breaks off and he begins to weep in earnest.

I spread the tea towels out to dry, look over at him and see the face of my little brother, six years old, hurt by some cruelty I've inflicted on him. I pick up the box of tissues and sit down across from him. "Here. Your nose is running." I push the box in his direction. "You know why Mom said that, don't you?"

Graham blows his nose, doesn't answer.

"For you, Graham. She wanted you to forgive Pascale for your own sake. Mom didn't want you carrying that stone in your heart for the rest of your life."

Graham raises his head and looks at me through swollen bloodshot eyes. "She took my money and my children. She took away my home. She ruined my life. I'll never forgive her."

I see that his hurt is as raw, as real, as on the day Pascale sued him for divorce. It's an open ulcer that eats him from inside.

"Eva's betrayal has been horrible," he says. "But I can forgive her everything. I still love her. I'll always love her." He blows his nose again. "I'm going to chastise my Eva once by email, but end with absolute forgiveness and sincere desire for friendship."

I leave him then, and go downstairs, wondering how the Slavic princess will take to chastisement by email. Not well, I think. But who among us could resist "absolute forgiveness?"

Vivian and David are sitting at the bar; the others are playing pool and the card game Lost Heir. I sit down beside Vivian. "Graham is still at the kitchen table. Pissed and hurting."

"He gave us a bottle of Pisse-Dru for Christmas again," says David, "even though he knows very well I don't like French wine. I tell him that, every year. Giving us that wine, it's like he's lifting his leg and pissing on us all."

"Sometimes I wonder if the old way was better," I say.

David frowns. "What do you mean?"

"The generation before us. When something bad happened to them, they thought it was God's will. They believed the bad thing had a purpose. They didn't know what it was, but there was meaning in it. Graham's had one loss after another, and now he has nothing and nobody to hold onto."

Vivian gets up suddenly: "Lexie, don't. Can we please all just stop talking about Graham. I've had it."

Later, I hear my brother's voice upstairs. He's demanding his car keys of Vivian, his tone belligerent. His horses will die if he doesn't get back to the farm and let them into the barn. Later still, Vivian comes down and says that Graham has passed out upstairs. She puts her hands to her head. "I'm exhausted. Mike and I are going to bed."

I decide to turn in as well. Julie and Yves and David stay up to talk. I can hear the rise and fall of their voices, but not what they're saying, as I lie in bed. The sound of my family. Imperfect as we are, messy as our lives can be, there's comfort in being together and in bringing our children together. Creating memories and a bond they'll have with their first cousins, once we're gone. Creating family lore.

The bedroom window pane rattles. The old Christian God is in decline but still active—in Huron County at least. Outside, He continues to shovel snow from the front steps of heaven. It plops down by the bushel basket. Plops, pours, sifts, blows, beats, floats, flies, swirls.

Blinds, obliterates, whitens.

Transforms.

Acknowledgments

Many thanks to the editors of the following literary magazines: *Grain* for publishing "Beyond Aunt Bea's Garden," *Prairie Fire* for publishing "Head-doors" and awarding it second prize in their national fiction contest, *Queen's Quarterly* for publishing "On Huron's Shore" under a different title, and *Freefall* for publishing "The Love Bites of Twenty-three Rogue Monkeys" and awarding it first prize in their national fiction contest, *Event* for shortlisting "This is History" for its national contest. Thank you to the then CBC Literary Contest for shortlisting the "You My Father" portion of "On Huron's Shore" for its national contest, and the then Hamilton and Region Arts Council for awarding several of the stories in *On Huron's Shore* the Best Published Fiction award, over a series of years. Thank you to Boheme Press for first publishing "The Sun is Out, Albeit Cruel" and "The Discovery of the New World" as part of *The Roseate Spoonbill of Happiness*. To the Banff Centre for the Arts, the Ontario Arts Council and the staff of Bryan Prince Bookseller, present and past.

Special thanks to Demeter Press and to its publisher, Dr. Andrea O'Reilly.

Special thanks to Georgina and Tijana of the Second Cup of Westdale, where much of this book was written.

Special thanks and love to my family, especially Dan Pilling,

Marie Gear Cerson and Larry Cerson. And to my writer friends, especially Linda Frank, Dick Capling, Ross Belot, Tim McKergow, J. S. Porter and John Terpstra. In loving memory of Gordon Sheppard.

Marilyn Gear Pilling lives in Hamilton, Ontario, and is the author of eight books of poetry and short fiction. Her fiction, poetry, and creative non fiction have been anthologized and have appeared in most of Canada's literary magazines. Her work in all three genres has won and been shortlisted for many national awards. Pilling has read her work in many venues, including Eden Mills, Harbourfront, the Banff Centre in Alberta, Vitteau, France, and at the historic Shakespeare & Company Bookstore in Paris, France. *On Huron's Shore* is set in Huron county, in the town of Wingham, and in the East Wawanosh area equidistant from Belgrave, Blyth and Auburn, fifteen miles inland from Lake Huron. Of the author's fiction, the *Toronto Star* said, "Pilling has a poet's gift for unlocking the strangeness beneath the familiar; her seductive stories reveal the secret flamboyance under the surfaces of our lives."